MATT GOLDMAN

BROKEN
ICE

FORGE®

A Tom Doherty Associates Book / New York

This is a work of fiction. All of the characters, organizations, and events portrayed in this novel are either products of the author's imagination or are used fictitiously.

BROKEN ICE

A Forge Book
Published by Tom Doherty Associates
175 Fifth Avenue
New York, NY 10010

www.tor-forge.com

Forge® is a registered trademark of Macmillan Publishing Group, LLC.

ISBN 978-0-7653-9134-6

Our books may be purchased in bulk for promotional, educational, or business use. Please contact your local bookseller or the Macmillan Corporate and Premium Sales Department at 1-800-221-7945, extension 5442, or by email at MacmillanSpecialMarkets@macmillan.com.

First Edition: June 2018
First Mass Market Edition: May 2019

Printed in the United States of America

0 9 8 7 6 5 4 3 2 1

BOOKS BY MATT GOLDMAN

Gone to Dust

Broken Ice

The Shallows (forthcoming)

For my mother, Helen,
who put a book in my hands
whenever I set down my baseball mitt.

BROKEN
ICE

1

I saw Roger Engstrom three times—the second two he was dead. But the first time he sat on a tufted leather chair in the Saint Paul Hotel's Harold Stassen Suite with a Yorkshire terrier on his lap. The dog was the result of neither intelligent design nor natural selection. Man created the Yorkshire terrier, and Man had made a terrible mistake. If your full-grown dog fits in a bag designed to carry keys and a wallet, it's not a dog you're toting around—it's an accessory.

Roger had curly blond hair threaded with silver, was tall and lean except for a soft belly that hung over his belt. He wore a navy long-sleeved polo tucked into khaki pants that rode up his legs revealing socks festooned with images of computer chips. Duck boots covered his feet, protection from Minnesota's March slush.

He scratched between the little creature's ears and said, "Thank you for seeing us on short notice, Nils." His voice was high-pitched and soft. "The Missing Persons unit of the St. Paul police are doing everything they can, but we know about your success in Duluth and then again last year in Edina. We hear you're the best there is, Nils. And our Linnea deserves the best."

Roger referred to murder cases, not missing persons, but I kept that to myself. "When did you first notice your daughter was missing?"

Roger looked to my right. His wife, Anne, sat on the loveseat beside me. I thought it strange Roger chose not to sit next to her but rather in the lone chair. It was his meeting, I supposed, and he was going to run it.

Anne wore hiking boots, canvas work pants, and a plaid flannel shirt of reds and blues. She was dressed like a roofer but was far more feminine than her not-so-masculine husband. Her gray eyes looked out from behind oversize eyeglasses. The lenses were so big I worried birds would fly into them. She had shoulder-length chestnut hair with bangs that brushed the top of her glasses. Her hair color looked expensive and almost real.

Anne said, "Linnea's curfew was 11:00, but we fell asleep in the bedroom, so we don't know if she came back or not."

"What did she do last night?"

"She went to the hockey game. We all did. It's why most of Warroad is here."

Warroad, Minnesota, lies six miles south of the Canadian border. Its citizens and a few others refer to it as Hockeytown USA, a deserved moniker considering the population is fewer than two thousand people, but no United States Olympic Hockey Team has won a gold medal without a player from Warroad on its roster. The tiny town has sent several players to the NHL and won four Minnesota State High School Hockey championships competing against Twin Cities–area powerhouses and the hockey-centric Duluth schools.

Anne said, "Linnea sat in the student section with her friends. After the game, they all walked to dinner at Burger Moe's to celebrate the victory, and somewhere between the Xcel Center and the restaurant, Linnea disappeared."

"So Linnea never made it to Burger Moe's?" I said. Anne shook her head. "That's not even a two-block walk. No one noticed her leaving the group?"

"We've spoken to Linnea's friends," said Roger. "They all said the same thing. She was there. Then she wasn't. There were over eighteen thousand fans last night and they all poured out of the arena at once. And no one saw anything unusual. That's why the police are treating Linnea as a runaway. That and she's still seventeen."

"But they're treating Haley Housh as a missing person," said Anne.

"Who's Haley Housh?"

"Another senior from Warroad. She's missing, too."

Anne relayed the information as if it were happenstance, as if she were talking about the weather or what they'd eaten for lunch that day. "Were Linnea and Haley together?" I said.

"No," said Anne. "Haley and Linnea aren't close. They didn't sit near each other at the game, and Haley's group wasn't headed to Burger Moe's. All anyone knows is Haley disappeared from the crowd outside the stadium like Linnea did. But Haley's eighteen, so they can't consider her a runaway."

Two girls from the tiny town of Warroad go missing at the same time. Only insular parents would believe that's a coincidence. The police wouldn't, and I sure as hell didn't. "Do you have a picture of Linnea?"

Anne found a photo on her phone and handed it to me. If Anne had told me I was looking at a picture of her at seventeen, I would have believed her. The same chestnut hair. The same gray eyes. Only Linnea's were playful instead of resigned. Maybe more than playful. Maybe a little wicked. A girl with Linnea's looks would have an array of trouble offered to her. I turned toward Anne. "Do you think Linnea ran away?"

"No," Anne said. "Linnea's a happy girl. Popular in school. The only possible reason I can think she'd run away is to take off with her boyfriend. But he's not going anywhere."

"Why not?"

Anne looked at me with indifference or fatigue or perhaps numbness over her daughter's disappearance. "Luca Lüdorf? He's Warroad's star player."

"Have the police questioned Luca?"

"Yes," said Roger. "We talked to him, too. He's devastated. He has no idea where Linnea could be. Hasn't heard a word from her."

"What happens when you try her cell phone?"

"Straight to voice mail," said Roger. "Texts don't register as delivered. And the police have had no luck tracking it."

There was a knock on the door. Roger got up to answer it.

I lowered my voice and looked at the cold eyes under the chestnut bangs. "How long have you lived in Warroad?"

"Five years. We moved up from Minneapolis so Roger could start NorthTech."

Roger opened the door. A tall man, nearly forty with blond hair and a boyish face, stood in a navy-blue suit he couldn't break the habit of wearing.

"Can I help you?" said Roger.

"I'm sorry to bother you. I'm a colleague of Nils's."

"Of course. Please come in."

"Roger and Anne," I said, "this is Anders Ellegaard. He works with me." I would have said works for me, but that's not how it is. If anything, it's the opposite. Before Ellegaard, I was on my own and worked out of my shit-box house and aged Volvo. But nine months ago, Ellegaard resigned from Edina PD and used his connections to secure start-up funding. Now we have an office downtown and a junior investigator and an assistant and, worst of all, a website. My life, as I knew it, went to hell the day Ellegaard leased us a copier. But I'm making a steady living for the first time, have health insurance, and an IRA. And Ellegaard doesn't complain about me too often, so I try to keep my complaining about him to a minimum.

Roger and Anne said a grave but pleasant hello to Ellegaard, then Ellie asked if he and I could talk in private. The Engstroms made a fuss about stepping into the bedroom, but I insisted Ellie and I leave the suite. We did and walked down the hall lined with silver room service trays piled with mostly eaten breakfasts, empty coffee cups, and spent napkins.

When we were far from the Engstroms' eavesdropping range, Ellegaard said, "Have you accepted the case?"

"Not yet. Why? Did St. Paul PD turn up anything?"

"Yeah." He looked down, shook his head, then looked back up. "The other kid, Haley Housh, they just found her body in a cave along the Mississippi River."

"Jesus."

"It's about to leak. Thought you'd want to know before deciding on the Engstrom case."

"Anybody else in that cave?"

"No. St. Paul PD's forensics people are setting up now to comb through it." Ellegaard and I stood in silence for a full minute. Then he said, "Too tragic." I thought he might cry. "I don't know, Shap. Maybe we should leave Linnea Engstrom to the police."

"What?"

"Hey, I have three daughters. I can imagine all too well what the Engstroms are going through. But this smells like a runaway to me. If the kid doesn't want to be found, it will be hard to find her. Mostly likely, she'll come back when she's ready."

"Or she's dead like Haley Housh. Or has been raped. Or drugged and kidnapped into trafficking."

"Don't do this, Shap. Don't make it seem like I don't care about a seventeen-year-old girl. That's malarkey and you know it."

"Don't say malarkey. That's not a word anymore." Ellegaard never swore. Or drank. Or jaywalked. He looked uneasy. I said, "You want to stick me on BrainiAcme."

"It's a solid case, Nils. It's lucrative. It'll help build the firm's reputation."

I looked up at Ellegaard's blue eyes—they weren't ice blue or gray like Anne's—they were blue like a baby's. The goodness in his veins must have preserved them that way. When he was a cop he could always be the good guy. You would've never seen him on YouTube abusing his power. He wore a gold shield that protected his moral code. Now he wore a businessman's getup, and his code was exposed and vulnerable. He needed me to help defend it. "Give me a week on this, Ellie. If Linnea doesn't turn up by then, I'll work the BrainiAcme case."

A maid pushed a cart of towels and toiletries toward us. We stepped aside so she could pass, and I helped myself to a sewing kit. You never know when you'll need one.

Ellegaard said, "All right. What's your gut?"

I smiled at the tall man in the navy-blue suit, not because I had a gut feeling about Linnea Engstrom, but because Ellegaard asked for it.

2

I took the case. Roger and Anne Engstrom shook my hand, and Ellegaard slipped a check for five thousand bucks in his suit coat's breast pocket. I wouldn't have asked for up-front money from the parents of a missing teenage girl, but my partner has something I don't have, a head for business. I helped protect Ellegaard's moral code. He helped me survive in this world.

We assured the Engstroms of our diligence, said our good-byes, started out the door, then heard an odd thwacking sound. I turned just in time to see the last quarter bounce off the glass dining table. Neither Anne nor Roger Engstrom had thrown quarters. No one else was in the suite. I looked above the table. A mostly crumpled dollar bill was stuck on the fifteen-foot-high ceiling. It was an old bar trick and inadvertent two-dollar tip. Stick a thumbtack through George Washington then place four quarters on George's face and crumple the dollar around them. Throw it up just right, and the weight of the quarters forces the thumbtack into the ceiling.

Hours or days later, gravity calls the quarters home, the folds in the bill loosen, and the coins fall out. You've tipped one dollar. But the tack keeps the dollar on the ceiling. When there's enough of them up there, someone who works at the bar knocks the dollars down. You've tipped a second dollar.

I said, "How long has that been up there?"

"I didn't know it was," said Roger.

"I've never noticed it before," said Anne.

We called maintenance. Two men arrived with a ladder. One braced it while the other climbed up and pried the tack from the ceiling with a flathead screwdriver. Ellegaard told the man to let the dollar and tack fall without touching either. My partner grabbed a plastic spoon from a cup near the in-room coffeemaker and used it to lift the quarters, half crumpled dollar, and the thumbtack to the table. He then called the front desk and asked for hotel security.

"What does that dollar mean?" said Anne.

"I've seen that in bars," said Roger. "It could have been up there for days. What a strange thing to find in a hotel of this caliber."

I said, "Don't touch the quarters. The police may be able to get clean prints off them."

A dark-skinned African American woman, about five foot seven, showed up looking like a tourist. She wore jeans, a red Duluth East sweatshirt, and Red Wing work boots. She introduced herself as Rosamond Pinkney, Saint Paul Hotel security. She showed us her ID and badge.

I said, "Nils Shapiro," and shook her hand. Ellegaard did the same and gave her our Stone Arch Investigations card.

Rosamond had met the Engstroms earlier that morning. I explained how we'd discovered the dollar in the ceiling, and that the police should dust the bill, tack, and quarters for prints.

Rosamond said, "I've seen a few things in this hotel. I've never seen this."

She used her cell to call the police. I used mine to photograph the tack and quarters and dollar with my iPhone, flipping the dollar over with the spoon to capture both sides.

Rosamond said a St. Paul detective was on the way. "And just before you called I finished reviewing security camera footage from six o'clock last night to just a few minutes ago. No sign of Linnea entering the hotel. I'm sorry." Anne removed her giant glasses and wiped her eyes.

Ellegaard and I headed to the parking garage, where he hung his suit on a hanger in the backseat of his Lincoln Navigator. I pulled my old Sorels out of my new Volvo wagon, which was the envy of every hockey mom in the state. It had all-wheel drive and nav and smelled like Sweden. Ellegaard insisted I get something new, that as principals of our firm, we needed to make a good impression. Maybe that was true, but I didn't care for it. A car is like a relationship. When it's new and perfect, it causes more anxiety than comfort. You're just waiting for that first dent or a scrape to put you back on nature's well-trodden path to chaos and disorder so you can relax.

We left our new and perfect cars at the hotel and walked over the Mississippi River on the Robert Street Bridge. It was the first week of March, and the big river flowed swollen and stained with runoff. The temperature had hovered just north of freezing for days, and the snow was mostly gone save for the small mountain ranges of dirt and ice the plows had made in corners of parking lots. It was, no doubt, spring's tease. A warm week for the hockey tournament, then next week, during the state basketball tournament, when athletes wore shorts and sleeveless shirts, the first of the March blizzards would pound the town white.

"You'll have to take the brunt of this case, Nils," said Ellegaard as our feet crunched road salt and sand. "I'll help interview the friends and parents and teachers. I just—"

"You don't like this case—you don't have to explain it."

"It's not just that. Last week, Emma got her period for the first time. It's messing with me a little."

"I bet." I'd known Ellegaard's three girls since they were born. I've watched him change a diaper, bundle a toddler for the sledding hill, placate the three of them in a slow restaurant by having them guess what color packet of sweetener he held in his fist. I made mental notes of Ellegaard's parenting skills because I assumed I was right behind him. But it hadn't happened. Not on purpose. Not by accident.

Ellegaard and I stepped off the bridge then followed a gravel path. A few minutes later, we stood outside the entrance to one of St. Paul's caves. Most are natural. Some are man-made, carved out of the sandstone bluffs along the Mississippi. The caves have been used for growing mushrooms and making blue cheese and housing hundreds of homeless during the Great Depression. During Prohibition, bootleggers made and stored liquor in the caves. They set up a speakeasy and even a dance hall.

When I was in high school, kids talked of exploring the infamous St. Paul caves, but, as far as I knew, it never amounted to anything more than talk. Most of the entrances had been sealed off in the 1970s to discourage exploration. Too many bad things had happened over the centuries, the worst being cave-ins due to the caves' soft sandstone walls and ceilings.

Ellegaard and I arrived before the press. A handful of St. Paul cops and forensics personnel gathered inside the yellow tape near the mouth of the cave. A trio of gas-powered generators roared electricity into snaking cables. St. Paul cops have a reputation for community policing, the only problem being it's based on their definition of community. We certainly weren't included in that definition, and that's the look we got from a heavy-set uniform who stood six foot four and had a face so fat his ears looked like an afterthought.

"This is an SPPD investigation, guys," said the cop, whose name tag identified him as Officer Terrence Flynn. "We're not ready to talk. Go on home." The *o*s in *go* and *home* were harder than calculus. Terrence Flynn was blue-collar St. Paul all the way.

"We're not press," said Ellegaard. He handed the cop our business card.

The cop read it. "Jesus Christ. Privates. You got to be fucking kidding me. Will you let us do our jobs here?" The cop looked us over and seemed to recognize me. I avoided eye contact and let Ellegaard do the talking.

"We have no intention of getting in your way. Until a few months ago, I carried the badge myself. I'm sensitive to what you're dealing with here. It's just we're working for the parents of Linnea Engstrom, the other missing girl from Warroad. As you can imagine, they're a wreck. They know you're doing everything you can, but they hired our firm just to make sure they're doing everything they can. You can't blame parents of a missing girl for that."

Flynn said, "You got any information that can help us out?"

"Not yet."

"So what do you want?" said Flynn. "I can't let you in there. They're still processing the scene."

"Just a quick look around, Officer," I said. "I'll stay out of the way."

"Hold on just a mother-fucking minute. Jesus Christ. You're that guy. That guy from the news. Who solved Duluth and Edina and made all the cops look like idiots. No fucking way, buddy. No fucking way I'm letting you in there."

"Officer Flynn," said Ellegaard, "I'd like to introduce you to my colleague, Nils Shapiro. The police in both Duluth and Edina were grateful for his help. I should know. I was one of them."

"Shapiro, that's it," said Flynn. "Yeah, Nils Shapiro." He smiled, and his fleshy cheeks expanded. "Take a walk."

"Nice to meet you, Officer." I extended my hand to the big man. He didn't take it.

"Turn around guys. I'm not fucking around here."

A March wind pushed from the south. A male cardinal clung to a high, skinny branch in a birch tree and tweet-tweeted the coming of spring. A car behind us on Shepard Road disagreed with the cardinal's forecast, its snow tires screaming on the pavement that winter would return.

Ellegaard stepped closer to Flynn and lowered his voice. "Listen, Flynn. Nils here was all over the news last year. But it wasn't his doing. Did you ever see him interviewed? You did not. Because he wouldn't consent to an interview. Not for the *Strib*. Not on TV. Not even for the radio. But we still get calls every week begging for one. Someone in this town gets killed, the press wants to know what Nils Shapiro thinks. But every time they call, what do you say, Nils?"

"I say no."

"You hear that? Nils says no to every request he gets for an interview. But guess what's going to happen if you don't let him take a peek in that cave." Officer Terrence Flynn looked as if he'd just stepped in dog shit. "On TV, Nils will say the town of Warroad is suffering because teenage girls just disappear off St. Paul streets during the hockey tournament. In the newspaper, he'll say the town of Warroad, which has already lost one of its girls, could very well lose another because St. Paul police bungled the investigation. On the radio, Nils will say that, despite his solving murders in Duluth and Edina, the St. Paul police are so worried about their precious reputation that—"

"I'll run it up the ladder," said Flynn. "Just keep your fucking panties on." The cop walked away.

Ellegaard smiled, quite proud of himself, then his eyes caught sight of something, and his smile disappeared. I looked over my shoulder and saw two police officers escorting a couple about my age toward the entrance of the cave. They wore matching green windbreakers. The woman was red-faced and crying. The man appeared grayish white and walked with a stumbling gait. The parents of Haley Housh seemed to be in separate hells but found each other's hands as a uniform briefed them before entering the cave. The back of their matching windbreakers said CRAIG'S BAR & GRILL.

The mouth of the cave looked like the mouth of an unpleasant person, a horizontal grimace, twisted and contorted. The police had covered the ground in tarps. The uniform led the Houshes by crawling into the mouth first. The poor Houshes had to forfeit the simple dignity of walking upright to identify the body of their dead daughter. They followed the officer into the cave on hands and knees. A few minutes later, the mouth spit them back out. Mr. Housh's face had turned red and wet like his wife's. He labored to breathe. His sobs carried in the cool air. They walked away from the police unescorted, back toward Shepard Road.

Ellegaard didn't say a thing. We caught each other's eyes and understood the plan. He raised his voice toward Flynn, who was on his cell near the entrance of the cave. "What's the holdup, Officer?! I'm about to make some calls. And you do not want me to make those calls!" All eyes turned toward Ellegaard, and I feathered into the shadows of the birch trees.

3

"Excuse me, Mr. and Mrs. Housh." They stopped and turned and looked at me. Haley's father's corn silk blond bangs danced in the breeze over pale blue eyes. His wife stood short and heavy under a home perm. Her blue eye shadow looked like it was imported from Chernobyl. Cursive stitching over the left breast of their matching Craig's Bar & Grill windbreakers told me their names were Mike and Connie. I said, "I'm sorry about Haley." Connie buried her head in Mike's chest.

"Yeah, thanks," said Mike, a Minnesotan on auto-polite. His voice shook. Then he steered his wife back toward the road.

"My name is Nils Shapiro. I'm a private investigator." They stopped. I saw a vague recognition in their eyes but they said nothing. "I'm working for Roger and Anne Engstrom." If the parents of a dead child can be knocked down even harder, hearing the name "Engstrom" did just that. Mike's face soured, giving him a gestapo-like appearance, and Connie's lower jaw jutted forward like a bulldog's. "I'm sorry. I didn't mean to upset you further."

"Warroad's been shit since the Engstroms moved to town," said Mike. "And now it's a whole lot worse than shit."

"No offense," said Connie, "but we sure as hell ain't gonna help you help them."

"I'm not asking for your help. I'm offering my services. Free of charge. Losing your daughter is tragic. I can't make it any better. But I can help the police figure out what happened."

It was supposed to be a sales pitch, and maybe that's how it came out, but the words felt genuine when I heard them. I wasn't immune to the Houshes' pain. I'd seen it before in the early days of my solo career, taking money parents didn't have to help find their missing kids. Mostly teens. Mostly runaways. The only difference being those parents' anguish was swirled with hope.

The Houshes had just left the last of their hope in a cave. Legally, Haley Housh died as an adult. But in reality, she was a child.

I did want Mike and Connie's help finding Linnea Engstrom. They knew it, but they welcomed any chance of relief. Learning how Haley spent her final hours *might* provide the slightest bit. They looked at each other. They didn't need to discuss it. Then Connie turned toward me and said, "That's a kind offer, Mr. Shapiro. Thank you."

"I only have one question at the moment." They didn't object, so I continued. "Did Haley have a boyfriend?"

"She did," said Connie. "At least that's what she called him. Ben Haas. He lives in Woodbury."

"Her boyfriend lives in the Cities?"

"Ben worked at a summer camp near Warroad," said

Mike. "They met when Haley was working at the Dairy Queen. They somehow made the distance work, you know with the video chat and all."

"Do you know if they saw each other last night?"

"They were supposed to after the game. I don't know if they did. The police are looking into it."

"Thanks. I'll be in touch after you give your statements to the police." I handed them my card. "And don't hesitate to call. For any reason."

As I walked away I thumb-typed a note on my phone. *Ben Haas: Haley Housh's Boyfriend-Woodbury.* Then *Luca Lüdorf: Linnea Engstrom's Boyfriend—Warroad.* And finally, *Craig Housh: "Warroad's been shit since the Engstroms moved to town."*

When I returned to Ellegaard, Officer Flynn stood next to him. The fat cop said, "No one's fucking happy about this, especially the brass. So here's how it's gonna go. Our PR department is telling the press we've hired you, even though we're not giving you a fucking nickel. And you're going to go along with it or else we'll be giving the interviews and say you're more worried about stuffing your wallet than finding missing girls."

"That's fair," I said.

Terrence Flynn raised the yellow police tape and said, "That's bullshit is what it is." I ducked under. Ellegaard stayed where he was. "What," said Flynn, "the ex-cop too high and mighty to look at a dead girl?"

"Nothing like that, Officer," said Ellegaard. "Just no need for a crowd."

Terrence Flynn shook his head then walked me to the cave and handed me to another uniform. Officer Julia Mason had orange hair, freckles, a pug nose, and big gums that looked like the result of unfortunate genetics rather than poor dental hygiene—her teeth were new sneakers white. Her blue polyester cop pants shined at the hips and knees from wear. She led me into the crooked mouth. I wanted to say something about her taking me in because fat Flynn couldn't fit, but kept it to myself. The story of Ellegaard's strong-arm tactics had spread. I was less welcome at the scene than dead Haley Housh. I had to behave like a big boy if I wanted even a token attempt at cooperation from SPPD.

I slipped into the cave then stood. LED floods lit up the sandstone walls and ceiling. Graffiti was everywhere, not the artistic kind, but the kind akin to what's on the stall doors in a middle school bathroom. I learned "The Packers Suck!" and "Andy fucked Patti in the mouth!" and "Javier is a fag!" The proliferation of exclamation points . . . They just don't have the impact they used to.

Artists had carved into the soft sandstone walls creating images of penises, flaccid and erect, dripping with something penises should or shouldn't drip with. The floor was made of sand and was littered with beer cans, schnapps bottles, fast-food wrappers, spent hypodermic syringes, an overturned shopping cart, underwear, and used condoms.

I live in one of the most beautiful urban environments in the world, seemingly because every bit of its literal and metaphorical ugliness had been swept into that cave.

A dozen crime scene investigators took molds of footprints, sifted sand for genetic material, and collected trash in labeled plastic bags. It was a futile effort. The cave had collected centuries of human DNA. Even if a suspect was identified and his or her DNA was found in that cave, if it wasn't in one of Haley Housh's body cavities, its proximity would be circumstantial.

Haley Housh lay on her side in the sand near the cave wall, a wet mush inches from her head, a phone near her hips. She had long, dark hair and gray skin and wore a black-and-gold Warroad Warriors letter jacket, a scarf and mittens.

The Ramsey County medical examiner knelt over her body. The M.E.'s name was Char Northagen. She stood six two and was prettier than autumn. Fifteen years ago, she was a torn ACL away from making the U.S. Olympic volleyball team. Now, to every straight male cop's dismay, she played for another team.

"Is the kid's phone dead?" I said to Big Gums.

"I wouldn't know," she said.

"Mind if I ask?"

"Apparently, Mr. Shapiro, you can do whatever you want."

"Nils," I said, extending my hand to her.

"Whatever." She walked away.

I stepped to the edge of the tarp and watched a forensics person of Hmong descent sweep the cave floor with a metal detector. He wore headphones and a jumpsuit and looked like the Mine Sweeper Green Army Man of my youth. He passed by without taking his eyes off the cave floor.

No one paid any attention to me, so I followed a taped-off path to Char and dead Haley Housh.

"Nils Shapiro," she said without taking her eyes off her work. "You probably didn't even have to duck to get into this cave."

"With a tongue that sharp, I'm surprised the ladies let you go down on them."

She stopped and looked up at me. Haley's body temperature must have lowered a full degree before Char smiled. "That was good. That was very good. Except I don't have a sharp tongue. I have a quick tongue."

"I stand corrected."

She refocused her attention on the dead body. "Heard you're working for the Engstroms."

"Small cave. Word gets around fast. Any idea what that one was doing in here?"

"Not yet, but she died between 1:00 and 2:00 A.M. That right there is vomit. Don't step in it."

"Good advice."

"I try. No evidence yet of foul play. Rapists don't redress their victims down to the hats, scarf, and mittens."

"Carbon monoxide?"

"That's my guess. I'll know for sure when I run toxicology."

Haley Housh probably didn't know most of the St. Paul caves were connected to others. A fire burned for warmth and light in a nearby cave. The air in her cave grew poisonous, but all she felt was sleepy. A couple dozen people die of carbon monoxide poisoning every Minnesota winter. Five hundred are hospitalized. A faulty furnace. A clogged chimney. Lighting charcoal briquettes inside the home. I'd seen my share of it in my early investigator days when I tracked down prostitutes and drug dealers for even less respectable clients.

Haley wore a boy's letter jacket with a hockey emblem on one sleeve. The name embroidered into the jacket was GRAHAM.

I crawled out of the cave. Ellegaard waited for me outside the police tape. I told him all signs pointed to CO poisoning.

He said, "Any sign of Linnea Engstrom?"

"Not yet."

"Do you think she was in there?"

"I have no idea. But I know who we need to talk to

next. By the way, we're working pro bono for the Houshes."

I heard it before I felt it. At least that's what I remember. I don't know if the horror on Ellegaard's face was in reaction to "pro bono" or because he saw the arrow lodge into my shoulder.

4

Arrows and bullets kill in different ways. Bullets mushroom on impact with such velocity they penetrate the body to crush bone, muscle, and organs. Arrowheads, at least broad-head arrowheads, kill by slicing through blood vessels. This causes an animal or private investigator to bleed out in minutes. And that's exactly what would have happened if Char Northagen hadn't just crawled out of the cave for fresh air.

Ellegaard yelled, "Shap!" Char looked toward us, saw the arrow's bright red shaft and yellow fletching, then ran to her van.

I was down half a quart when she sat me on the ground and opened her medical bag. She'd brought Big Gums to assist. I couldn't see what the redhead was doing but I heard the pop and hiss of a gas torch being lit. Then Char said, "Give him something to bite down on." Char stripped the fletching off the arrow then swabbed the shaft with rubbing alcohol. Ellegaard rolled up one of his leather gloves and stuck it in my mouth. "With almost any other puncture wound we'd leave the object in. But you're too sliced up inside. We have to remove the arrowhead then try to stop the bleeding. The arrow can't come backward, so it has to go forward, hopefully north of your subscapular artery. Shut your eyes."

I did not shut my eyes. I looked into Char's and focused on a speck of gold in her right iris, a tiny aberration that floated like a prospector's find in a blue mountain lake.

"Do you want me to knock him out?" said Ellegaard.

"No time," said Char. "Ellegaard, brace his back." Then Char Northagen pushed the arrow forward. Pain is like depression, when you feel it you know you're alive. It may not be good that you're alive, but you definitely know you are. Ellegaard moved aside as Char stepped behind me and pulled. I shut my eyes as I felt the arrow's shaft slip through, the alcohol stinging my flesh as it passed. Then Big Gums went to work.

There's nothing like the smell of your own burning flesh to make you faint, but I did not. I opened my eyes and saw Big Gums pushing a straightened, red-hot metal coat hanger into my shoulder. I think she liked it. Ellegaard tried to joke that I smelled delicious but needed a few more minutes until I was done. I wanted to laugh but couldn't. I looked at Ellegaard for the first time since Char arrived. I saw fear.

An ambulance appeared, and soon after, morphine warmed my veins. It still hurt like fuck but I didn't care. The morphine submerged me in amniotic fluid. I floated, cushioned and buoyant. Noise grew faint and distant. I remember conversations, or maybe they were just dreams. Paramedics lifting me into the ambulance. Ellegaard riding in back with me. Hours of hazy images, but St. Joseph's is only a mile away from the cave, so it must have been minutes.

I awoke from surgery shivering. A nurse put another blanket on me, and my world went dark again. The next time I woke I was in a hospital room aglow in lamplight. The harsh overhead fluorescents were off. No one noticed when I first opened my eyes. I saw flowers and Mylar balloons and heard hushed voices. I shut my eyes and listened.

Ellegaard spoke with Micaela, my ex-wife. I hadn't had any contact with Micaela for over a year. It's not that we didn't get a long—we did, a little too well. After divorcing we agreed to joint custody of whiskey and sex and emotional support. Somehow, all that wasn't enough to make the marriage work, but it was more than enough to make a friendship work, a friendship that anchored me from going anywhere else. Last spring, I cut Micaela out of my life in hopes of getting over her. It didn't work. I tried to hide the failure from my current girlfriend, Lauren, whom I heard talking to a nurse about my prognosis.

Everyone dreads running into an ex with their current partner. It's awkward for all parties. Most people smile their way through it. Others pretend they're unconscious despite a room full of people waiting for them to wake up.

I opened my eyes a second time and saw a vase filled not with flowers but with a stunning arrangement of arrows. I knew then I was going to make it. You don't send a bouquet of arrows to someone who was shot by an arrow unless you're certain they're going to live. That's what makes it funny. I guessed they were from St. Paul PD. But they could have been from Minneapolis PD, too. Some of the older Minneapolis cops still held a grudge against Ellegaard and me for never rejoining the force after getting laid off. In our defense, the mayor laid off all the new hires in a political display of cost cutting. They said it was a formality, that we'd be rehired right after the election. But Ellegaard and I decided not to wait around. He went to work for Edina PD. I went to work for myself. Seventeen years later, we were back together again.

I must have glanced at the vase of arrows too long because Lauren said, "He's awake." Then she, Ellegaard, and Micaela gathered around my bed. Micaela took my hand.

"Welcome back," she said. I hadn't seen her in a year. Her strawberry blond hair still frizzed well past her shoulders. Her pale skin looked like it hadn't seen the sun since September. Her annual spring trip to Aruba or St. Barth must have been a week or two away. The lamplight was her doing. She knew I hate fluorescents and probably sent an underling lamp shopping on my behalf. "How you doin'?" she said with a half-smile. Her round, gray eyes shined.

"Well, you know," I said, "I got shish kebabbed." My mouth felt like dryer lint. Lauren poured me a glass of water. "What time is it?"

"It's 7:30," said Ellegaard. "At night."

"Fuck. I lost most of a day."

"Don't worry about it, buddy."

"How's the pain?" said Lauren. She was an oncology nurse, but this was the first time I'd benefitted from her bedside manner. Long dark hair, olive skin, and emerald eyes. She'd lost weight since we met. Men turned their heads. It ignited nothing in me. I wish it did. I wish I loved her like that. But I didn't.

"The pain hurts," I said. "But that would be weird if it didn't, right?"

"I suppose it would," she said. She took my free hand. "You'll have to wear a sling for a while. Your left arm won't be much use."

Not what a left-handed guy wants to hear.

The remainder of Stone Arch Investigations entered. Ellegaard introduced Leah Stanley and Annika Brydolf to Micaela.

Leah Stanley's a twenty-three-year-old African American who grew up in North Minneapolis and graduated from Macalester College with a degree in cognitive science. I'm still not sure what the hell that is. Ellegaard and I knew her dad, a retired Minneapolis cop who helped train us when we were cadets. He sent his daughter to us out of respect or revenge. We hired her for one year so she could pad her résumé and bank account before going to law school.

Leah's short with medium dark skin, curves, golden eyes, and a teased-out Afro. She wears big earrings and skirts and button-down oxford shirts under sweater vests in the winter and without sweater vests in the summer. Ellegaard takes a mentor tone with her, and I belittle her for wanting to waste her life as a lawyer. She responds to both of us with indifference because she thinks she's smarter than us and she's right.

Leah said, "You look worse than usual."

"If I'd known you were coming, I would've made myself pretty."

"You just keep believing anything's possible." She did not smile.

"I think you look great, Nils." Annika Brydolf is a thirty-five-year-old single mother who always wanted to be a cop but circumstances intervened. She's my height with long, black hair, white skin, and glacier blue eyes that won't look at you very long. She's thin and wears silky shirts and bell-bottom jeans that go all the way to the ground over wedged shoes, which is a bit white trash, walks her around at five eleven, and makes her attractive the way you think girls are attractive when you're thirteen.

Her right eye droops at the outside corner from nerve damage courtesy of her ex-husband's fist. She limped into our office days after we'd opened because the police didn't have the manpower to enforce the restraining order on her ex-husband. We did a little digging and learned he was into a few things that could send him to jail. He just needed a little nudge, and we were happy to give it. Annika couldn't afford to pay us, so we cut a deal with her to work undercover on another case.

Despite her adolescent sense of fashion, Annika Brydolf is a beautiful woman. When you first meet her, you notice her droopy eye, which makes her beauty less intimidating and gives stupid men the idea they have a chance with her. So we sent her into a bar to distract one particularly stupid man while we wired his home with surveillance equipment to prove he was stealing trade secrets from his employer. She handled herself and the stupid man well, is good with a camera, and available to work stakeouts during school hours. So we gave her another case and then another then made her our full-time investigator-in-training. Another five thousand hours on the job, and the State of Minnesota might grant her a license.

Annika said, "How's the food in here? Want us to get you a pizza?" She touched my cheek like a mother checking her kid's temperature.

Leah said, "Yeah. Whatever you need. We'll get it. No need to get up and show us your ass hanging out the back of that gown."

I said, "Whatever they're dripping into me, tell them to increase the dose now that Leah's here."

Leah finally smiled.

Lauren said, "The drip contains antibiotics and Oxy-Contin. So far you don't have an infection. They'll keep a close eye on you the next few days to make sure."

"No, they won't. I got to go." I hadn't intended to say it out loud, but I did.

"Not happening, buddy," said Ellegaard.

"Nils," said Annika, "you're staying put."

They all looked at me as if I were a dog on a chain. Sure, I didn't like it, but at least I wouldn't run into the street and get myself run over. "Do you mind giving me a moment alone with Ellie. My partner and I need to talk."

Lauren said, "Talk as long as you want. You have days."

Micaela leaned over and kissed me on the forehead. Lauren kissed me on the lips. Then Annika kissed me on the forehead. Leah slugged me on my right shoulder. The nurse entered. "Welcome back, Mr. Shapiro. I just want to—" Lauren stopped her with a look. The nurse turned around and exited with Lauren, Micaela, Annika, and Leah.

Ellegaard said, "The police will find who did this to you."

"I'm their favorite. They're probably going house to house right now, combing the city for someone who looks like Robin Hood."

"Well if they don't, we will."

"Let's go."

"I'm not letting you out of here," said Ellegaard.

"One teenage girl is dead. Another is missing."

"The police will find her. Or they won't. But you're staying here."

"The jacket said *Graham*."

"What?"

"Haley Housh died wearing the letter jacket of a War-road player."

"So what? It was her boyfriend's."

"No, it wasn't. Haley was dating a guy named Ben Haas from Woodbury."

"Big deal, Shap. Guys let girls wear their letter jackets all the time. Especially on game day. Besides, the police know about it. They're—"

"Don't make me explain it, E. Don't—" Fatigue pushed me hard into the bed. "I don't have the energy to fight you on this. Just let me win."

"The letter jacket did it to you?"

I nodded. Ellegaard had witnessed it enough times to know he couldn't ignore it. It has nothing to do with psychic ability. I think of it more as the total sum of my thoughts and experiences being thrown into a massive equation that some part of my being comprehends but my mind can't yet process. So I only get the feeling, not the knowledge. It's like in baseball when the batter makes contact with the ball, the outfielder takes off running to the spot the ball will land. How, in that instant, does the outfielder know exactly where to go? I have no fucking idea. It's not a conscious process. The math gets calculated someplace else.

Ellegaard stared at me for a while then said, "I suppose I could say we're worried about a hospital-borne infection."

"That's good. I like that."

"Only if Lauren moves in for a week or two to redress your shoulder and keep an eye on you."

"I don't think that's a good idea."

"Oh, Shap," he said. "Really? I like her."

"So do I."

"Then why?"

Char Northagen entered without knocking. She wore jeans and a navy Patagonia shell over a lavender cable-knit sweater. She carried an opalescent gift bag tied at the top with curled ribbons of green and gold. "Hey, guys. Hope I'm not interrupting you two declaring your love or anything."

Even Ellegaard, the overgrown Boy Scout, the dedicated husband and father of three girls, stared a little too long at the statuesque queen of the morgue. "Uh, no," he said. "Nothing like that."

"I brought you a present, Nils." She handed me the gift bag.

"About time," I said. "Did you think I was going to let you off with just saving my life?"

"My intention wasn't to save your life. That was a good arrow. I wanted it."

I tried to untie the ribbon with my right hand. I failed. Char took the bag from me, untied the ribbon, opened the bag, and handed it back to me. I stuck my right hand in and removed a block of resin. An arrowhead floated inside the clear plastic. It looked like a surgical instrument made of two, crossed stainless steel razor blades that converged at a lethal point. A half-inch of threaded rod was opposite the point so the arrowhead could screw into a shaft. The signature of Ed Ashby was engraved onto the edge near the bevel.

Ellegaard said, "Holy Mother."

"Who the hell is Ed Ashby?" I said.

"Ed Ashby designed the arrowhead," said Char. "His signature is on all of them."

"But this is the one that sliced through my shoulder."

"The one that sliced through your shoulder is being

held for evidence. This is just like that one. From my own personal stock. And be impressed. It's called a Grizzly-Stik. It's 440c stainless steel with a straight edge, much better penetration than a convex edge. It's razor sharp right out of the box. Whoever shot you wasn't screwing around. These arrowheads run a hundred thirty-five bucks a pop."

"What?" said Ellegaard.

"They're designed for big game. Moose and polar bears. Even elephants. You're lucky it hit you where it did, Shap. And that you don't have much muscle to slice through."

"What's with the cheap shots, Northagen? What did I ever do to you?"

She smiled. "I find it ironic, to tell you the truth. The quality of the arrowhead may have been what spared you. Because you're so slight, I only had to push a quarter inch for it to exit out your back. The thing's designed for big game. What are you, five seven, a buck fifty?"

"I'm five nine. One sixty-five."

"In heels and a parka maybe."

"So, Char," said Ellegaard, "was it your idea to send the bouquet?"

"I'm a county medical examiner, not a heart surgeon. I can't afford to part with an arrowhead like this and send flowers."

"I'm not talking about flowers," said Ellegaard. "I'm talking about those." He pointed to the arrows in the vase. The shafts stood, fletching end up.

"No," said Char, "I didn't send those. Who are they from?"

"I assume the police. I don't know. They were delivered right before Shap woke up." Ellegaard pulled the card from the bouquet. "The envelope says *To Nils Shapiro from your favorite men in uniform.*"

"Minneapolis or St. Paul?" I said.

Ellegaard opened the envelope and pulled out the card. He looked confused.

"What is it, E?"

He read, "*Even good shots miss sometimes. The next one won't. Compliments of the Warroad Warriors.*"

Char Northagen pulled two purple latex gloves from a wall-mounted box and snapped them on with the ho-hum perfection of a medical examiner. She lifted the arrows from the vase then turned them over to get a look at the arrowheads. They were all tipped with GrizzlyStiks, just like the one she pushed out my back.

"Man," said Ellegaard.

"An even dozen?" I said.

Char counted. "Eleven. One's missing."

"Gee, I wonder where it is."

"This is an expensive message," said Char. "Almost fifteen hundred dollars if my math is right."

Her math was right.

5

Around 9:00 P.M. an orderly wheeled me out of the hospital. Ellegaard helped me to my feet, and I stood near the curb. My shoulder had stitches in front where the arrow entered, stitches in back where it exited, and whatever was in between had either been cauterized or sewn together with what felt like razor wire. Pain shot through the upper left side of my torso every time I blinked. The Oxy had worn off. I refused more—I needed to keep my head clear.

I scanned the parking lot like a deer stepping into a meadow. Whoever stuck me could try again. Ellegaard became my Secret Service agent, pacing in front of me, his eyes like mine, panning the perimeter. Apparently, someone didn't want us investigating Haley Housh's death or looking for Linnea Engstrom. Or both. SPPD had called Ellegaard to ask if either of us had seen anything prior to the arrow. We hadn't. Ellegaard said the only thing he'd seen was a hostile attitude from the St. Paul Police.

Lauren pulled my new Volvo in front, got out of the car, and opened the passenger door. "This isn't right, Nils. You should stay in the hospital for at least five days."

Micaela approached with a St. Joseph's Hospital tote filled with white wound dressing, antibiotics, and pain medication, as if I were on my way to run with the bulls. "Lauren's right, Nils. This is ridiculous."

"I know," I said. "Ellegaard should drive."

Lauren said, "Forget it, Nils. You're not working tonight."

"We just have one quick stop a few blocks from here. Then I'll go straight home to bed."

My ex-wife and current girlfriend couldn't win if they played by my rules, so they invented their own. Micaela turned to Lauren and said, "Are you okay staying with him for a few nights?"

"Of course," said Lauren.

"I'm happy to drop in on him once or twice during the day," said Micaela.

"That would be great. I usually work from 6:00 A.M. to 3:00 P.M."

"Perfect," said Micaela. "Let's exchange numbers."

Micaela and Lauren exchanged numbers. Ellegaard saw my misery and did his best not to laugh, but his best wasn't good enough. For most people who get shot by an arrow, the worst part is getting shot by an arrow. But for me, the worst part was watching Micaela and Lauren team up to oversee my recovery.

I let them finish and told Lauren I'd be home before 11:00. Ellegaard said it'd be closer to 10:00. He was wrong, but I didn't correct him.

The Warroad Hockey Team was staying at the Wabasha Riverfront Hotel. It sits near the corner of Kellogg and Wabasha, two blocks from the Saint Paul Hotel where, earlier that day, Roger and Anne Engstrom hired me to find their missing daughter. The building faces the Mississippi River and the north end of the Wabasha Street Bridge. The south end of Wabasha Street Bridge is a minute's walk to dead Haley Housh's cave.

High school hockey fans crowded the lobby on their way to and from restaurants and bars. I scanned the faces for Linnea Engstrom. Maybe she wasn't really missing but just switched allegiances and was running with another team, disguised as a Minnetonka Skipper or Duluth East Greyhound. No luck.

Ellegaard and I approached the front desk. A young woman with a lifetime membership to an all-you-can-tan salon stood behind the desk mustering as much authority as her hospitality services degree would permit. She wore an ill-fitting black blazer and white shirt. A name tag pinned onto her lapel through presewn holes read: JILL—GUEST RELATIONS SPECIALIST. Jill greeted us with a smile I knew wouldn't last long. I had told Ellegaard to follow my lead. Carrying a badge gives a detective authority and access. Ellegaard was still learning how to replace his badge, although he'd done a damn good job with Officer Flynn outside the cave.

"Good evening," said Jill. "Checking in?"

"No," I said. She glanced at the sling holding my left arm to my chest. I had ditched my jacket in the car in the hopes of getting just that look. You use what you can. "We're here to see Gary Kozjek."

"Is he expecting you?"

"No. We were hoping you could tell us what room he's in."

"I'm sorry," she said, maintaining her smile. "I'm not at liberty to give out guest room information."

"Huh. Well . . ." I paused. My entire left side felt like

it might fall off. "Can you please call up to the room and tell Coach Kozjek that Nils Shapiro and Anders Ellegaard are here to talk to him about Linnea Engstrom?"

Her smile vanished. She recognized the name Linnea Engstrom. The missing teen was all over the news and social media. "Are you police officers?"

A thick woman who also wore an ill-fitting Wabasha Riverfront Hotel blazer appeared behind the desk. Her name tag said: PATTY—MANAGER. She must have been eavesdropping from wherever hotel desk clerks lurk before they appear.

"Hello. I'm the manager. How can I help you?"

Jill said, "They'd like to see Coach Kozjek from Warroad." She whispered, "It's about the missing Engstrom girl."

The manager of the three-star hotel didn't have much practice exercising discretion. Its most important guests were high school hockey coaches like Gary Kozjek and lobbyists from the Red River Valley Sugarbeet Growers Association or the Minnesota Turkey Growers who were in town for business at the capitol.

"Can you call him?" said the manager. "Do you have his cell phone number?"

"No, we don't. Could you please call up to the room for us?"

"I'm sorry," said the manager. "Normally I would, but Mr. Kozjek has left strict instructions not to be disturbed."

I touched my sling with my right hand and said, "I know you're in a sensitive position, but I can approach anyone in this lobby wearing a Warroad jacket and tell them we need to discuss Linnea Engstrom's disappearance with Gary Kozjek. Warroad's a small town. Everyone knows him. They'll get him the message. That'll save you the trouble of telling Gary we'd like to see him, but then you'll be responsible for everyone in Warroad knowing his business."

"Your call," said Ellegaard.

Patty the Manager looked to her guest relations specialist, Jill. The latter shrugged. Life sure is complicated outside the tanning booth.

Then Patty said, "Nice try, guys. I'm not disturbing Coach Kozjek."

I looked at the ceiling and saw a shiny black half dome and hoped the camera inside wasn't high resolution. I said to Ellegaard, "Give them our business card."

Ellegaard held out business cards in each hand. A folded hundred dollar bill was on the face of each card. The manager and Jill looked at each other, then the manager said, "I'd hate for Coach Kozjek's privacy to be violated." Jill nodded in agreement then led us up to the fifteenth floor in a service elevator lined with padded blankets.

Ellegaard and I stepped out of the elevator and rounded the corner toward Gary Kozjek's room. He stood waiting in the open doorway with arms crossed, his back pressed against the doorjamb, a plastic toothpick in his mouth. He wore a Warroad Warriors black turtleneck, blue jeans, and flip-flops. He had close-cropped gray hair and an assortment of facial scars that shined in the corridor's fluorescent light. The most prominent scar was over his right eye, plastic-looking under the eyebrow. A close second traversed his chin. Both were courtesy of Kozjek playing nineteen years in the National Hockey League.

I had never met the man, though I knew him intimately as Kozy, the former Minnesota North Stars defenseman whose poster covered my childhood bedroom door, whose hockey card lived in the ID window of my cowboy wallet, and whose name echoed in my head when I skated in pickup games on the rink in Lions Park. I idolized the man, mostly, because he was small like me. A five-foot-eight player is an anomaly in the NHL but practically unheard of for a defenseman, who are normally the largest and most brutish players in an often brutish sport.

Kozy grew up in Warroad, and its favorite son had returned to coach high school kids to greatness. He was not a god but *the* god in Warroad, and had achieved all his dreams except two. He went pro in 1979, disqualifying himself from playing on the 1980 Olympic team that stunned the Soviet Union and went on to win the gold medal. And he had yet to coach Warroad to a Minnesota State High School Hockey Championship.

Gary "Kozy" Kozjek looked up at Ellegaard then straight ahead at me, moved the toothpick from one side of his mouth to the other, then exhaled contempt. He saw how old we were, a couple of Minnesota boys who no doubt idolized him. Yet we'd interrupted him from his game-planning. Or rest. Or something else he didn't want interrupted. Without saying a word, he lifted his back off the doorjamb and turned into his room. Ellegaard and I followed.

Kozy's suite had been retrofitted into a war room. Eight chairs surrounded a conference table. Forty-two-inch video monitors were mounted onto three rolling stands. Whiteboards lined the walls. At least I assumed they were whiteboards—sheets covered them—you never know if a maid or bellhop or private investigator is working for the other team.

Kozy sat at the head of the table and spoke without looking at either of us. "What do you guys want?"

Ellegaard slid him our card. Kozy pushed it back without looking at it. I said, "We'd like to talk to Luca Lüdorf and Graham Peters."

"Can't help you. Lights-out was twenty minutes ago. And both boys have talked plenty to St. Paul PD. Why don't you just ask the cops what they said?"

"We will," said Ellegaard. "But we're working for Roger and Anne Engstrom. It's in Linnea's best interest if we question the boys directly."

"Well," said Kozy, running his fingers over his scarred eyebrow, "we all hope Linnea turns up soon. But the Engstroms are not Warroad blood. And distracting Luca and Graham, after they've already talked long and hard to the police, that's not in the best interest of Warroad."

My first encounter with my childhood hero wasn't going as well as I'd hoped. "So what you're saying, Coach, is that winning tomorrow's game is more important to Warroad than finding Linnea Engstrom."

Kozjek removed the toothpick from his mouth. It was the expensive kind tipped with what looked like a tiny pipe cleaner. I don't know how many teeth in Gary Kozjek's mouth were real after his five-plus decades of hockey, but he seemed intent on keeping whatever was in there clean. "The people of Warroad make windows. That's what keeps the town alive. But when the economy dips, Americans quit building houses. That's not good for the window business. Things are getting better, but the great recessions hit Warroad hard. People lost their livelihoods. And some people lost a lot more than that. But if Warroad wins the state championship for the first time in over a decade, that'll help rebuild hometown pride. I don't expect you boys to understand that, you not being from small towns. No offense. You just don't look the type. Trust me, a new state championship banner will help us more than finding the Engstrom girl. Nothing against Linnea, but her parents are not a good addition to the town."

There it was again. First Mike and Connie Housh with "Warroad's been shit since the Engstroms moved to town," and now Gary Kozjek saying the Engstroms weren't a good addition to Warroad. I wondered how many more people from Warroad felt that way. I wondered if Anne Engstrom agreed. Maybe Linnea Engstrom did, too.

Ellegaard said, "Do you hunt, Gary?"

"What kind of question is that?"

"A simple one. Do you hunt?"

"Of course I do. Why?"

"Deer? Pheasant? Waterfowl?"

"All of them."

"What's your deer gun?"

"What's that got to do with anything?"

"You hunt bow season?"

"Yeah. So what? Rifle season conflicts with hockey season."

"Did you bring your bow down to the cities?"

"What the fuck is this? I didn't do anything. You fuckers got a lot of nerve. You're not even cops."

Something about Gary Kozjek rubbed Ellegaard the wrong way. Maybe it was Kozy's cavalier attitude about a missing teenage girl. Maybe it was something more than that. "Put us in a room with Luca and Graham right now, or I'm going to the St. Paul police and tell them we suspect you of shooting Nils Shapiro with an arrow."

"What?!" said Kozy. "Who the fuck is Nils Shapiro?"

"I am," I said and glanced at my sling.

Kozy looked at Ellegaard. "And you suspect me of shooting him with an arrow? Are you out of your fucking mind?"

I looked at Ellegaard. He wasn't out of his fucking mind. He had simply found a substitute for his badge. "We'll have your boys back in bed by 10:00," he said. "It's either that, or their coach spends the night being questioned at police headquarters. I don't imagine that'll help the Warroad Warriors hang another banner above the red line."

Kozjek rubbed his forehead. Then, for the first time since I entered his suite, he looked at me. "Someone shot you with an arrow, huh? Can't imagine why."

That hurt my feelings.

6

Luca Lüdorf and Graham Peters traipsed into Kozy's suite wearing black Warroad hoodies and gold sweatpants. Both boys grew up in Warroad. Both played hockey. Graham stood six foot four, Luca six foot two. Both were eighteen, so no need for parents to be present. That's where the similarities between Luca and Graham ended. We shook hands and lied about how nice it was to meet one another, then Graham, Luca, Kozjek, Ellegaard, and I sat at the table.

"You got ten minutes," said Kozy.

I said "Thanks, Coach," then turned to the boys. "Hope we didn't wake you guys up."

"Seriously?" said Graham. He smiled, exhaled a "puh" and leaned back in his chair, his long black hair falling past his shoulders. Graham had hockey hair. Hockey hair varies in style from year to year, but its defining characteristic is it's too long in the back or too short in the front, depending on how you look at it. Some years hockey hair means a full-blown mullet, other years the front/back disharmony is less pronounced. But less pronounced doesn't mean subtle. Hockey hair is hockey hair—it doesn't take an expert to know it when you see it.

"So lights-out doesn't mean lights-out?" said Ellegaard.

"Nah," said Graham. "Most guys listen to music or screw around on their iPad." He scratched his beard—it was full and teased out Appalachian style. Graham added something about them not being babies and they couldn't be put to bed, but I kept my eyes on Luca.

Luca Lüdorf had blond hair, straight but coarse and a clean-shaven face. His hockey hair was less severe than Graham's. Its most hockeyish feature was it spread out like a dove's tail in back. Graham could pass for twenty-five, but Luca looked like an overgrown twelve-year-old, his lithe body just a stick to hold up his round, soft face. Luca looked down at the table and squirmed in his seat. I thought he might throw up.

I turned my body toward Luca. A wave of pain pierced my shoulder. I gasped, and my eyes teared over.

Kozjek said, "Play with pain, pal. Or go home."

I winced a smile at him, then said, "So guys, I know you've been over this with the police, but where were you after the game last night?"

"Team came back to the hotel for dinner," said Graham. "Wanted to go out, but Coach has a super strict tournament policy, right, Coach?" Kozy nodded. "Here we are in the big city, but gotta keep it tight 'til we win the championship."

Ellegaard said, "You were at the dinner, too, Luca?"

Luca nodded. And what I initially assumed was nausea now appeared to be sorrow.

"Talk to the gentlemen, Luca," said Kozy.

"Yeah," said Luca. His voice shook. "I was at the dinner."

"And what about after dinner?" I said. "Do both of you have alibis through the night?"

"Whole team watched film on Wayzata," said Kozy. "We play them tomorrow. The boys got a bunch of alibis for that. Then everyone retired to their rooms. Graham and Luca room together. They're each other's alibis. At least from about 11:00 P.M. to 7:00 A.M."

"Really," I said. "Either of you two wake up during the night?"

"I didn't," said Graham. "And, dude, the police asked us all this. They swabbed our cheeks and kicked us out of our room and took our sheets and towels and a bar of soap from the bathroom. They even took the fucking garbage from the garbage can." He turned to Kozy. "Sorry for swearing, Coach."

Kozy nodded, accepting Graham's apology.

"What about you, Luca?" said Ellegaard. "Did you sleep through the night?"

"Uh-huh."

"Really?" I said. "No one got up to pee? Check their email? Texts? Facebook? Snapchat? Jerk off? Hey, I remember eighteen. Volume management is a constant job."

"Keep it clean, Shap," said Kozy.

"What?"

"You heard me. Keep it clean."

I looked at Ellegaard, but his eyes were on Luca. "Sorry, Coach." I waited for Kozy to accept my apology just like he had Graham's. But the acceptance didn't come. Some hero. I'd have to find a new one. "So, Graham, why was Haley Housh wearing your letter jacket?"

"Oh, man," said Graham, as if I'd just asked him to mow the lawn, "because she asked if she could wear it."

"When?"

"Last week before we came down here. It's a thing, okay? Girls ask to wear guys' letter jackets."

"Who's wearing your letter jacket, Luca?"

"Linnea," he said into the table.

"Graham, what was the nature of your relationship with Haley?"

"Oh, dude. Why you gotta ask me this? Ask the police. I told them. I don't want to repeat it." Graham looked to his coach. Kozy gave him a nod to continue. "All right. We had sex, okay? Since we were fifteen."

Ellegaard said, "I thought Haley was dating a kid named Ben Haas from Woodbury."

"She was. Relationships didn't get in the way of our thing. We had an FDR."

"What's an FDR?" said Ellegaard.

"Full disclosure relationship. We can, you know, have sex with each other, but also see other people and talk about those relationships. Everything's out in the open. Full disclosure."

"Does it work both ways?" I said. "Did Haley fully disclose her relationship with you to Ben Haas?"

"I doubt it, because Haley didn't have an FDR with Ben. She had one with me."

"Why can't someone have more than one FDR?"

Luca pounded his fist on the table. His voice shook. "Can we stop talking about Haley?! Nothing we can do will help Haley! You need to find Linnea! That's why you're here, isn't it?"

Graham got small, or at least feigned it, as if the coach had just yelled at the team after skating a terrible period.

"Luca," I said. He stared at the table. "Luca," I said

louder. He looked at me. His eyes were wet. "I know this isn't a new question, but do you have any idea where Linnea could be?" He shook his head. "Just take a second and think about it. No pressure. We're not the police." The boy with straight blond hair seemed to relax. "Did she ever mention friends in the Cities, people she knew before she moved up to Warroad and maybe kept in touch with?" Luca shook his head again. "Did she ever mention doing anything that wasn't hockey tournament related? Going to a favorite restaurant or mall or park? Anything?" Again Luca shook his head.

Then the tears came hard. Luca tried to hold them in. His failure angered him. "Why can't anyone find her?! What's wrong with the police? Don't they have cameras everywhere? Doesn't her cell phone leave a trail? Or credit cards? What the hell is wrong with everyone?!" Luca cried like the boy he appeared to be. He put his forearm on the table and rested his head on it. Kozy glanced at me. His face said, are you proud of yourself? Graham looked at the crap painting over the in-room refrigerator.

We listened to Luca sob, then Kozy said, "Two more minutes."

Ellegaard said, "When did you all first hear Haley and Linnea were missing?"

"I heard this morning," said Kozy. "A little after 7:00 A.M. I guess around 6:00, Roger woke up and noticed Linnea wasn't in their suite. He started making calls."

"Yeah," said Luca, wiping his eyes with the black sleeves of his hoodie. "Mr. Engstrom called me at 6:30. He thought Linnea might be with me."

"Mrs. Housh texted me about Haley last night," said Graham. "I told her I hadn't seen her and said she was probably with Ben Haas, but I didn't have his number. She didn't either and was pretty mad 'cause Haley wasn't answering her phone or responding to texts. Said something about Haley being in big trouble and sending her back to Warroad." Graham half smirked. "Guess, in a weird way, that's what she's going to do." Graham combed his beard with his fingers without a hint of sorrow in his eyes. It was all matter-of-fact to him. The only emotion he had shown was in reaction to Luca's outburst. And that wasn't exactly sadness. It was closer to embarrassment for his teammate and friend.

"You heard Luca," said Kozy. "Both boys were woken up early with this. It's time for them to get to bed."

"Almost done, Coach," I said. "Graham, I know you had an FDR with Haley, that you were seeing other people, but I got to tell you, you don't seem too upset she's dead."

Graham nodded. "Yeah," he said and nodded some more. "I can't fake it. Not in my DNA, you know? I'm not upset. I'll be honest with you—I never liked Haley Housh. I liked her body and I liked that she was willing to share it. But the rest of her I could have done without."

"Why's that?" said Ellegaard.

"She was a climber. Nothing in Warroad was ever good enough for her. That's why she slept with me—I'm a ticket out of there. Same reason she was sleeping with Ben Haas. His parents are rich. His mom's some BFD at 3M. And his dad's a bigwig architect. Dude's going to Stanford. Haley had him wrapped. Dude would have married her if she wanted him to, and I'm not just saying that. She told me they talked about it. Messed up, I know. But Haley knew the right time to ask for stuff, if you know what I mean."

"Do you mean in bed?" I said.

"Well, usually it's in the backseat of a car, but yeah," said Graham, like I was an idiot.

"Did you tell the police about Haley being a climber?" said Ellegaard.

"Nah. It never came up."

"What about you, Luca?" I said. "What is your relationship with Linnea like?"

Luca took a breath to calm himself and said, "I love her."

The poor kid. When love has its grip on you, you shouldn't make financial decisions, operate heavy machinery, or play contact sports. "Does she love you?"

Luca nodded and sniffled. Kozy pulled a Kleenex from a box on the table and handed it to him.

"Does she tell you that?" I said.

"Every day."

"Is the relationship sexual?"

Luca nodded.

Ellegaard handed Luca and Graham business cards and told them to call or text if anything else came to mind. The boys left with the same loping gaits they walked in with, Graham's big hockey hair just inches under the top of the doorframe. When they were gone, Kozy said, "That's it. No more questions for these guys 'til after the tournament."

"Thanks for tonight," I said. "One more thing: Did you or one of your assistant coaches check in on the boys last night?"

"What do you mean?"

"Does anyone check in to make sure the boys are in their rooms at midnight or whenever?"

"No. Why would we do that?"

"I remember going on class trips in junior high and high school. Sneaking out was always our main goal."

"This isn't a fucking trip," said Kozy. "It's a hockey tournament. It's *the* hockey tournament. These guys have been going to 'em since they were eight years old. Their goal isn't to sneak out. It's to skate their asses off and win. You know how many college and pro scouts are here? They're not going to jeopardize this team or their town or their futures to sneak out and fuck around."

I heard him loud and clear, but didn't feel like telling him.

Ellegaard said, "So what are Graham's and Luca's futures, do you think?"

"Come on, guys," said Kozy. "Do your homework. It's common knowledge. Both boys are playing college. I don't know for how long—either one could leave for the pros—but they'll both be skating Division I next year."

"Where are they going?" said Ellegaard.

"University of Minnesota and Harvard."

I said, "Luca Lüdorf got into Harvard?"

"Luca's skating for U of M. Graham's going to Harvard. He's off-the-charts smart—2350 on the SAT, 35 on the ACT."

Technically, that was on the charts, though I didn't feel much like mentioning it. But I had to make sure I understood him correctly. "Graham is going to Harvard? The big defenseman with the beard?"

"Yeah," said Kozy. "The big defenseman with the beard."

"But if Graham could play pro, shouldn't he play for a better college team, like U of M?"

"Harvard's one of the best teams in the country," said Kozy. "Better than Minnesota the past few years. And it's a perfect fit for Graham. The kid's got some serious brainpower, like nothing I've ever seen."

Of course it's like nothing you've ever seen, I thought. *You're a hockey player.*

"Now get the hell out of here," said Kozy. "I'm about to have a 911 in the shitter."

We said our good-byes without merriment. Ellegaard and I returned to the lobby then walked out into the night air. The temperature still hadn't fallen below freezing. The day's snowmelt had evaporated into an icy fog. A similar fog hung in the air last night, ideal conditions for a teenage girl or two to disappear.

It was eerie quiet, but that's the way St. Paul sometimes is. Like there just aren't enough people to give the city a heartbeat. It's a facade, of course. St. Paul's heart beats in its tree-lined neighborhoods, in the granite foyers of its historic buildings, in the chests of its citizens who watch Minneapolis get most of the attention only because Minneapolis makes most of the noise. St. Paul moves forward with a quiet confidence, like the subdued kid in high school who has no need nor interest in sparkly, squealy bullshit.

"He called me Shap," I said.

"What?" said Ellegaard.

"Kozy. When I asked the guys if either of 'em jacked off last night, Kozy said, 'Keep it clean, Shap.'"

"So?"

"So you introduced me to Kozy as Nils Shapiro. Not Shap. You never once called me Shap in front of him. And yet he made a fairly big stink about not knowing who I was. Remember? You threatened to tell the police you suspected him of shooting Nils Shapiro with an arrow? And he said something like who the fuck is Nils Shapiro after we'd been sitting there for a while."

"But he called you Shap," said Ellegaard.

"Yeah. Gary Kozjek knew exactly who I was. So why did he pretend he didn't?"

7

I lowered myself into the Volvo, and the pain ripped through my shoulder as if it were making pulled pork. A sound came out of me I hadn't heard before. I sat breathless and glassy-eyed. The windshield and cars beyond refused to come into focus. The streetlights starred like quasars. I shut my eyes and felt a tear roll down my right cheek. I was a man experiencing pain like a boy.

"Let's get you home," said Ellegaard. "You can medicate for the night."

I wiped the tear with the sleeve of my jacket. "We need to see Ben Haas. I called in a favor. Got the address texted to me a few minutes ago."

"It's after 10:00, Shap. You should be in bed. Besides, it's too late. Ben Haas is a high school kid."

"Good. He won't be expecting us." Ellegaard started the Volvo but kept it in park. He was thinking hard when I said, "Linnea's been gone over twenty-four hours, and we have nothing. There's a hell of a lot more we should do right now than talk to Ben Haas. But after that we'll call it a night. I promise."

"Ben Haas dated Haley Housh. Our job is to find Linnea Engstrom."

"Two missing girls from Warroad can't be a coincidence."

"It can, Shap. It absolutely can. You know better than to base an investigation on an assumption. Let's go home and get some rest and tomorrow we'll talk to Linnea's friends and teachers while everyone's still in St. Paul for the tournament."

"You don't have to go, Ellie. I can Lyft from here."

Ellegaard looked at me. He'd lost and knew it. He put the car in gear and drove east on Warner Road paralleling the Mississippi, which for most of the river's two thousand-plus miles, runs north-south. But not in St. Paul. In St. Paul, the Mississippi runs south-north, then east-west, for a bit then returns to its journey toward the Gulf. It's all over the place.

A truck in the oncoming lane sent a wall of water into the Volvo's windshield. Ellegaard searched for the wiper controls, but the car's sensors took over and started the wipers for him. We drove through Indian Mounds Park. The fog hung in the trees and undulating swells, comfort for the Native Americans buried there, I'm sure.

Driving toward Ben Haas eased the pain. Pursuit is nature's anesthetic. It works wonders on skewered shoulders and roughed-up hearts. It slows racing minds and dulls unpleasant truths. Pursuit works like whiskey or electronic gadgets but without emptying your wallet.

Fifteen minutes later we arrived in Woodbury, Minnesota, St. Paul's farthest suburb, only thirteen miles from the Wisconsin border. Overbuilt homes sat on acre-plus lots landscaped to create the illusion Man has bested nature. As if saplings naturally grow out of concentric circles of white rock and boulders lie in perfect balance with one another. The production is set on land that grew corn and soybeans twenty years ago.

Ellegaard parked my Volvo on Crestmoor Bay, which is not a bay but a cul-de-sac where Ben Haas and his mother lived in a two-story behemoth sided with faux brick and boasting half a dozen columns of no structural value. The place reeked of new money, which displays worse than no money at all.

We walked up the driveway between a blue Toyota Highlander and a black Jaguar. I rang the bell at 10:32 P.M., three hours past Minnesota's polite time to pay an unannounced visit. Lights turned on behind the windows' sheer drapes. A security camera over the door panned to Ellegaard and me, then the amplified voice of a woman said, "Hello. May I help you?"

I didn't see where the voice came from so I spoke to the mammoth wooden door that was, most likely, not made of wood but fiberglass. "We're sorry to bother you so late. My name is Nils Shapiro. I'm with Anders Ellegaard. We're private detectives looking for Linnea Engstrom, a missing girl from Warroad. We'd like to speak to Ben Haas, please."

No response. We stared at the door. I felt Ellegaard's eyes and looked up at my partner, who stood a full head taller than me. He glanced down with eyebrows raised and lips pursed. He had told me so. I was about to concede defeat when the disembodied voice said, "Are you the Nils Shapiro?" Ellegaard's eyebrows fell in disappointment.

"I'm afraid so," I said. "And sorry it's so late."

The door swung open. "I understand. You have a job

to do." Winnie Haas wore flannel pajamas of baby blue and gray plaid. She'd tied her blond hair back in a ponytail, exposing the muddy roots. She looked older than me, maybe forty-five, and her face was clear and smooth. Her expression was neutral, as far from a smile as she could get without frowning. Another blue-eyed Minnesotan, though hers sparkled more than most. I thought maybe it was the halogen bulbs in the chandelier, the kind jewelry stores use to make their gems dance. I glanced at Ellegaard to see if his eyes were sparkling. They were not. Winnie's neck and chest looked more sun damaged than her face. But she made no attempt to cover either, the V in her pajama top open down near her sternum. Her large breasts hung near her body without support. Her round hips topped her long legs, though she wasn't tall. Like everything beautiful in this world, Winnie Haas was about understatement and proportion. I glanced at her left hand. Her ring finger was empty.

"Please come in," she said in a voice soft and raspy. She wasn't slurring her words, but they weren't clear, either. I began to wonder if the sparkle in her eyes had a little help.

"Thank you," said Ellegaard, handing her our card. She put it in her robe pocket without looking at it. "I know who Mr. Shapiro is. I read everything about Maggie Somerville's murder. I didn't know her, but a colleague of mine went to high school with her, so I followed the case. I read about you, Mr. Ellegaard, as well." She walked toward the staircase with a slight limp. Her left knee didn't bend so well, so she used her hip to swing the leg forward. "Ben's been talking to the police all day. He's quite upset. And exhausted. My ex is visiting him now, but I'll explain why you're here. I'm sure Ben will cooperate." Winnie Haas turned and ascended an open staircase. She used the railing to help lift herself up the stairs.

Ellegaard and I said nothing for a couple minutes, then Ben Haas came down the stairs with his father. Ben wore a pink button-down oxford, khaki pants, and navy Jack Purcell sneakers. He looked like he didn't need to shave more than once a month, and at five foot four, the high school senior probably still bought his clothes in the boys' department. "So more questions?" he said with a voice too deep for his tiny body. He pushed longish, sandy brown hair away from hazel eyes.

"It won't take long," said Ellegaard. "And it'll probably be a lot of what you've already answered."

"That's okay," said Ben. "Whatever helps."

"Do you want me to stay?" said his father.

"No, Dad. But thanks."

Ben's father stood no taller than his son. He had no hair on his shiny head and perfectly maintained stubble on his face. He wore round glasses made of cobalt-blue plastic, a black turtleneck, faded blue jeans, and butterscotch leather shoes that I assumed were European because no American I knew would wear them. I took a wild guess that the black Jaguar in the driveway was his. Raynard Haas stood out like Anne Engstrom stood out. On purpose. A short, bald man who wanted recognition for something other than being short and bald. But that's an unwinnable game, like trying to describe a person who happens to be Chinese without saying they're Chinese. It's just easier to say what everyone notices first. "You know, the Chinese guy." Or "You know, the redhead." Or "You know, the fat guy." With Ben's father it was, "You know, the short, bald guy."

The short, bald guy stuck out his hand. "Raynard Haas. Sorry to meet you under these circumstances." We shook hands and introduced ourselves. Raynard gave his son a hug and told him to call day or night, whatever he needed, then left.

We moved into the great room. Huge windows looked out on the backyard, but there was nothing to see at night. The ceiling hovered two stories over walls of paneled wood. It felt like country club decor, except a country club would have had a real fireplace. Almost twenty years had passed since Minnesota Building Code permitted building a home with a real fireplace. Now fires have to burn natural gas through fake logs behind sealed glass. The fires kick out plenty of heat but look like they're on TV.

Ellegaard and I sat on a caramel leather couch facing two chairs upholstered in red velvet. Winnie sat in the left, Ben in the right. After some small talk I said, "Ben, did you see Haley last night?"

"I was supposed to but she didn't show up."

"You planned to meet?"

"Yeah. We played The 7th Street Entry at 10:00. She wanted to come but you have to be twenty-one, you know?"

"But the people in the bands don't have to be twenty-one?"

"No. I mean, if they ever catch any of us drinking we'll never play there again. And they kick us out right after our set unless it's an eighteen-and-over show. It's a good gig, you know? It's music history in that place. We've been playing there since we were fifteen, and sometimes we get to play in the main room. Earlier this year we opened for Trampled by Turtles."

"What's the name of your band?"

"The Fiveskins," he said, emphasizing the five, like in the word *foreskins*.

"Really?" I said. "I have *The Last Temptation of Eric*. Great album. I knew you guys were young but didn't realize you're still in high school."

"Yeah," he said, matching the friendly but unflappable detachment of his mother. "That's our first record."

"So is all your stuff newgrass?"

"Yeah. That's what we do, you know?"

"I do." I first learned of The Fiveskins when the androgynous barista at Dunn Brothers, whose hair changes color more often than bruises, passed by my table and wrote the band's name on the napkin under my scone. The androgynous barista at Dunn Brothers makes no bad suggestions. The Fiveskins are good.

"So when and where were you supposed to meet Haley?" said Ellegaard.

"Mickey's Diner at 11:30. I was there on time. She never showed up."

"You always hang out that late on a school night?"

"No, not usually. We try to only play on weekends, you know, but when The Entry calls, we're there. It takes time to wind down after a show. Plus, Haley is—Haley was—in town. That didn't happen often on weekdays, you know?"

I liked the kid, but when he said *you know* it was hard to restrain myself from getting up and slapping him. "What do you mean 'on weekdays'? How often did Haley visit?"

Ben looked to Winnie. She nodded. He said, "A bunch of times."

"Did her parents know?"

"I don't think so."

"That's a six-hour drive. Each way. How did Haley manage to be away so long without her parents knowing?"

"I don't know," said Ben. "She'd drive down Friday night and go back Sunday. I asked Haley about it, you know, but she just said her parents are clueless."

"Whose car would she drive?"

"Hers. She had an old Rav4."

"And no one noticed her putting over seven hundred miles on the odometer in one weekend?"

"Guess not," said Ben. "It was her car. I don't know if anyone was paying attention."

"Where would she stay when she was down here?" said Ellegaard.

"Here," said Winnie. "Kids are going to do what they're going to do. I prefer that they're home safe." She offered a slight, self-congratulatory smile. I didn't hold it against her.

"So, Ben," I said, "was that the plan for last night? You and Haley were going to come here after Mickey's Diner?"

"For a little while, yeah. But Haley's parents are in town, so she had to get back to the hotel, you know?"

"Were you two sexually active?" said Ellegaard.

"Yeah."

"Exclusively?" I said.

"No. We had an FDR."

"What's that?" said Winnie, her forehead scrunched, but her eyes still sparkled.

"Full disclosure relationship," I said, as if I'd known for more than half an hour. "They sleep with other people, too. And fully disclose what they're doing."

Winnie looked at her son with something between disappointment and curiosity. "Apparently, my son doesn't tell me *everything*."

"Well," said Ben, "we lived three hundred and fifty miles apart. I'm going to California next year. She's not. There was no sense getting all tied up in something."

"How grown-up of you," said Winnie in a flat, unreadable tone.

Ellegaard said, "Ben, are you sleeping with someone else?"

"No. But I could. That's the idea."

"Whose idea was the FDR?" I said.

"Haley's. But I was all for it, you know?"

"You didn't love her?" said Ellegaard.

"Respect for the dead and all, but I didn't even like Haley all that much."

I told Ben we'd heard he and Haley had talked about marriage. Ben said that wasn't even close to true. Whoever said that was either lying or Haley had lied to them. Winnie listened and shook her head, her glassy eyes dancing with light.

Ellegaard said, "Why didn't you like her all that much?"

"She was more into the band than me. She mostly came down for the good gigs, the eighteen-and-over shows at The Entry or other clubs or private parties. She especially liked the private parties. Fraternities, mansions out on Lake Minnetonka, corporate Christmas parties. My dad's a pretty big architect. Sometimes we'd play for some of his rich clients."

I said, "Did he design this house?"

Winnie looked annoyed. "God, no. Raynard designs one-of-a-kind, *Architectural Digest*–type houses. Everything's custom built, even the furniture. He has to hold his nose just to enter this cookie-cutter McMansion, as he calls it."

Ben nodded. "He's remodeling a house for Graham Itasca up in Bemidji."

Ellegaard said, "*The* Graham Itasca? I thought he lives in L.A. now."

"I guess he spends half the year in Minnesota. He's got a recording studio and everything, you know? Huge house up north. I met Haley there for a party once. A bunch of famous musicians. Gold and platinum records on the wall. She was in heaven, you know? My dad was about to start an addition and remodel, so Graham let people draw on the walls and floors. It was crazy. Haley couldn't get enough of those kinds of parties. She didn't even try to pretend that she was interested in me. It was almost like we'd made a deal."

"Sex for access?" I said.

"I guess. Yeah."

"The sex must have been pretty good. Respect for the dead and all."

"I don't have a lot to compare it to, but yeah. I've talked to some friends about it. And to Mom. We have a pretty open relationship, right?"

"We do. Although, I did think you two had an exclusive relationship," said Winnie.

"Yeah," said Ben. "Sorry about that." He turned to Ellegaard and me. "Haley was different from the other girls I hear about. She'd just say 'what do you want tonight,' like I was ordering a burrito at Chipotle. It's not like she didn't enjoy it—she did. And she asked a lot of questions later. Did I like this? Did I like that? For Haley, the sex was definitely about the sex, not an emotional connection, you know?"

"How did you feel about that?" said Ellegaard.

"A little weird at first. But then I was okay with it. More than okay, actually. I was great with it. Experience, you know? Same reason Mom lets me have a beer or two when I'm home and not going back out. So I know what it's like. So when I go to college, I don't act like some idiot who just got released from prison."

"You're going away to college," I said. "Does that mean next fall's the end of The Fiveskins?"

"We don't know. They may replace me. They may play without a mando for a while and see how it goes."

"You don't want to be a rock star?"

"I don't know. Maybe. But right now I want to go to college."

There's a tradition of good boys in rock and roll. Paul McCartney, Jimmy Page, Dave Grohl. Nice kids with nice lives without a lot to rebel against. They just love the music. Ben Haas seemed to be one of those boys.

Ellegaard said, "What do you know about Haley and Linnea's relationship?"

"Haley never talked about Linnea. Ever. They knew each other. Warroad's a small town. But they weren't friends, you know?" Ben looked out the window again. "I met Linnea once at a party in Warroad last summer. That was it." Ben kept his eyes on the window, as if there was something to see out there.

Maybe Ben Haas wasn't such a good boy after all.

8

Ellegaard drove the Volvo into the loading dock. The old metal bay door had windows of frosted glass and chicken wire. He pushed the button above the rearview mirror. The door lifted, and Ellie drove us into the space I called home. He killed the engine, closed the dock door, then we got out of the car.

The former coat factory had thirty-foot ceilings and walls of yellow brick. City light filtered in through sections of glass block, each over an awning window that provided dry ventilation even in a downpour. The space was large and open, only the bedroom and bathroom had walls, and neither of those had ceilings. A long stainless steel countertop defined the kitchen. I'd salvaged it and the sink, refrigerator, and dishwasher from a failed restaurant on Nicollet. I mixed in furniture from my old place with Craigslist finds: worn and frayed Oriental rugs, mismatched lounge chairs, and a brown leather couch. A freestanding shelving unit filled with books created a wall between the sitting area and dining table.

And who says print is dead? The dining area had a table and chairs made of clear acrylic. I called it my Wonder Woman dining room.

I had lived there almost a year. A developer purchased the old factory with the intent of converting it into condos, but he'd hit a snag. I could have found out what that snag was but didn't. I was pretty sure it had something to do with money, asbestos, or lead paint. If I started nosing around, chances were I'd stir up something that got me kicked out, and I didn't want that. I loved my coat factory. How many people can drive right into their living room?

I climbed the four steps from the loading dock's cement floor to the worn wooden planks of the old factory floor and saw Lauren sitting up on the couch under a down throw, an open oncology journal on her lap. Her eyes begged for sleep. She offered neither smile nor word of welcome. She pushed off the throw, pivoted her feet onto the floor, and slid them into slippers that looked like bear's feet. She said, "Sit," then walked toward the kitchen, the plastic claws of her bear slippers clicking on the wood floor.

Lauren grabbed an infrared thermometer off the counter. "In a chair. Now. I'm not kidding." I sat on the couch and felt the warmth of her vigil. Ellegaard stood silent and unsure, the way a twelve-year-old watches his best friend suffer a parent's wrath. It's partly to support your buddy and partly to see the show and partly to feel grateful it's not you. Lauren sat down next to me and stuck the thermometer in my ear. A few seconds later it beeped— she read the display. "No fever," she said, her voice tired and angry. "You're fucking lucky, Nils." She stood up and turned away from me. I tried to remember if I said I'd be home by 10:00 or 11:00. I looked at my phone—11:33. But still. Her anger was in disproportion to the time. I hoped it was a nurse thing, but hope can be a shiny object to distract you from an unpleasant truth.

"Well," said Ellegaard. "I'd better get going. Glad to see Nils doesn't have a fever."

"This one's an idiot," said Lauren. "But you know better."

Ellegaard nodded, taking his scolding as I had. "I'll get a Lyft and talk to you tomorrow, Nils."

"No," said Lauren, "take Nils's car. He shouldn't go anywhere tomorrow other than back to the hospital. But if he does, you're driving him." Ellegaard looked at me for permission. My half smile gave it. He got in the Volvo, opened the garage door, and started the car. A wave of cold filled the space. With its thirty-foot ceiling and old single-paned windows and garage door opening to the elements, the place was as energy efficient as a paper box. Ellegaard backed out and drove off as the garage door returned to the ground. An eighty thousand BTU natural gas heater kicked in but did nothing to warm Lauren's demeanor.

"Take off your shirt," she said. "I have to change your dressing."

She went into the kitchen and returned with the bag of supplies Micaela had carried out of the hospital. I had put my jacket on my right arm en route to Woodbury and wore the left side like a cape over my sling. I hadn't taken it off since. I stood, held my right arm straight down and arched my back, hoping it would slip off my shoulder. It did not. Lauren sighed then proceeded to help. She stretched the elastic of my right cuff, then pulled the jacket off and held it up for me to see. The inside of the left shoulder was wet. "Goddammit, Nils." A clear, thick liquid had soaked through my shirt and the dressing underneath.

"Is that bad?" I said.

"Not if it's clear all the way down to the wound—it's your body healing itself. Despite the stupidity of its owner."

She unbuttoned my shirt down the front and at the wrists then removed it from my right shoulder and arm. With half the shirt off, Lauren focused on my left shoulder. She peeled the shirt away, as if trying to pull the label off a sweaty beer bottle in one piece. She separated my shirt from the dressing below. An odor reached my nostrils that I was in no hurry to smell again. She dropped the soaked shirt to the floor, opened a sealed plastic bag of scissors, and cut off the bandages.

"You may not want to look at this," she said.

I looked. The wound was buried under a gelatinous ooze that was clear to the skin. I could make out black stitches and burn marks from the hot coat hanger. Seeing the mess swirled my stomach. I focused on the open ceiling and let Lauren clean and redress the wound. When it was done she handed me a dull white pill shaped like a submarine, and a glass of water. "Take this."

"What is it?"

"Your antibiotic."

I washed down the pill.

"I picked up a carton of acidophilus. It's in the fridge. I'd drink some if I were you. And sleep with your shirt off. Give the wound as much air as possible." She packed up the supply bag and returned it to the kitchen. "I'm going to bed," she said. "You should take some Vicodin. I put the correct dosage on a paper towel near the sink. If you take it, no Irish. If you don't take it, drink all the Irish you want."

The bear claws clicked toward the bedroom. I let her

get halfway then said, "Where did you and Micaela go to dinner tonight?"

She stopped and looked back at me. "Who told you we went to dinner?"

"Your bedside manner."

The heater's flame hissed above. Headlights swept through the frosted glass bay door. "Bravo, Detective. Bravo." Lauren turned then continued into the bedroom and shut the door behind her.

I stood and felt the arrow return to my shoulder. I made it to the kitchen and poured myself a glass of acidophilus. I rejected the Vicodin on the counter and opened a bottle of fifteen-year-old single pot Redbreast.

A client had given me the bottle for tailing his wife for a month only to discover that all her excuses for being absent—triathlon training, extension courses at the U of M, volunteering at the Humane Society—were all true. I gave him a packet of photographs and time logs verifying her whereabouts. After reviewing them, he asked his wife why she chose to spend so much time out of the house.

She said she was disappointed in the man he turned out to be. She wasn't cheating on her husband. She simply wanted nothing to do with him. When he asked if she wanted a divorce, she said no. Their marriage had its function, and at fiftysomething years old, she didn't want another chance at love. If he wanted a divorce then fine, they'd get divorced. Otherwise, she was content doing what she was doing. The man was still in love with her, despite knowing the love would never be returned. So he kept her like I keep books, loving them but knowing I'll probably never open them again. He gave me the bottle of Redbreast as a departing gift with a note that said "When you need a warmth you can count on."

I quarter-filled a lowball and returned to the couch. I could have repaired the damage with Lauren. I could have gone into the bedroom and scooched up next to her. I could have told her I was sorry and that I loved her. I could have thanked her for taking care of me and putting up with me. But that would have just prolonged the breakup that was sure to come. We'd had a good first six months. But the last six we'd grown distant. Or maybe just I had.

I don't know what happened at dinner with Micaela, if Micaela said something or Lauren intuited it. Either way, Lauren walked out of that dinner realizing I wasn't all-in. I was capable of it, just not with her. So now I was the bad guy for fanning an ember that would never become a flame. The couch was the place for me. And I couldn't argue with that.

The whiskey warmed my body and calmed my head. After a day of looking for Linnea Engstrom, I knew little about her and a hell of a lot about Haley Housh. If my assumption was wrong, if Linnea's and Haley's disappearances were coincidental, then I'd wasted the crucial first day of the investigation. Linnea could have been anywhere, in a shallow grave in Swede Hollow Park or happily driving toward either coast.

This was a case for the police. They had the personnel to question everyone who knew Linnea both in Warroad, where she had lived the past five years, and in Minneapolis, where she had lived before that. The police had her cell phone records, her browser history, and would know the moment she used a credit or debit card and the exact location where it was used. St. Paul PD would gather all the puzzle pieces and put them together. They had smart people and less smart people, but it added up to a wealth of brainpower. And the police had incentive.

A missing seventeen-year-old girl. White and pretty and from Hockeytown USA. Along with Haley's death, it was a stain on the Minnesota State High School Hockey Tournament, the biggest event of the year in St. Paul. But the police were in a position to clean that stain. No sense sharing the glory with a private. I'd get no cooperation from my friends in blue.

Whoever launched the arrow into my shoulder was still out there. Maybe waiting for me to walk out my door. I could take precautions within reason. But I wasn't going to hide in my factory. If someone wanted to finish the job, sooner or later, they would. Another reason to walk away and let the police do their job.

I fell asleep knowing that wouldn't happen. I woke at 6:15 A.M. to a stiff, painful shoulder, full bladder, and a text on my phone.

Hello, Nils. It's Winnie Haas, Ben's mother. I would like to talk to you without Ben present. Please call me when you have time.

I went to the bathroom and saw the bedroom door was open. Lauren had left for work. There was a note on the stainless steel counter. "Take your temperature. Call me if you have a fever." No "Love, Lauren." No *x*'s or *o*'s. No smiley faces with puckered lips.

9

I made toast and two eggs sunny-side up because flipping them would've hurt. I spread butter and blueberry jam, ground salt and pepper, and dropped a purple capsule into the Nespresso machine. I ate standing up, put the plate in the sink, sat on the couch to finish my coffee and respond to texts. Then I fell back asleep until 8:00 when I woke to a pounding on the bay door.

I sat up and saw a figure standing on the other side of the frosted glass. The level of its head was above mine. The loading dock lay four feet lower than the factory floor, and I was sitting up on the couch. That put my visitor somewhere just shy of seven feet tall. Maybe it was Char Northagen in eight-inch heels, but I doubted it.

The figure pounded on the bay door again. I managed a dry-throated "Give me a minute" that had no chance of carrying outside. I walked over and lowered myself down the loading dock steps, leaning on the cold metal railing of chipped brown paint over safety yellow. I flipped the bolt on the service door and stuck my head outside and looked to the left.

"There you are," said a deep baritone from a black face under a mop of twisted curls and a fur-lined cap that had more flaps than an advent calendar. His cheeks puffed like dough left on the counter overnight and sandwiched his eyes under heavy lids. He had full lips over Crest Whitestrips–white teeth. Shaving bumps splattered his jaw and what I could see of his neck. He wore a Windex-blue jacket with narrow horizontal quilting, gray sweatpants, and chestnut man Uggs on his feet. "Oh, Micaela said you was cute and she wasn't foolin'! Sorry about all the poundin' but she said it's the only way to wake that boy up." He laughed. "Looks like she was right! You got sleepies in your eyes."

"What can I do for you?"

"You can let me in so I can do something for you." He patted a red canvas duffel that hung from his shoulder.

"You a doctor?"

"Nurse practitioner." He turned the bag toward me. It had the medical symbol with two snakes wrapped around a pole topped with wings. It had a big *N* for *Nurse* on the left side of the pole and a big *P* for *Practitioner* on the right. Some company full of Herman Miller chairs probably got six figures to conceive that logo. I wish someone had told me that was a job when I was eighteen and looking for a way to coast through the rest of my life. He patted the bag and said, "I got everything you need right here."

"Come on in."

The giant approached, handed me his card, and said, "That's for future needs. You call me anytime, day or night. I'm five minutes away." He removed a gray, fleece glove and extended his massive hand. I took it. It felt like a pillow with bones inside. "Jameson White. Pleased to meet you, Mr. Shapiro."

"I like anyone named Jameson," I said.

"Ha! I've heard that one before. And I like it. But I assure you, friend, I don't got a drop of Irish blood in me."

"That makes two of us."

"Then we already have something in common."

He walked inside. I was about to shut the door when I noticed a Latino kid on the sidewalk near the edge of my building. He sat on an overturned white plastic bucket with his back against the brick wall. Twenty at the oldest, wearing a Carhartt hooded jacket and jeans and yellow work boots. The hood was up and his hands were in his pockets. When I locked on his brown eyes, he looked away. No breath condensed in front of his hood. Another warm March day.

I went back inside and locked the service door behind me. Jameson White labored up the loading dock steps. "Pardon the creaky knees. Too many years on artificial turf." I tried to remember if there were any Minnesota Vikings named Jameson White but none came to mind.

He removed what must have been a size 5XL jacket, set it on the kitchen counter, and looked around. He wore a gray hooded sweatshirt that matched his sweatpants, the thick cotton kind that doesn't shrink and costs as much as cashmere. "You live in a factory. What do you make?"

"Trouble."

"How's it pay?"

"Not so good."

"Someone's got to do it though, right?" He laughed and sat me on the couch, kneeled on the floor, removed sanitary scissors from his bag, and began cutting at my bandages as if he were making a dress pattern.

"Who dressed this wound?"

"My girlfriend. She's a nurse at Park Nicollet."

"She did this just right. It's all about getting the blood moving under your skin and getting the air moving over it. Yes, sir. This is good. You hold on to that woman."

"I'll try," I said. Then I asked him how he knew Micaela. He said he didn't. She had called a doctor friend at Hennepin County Medical Center and asked who was the best trauma nurse in town. The doctor told her it was Jameson White.

"She asked me how much it would cost for me to take a two-week vacation and work full-time for you. I told her. She agreed, then put me up at the Loews Hotel a few blocks up on First Avenue and gave me a hundy a day for food. How rich is she?"

"Pretty fucking rich. And self-made. The tech industry."

"The goddamn tech industry. Wish I would've seen that comin'! I'd be rich, too!" He laughed then said, "You'd better write that Micaela a thank-you note. I am at your service twenty-four/seven for the next fourteen days." I couldn't see the expression on my face, but Jameson White got a kick out of it. "Oh, you got a stupid grin on your face, boy. She the girlfriend who dressed this wound?"

"No. She's my ex-wife."

"Oh no, that is precious. Precious! Oh, brother. She wants you to walk down that aisle with her again. That's what happened with my aunt Betty. Married the same man three times."

"How many times did she divorce him?"

"Two." He looked me in the eye then said, "Third

time? She shot him." Jameson White exploded with laughter so contagious I almost smiled. "I'm kidding! I'm kidding. I just couldn't resist!"

When he finished removing Lauren's dressing, he looked at the wound, front and back. "Huh," he said. "Never seen an arrow wound before. Probably 'cause I'm not a veterinarian."

I smiled.

"Oh, that one you like." He went to work cleaning and redressing the wound. "Who shot you?"

"No idea."

"What were you hunting?"

"I wasn't. I got shot in downtown St. Paul."

"Seriously?"

I nodded.

"Permission to speak freely."

"Granted."

"That's some fucked-up shit, brother. Fucked up. These times we live in. You can't fix 'em. The only decent and honest thing a man can do is make his way through the world not being part of the problem."

I tended to agree but didn't respond. I liked Jameson White. I didn't want to ruin that by getting into one of those sit-around-Starbucks conversations where the unemployed and out-of-the-know spew the answers to the world's problems despite having had to scrounge under their couch cushions for change to buy their caramel macchiato.

The big man finished dressing my wound, went over my medication schedule, packed his bag, and put on his coat. I asked if Micaela had given him my cell. He said she had, so I asked him to call me after he left and tell me if the Latino kid was still sitting on the sidewalk outside my building. He said he would and that he wanted to change my dressing three times a day. He'd come to wherever I was.

I thanked him and he left. A minute later he called and said the Latino kid was still sitting on the bucket. "Want me to make him leave?"

"No," I said. "You're a nurse practitioner, remember? You don't want to be part of the problem."

"That's right. I don't. Only trouble with being the good guy is it's kind of boring. Guess I'll just have to find my thrills elsewhere."

I hung up and texted a thank-you to Micaela. She didn't respond.

I put on a shirt and slipped my feet into a pair of Blundstones because I had one functional arm and they didn't have laces. I was thinking about moving the dirty dishes from the sink to the dishwasher when the loading dock door opened and my Volvo drove into the building. The engine died then the big door lowered as Ellegaard got out of the car. The passenger door opened and Anne Engstrom got out, a windshield over each eye and holding her sad excuse for a dog.

"Hope we didn't wake you," said Ellegaard as he led Anne Engstrom up the loading dock steps.

"Not at all. My new nurse just left."

The dog yipped. I considered my sink's industrial garbage disposal.

"We found her, Mr. Shapiro," said Anne. "We found Linnea."

10

Anne clutched the tiny dog and climbed up the loading dock stairs. She wore jeans rolled at the cuff over yellow Wellingtons and a 1970s ski sweater, black with a band of horizontal stripes in violet, royal, and powder blue. It was like she had a personal shopper who shopped only at garage sales. Between Anne Engstrom's clothes and giant glasses and severe bangs and the tiny creature she carried everywhere, the woman might as well have hired a spotlight to follow her around.

"The police called this morning," Anne said. "They asked us to come down to the station. Roger was at a business meeting. I tried to call him, but he didn't answer his cell. I was afraid the police might have terrible news. I didn't want to go alone, so I called your office. Anders offered to go with me."

"It was 6:30," said Ellegaard. "I wanted to let you sleep."

I said, "It sounds like the police didn't have terrible news."

Anne sat in the leather chair across from the sofa. "Linnea's in Madison, Wisconsin."

I wondered why Ellegaard drove Anne over to meet in person rather than picking up the phone, especially since he was so concerned about me getting enough sleep. This is real life, not a soap opera. People don't just drop by to have conversations they could have over the phone. I said, "Have you talked to Linnea?"

"Not yet," said Anne, "but I hope to soon."

"Who spotted her?" My skepticism must have leaked into my voice because Ellegaard remained standing and his mouth got small and defensive.

"We don't know yet," he said. "Her cell logged on to the Wi-Fi at a Starbucks on the University of Wisconsin campus. Linnea checked her Facebook page, logged into her bank, and then logged into her school account to check her midterm test grades."

"You both seem pretty confident it's Linnea, not just someone using her phone."

"That's just the thing," said Anne. "The bank app on her phone allows her to log in using her fingerprint instead of a password. And that's what she did. So it has to be Linnea."

"When was this?"

"Last night," said Ellegaard. "Logged into Starbucks' Wi-Fi at 9:24 P.M. Logged off at 9:36 P.M."

"Have the Madison police interviewed anyone to get a visual ID?"

"They're doing that right now. And there's surveillance video. Madison PD is sending us a clip covering 9:00 P.M. to 10:00 P.M. St. Paul should have it any minute if they don't have it already. That will give us a positive ID."

Then I understood why Ellegaard drove Anne over rather than call. The coat factory offered no place for a private conversation. No room where we could escape from Anne to discuss a grisly suspicion or shout it out with each other, something which, as respectable businesspeople, we'd never do in front of a client. That's where Ellegaard miscalculated.

I said, "So I suppose you two are here to tell me our investigation is over."

I wasn't going quietly. Ellegaard realized his plan had failed. "I know it's not the total win you like but—"

"Don't say total win. Don't buzzword me." I turned to Anne. "Did you call off the investigation without talking to Roger?"

"I—"

"Was it even your idea to call it off or was it Ellegaard's?"

"Shap," said Ellegaard, looking dead at me through the tops of his eyes, "don't do this."

"Don't do what? I'm not begging for work here, E. I have plenty of work thanks to you. I'd just like to know how the mother of a seventeen-year-old girl stops looking for the kid because her phone was detected in Madison. And even if the surveillance video does show it's Linnea, all that means is you know where she was eleven hours ago. Not now. She could be—"

Ellegaard cut me off. "We suspect the video is going to show Linnea with one of several friends who now attend Madison. Two are from Warroad. Five are from when the Engstroms lived in Minneapolis. That's how we'll find her."

"Have the police contacted those friends? Have you, Mrs. Engstrom?"

"Of course I have," said Anne. "And to be honest, I'm finding your attitude a tad on the difficult side."

"Let's not be honest about our attitudes—no one's going to walk away from that looking good. And you two are acting like I was investigating Linnea's disappearance then just by coincidence tripped and fell on an arrow. Well, that's not what happened. It wasn't a coincidence. So maybe I'm looking for more than a seventeen-year-old girl." Anne sat back in the chair and looked about as big as her goddamn dog. I let her discomfort fester then said, "So what did Linnea's Madison friends say?"

Anne sighed, scratched between the Yorkie's ears and said, "Well, of course, they denied seeing Linnea or knowing anything about where she is. But that's what you'd expect them to say, isn't it?"

"Depends what kind of friends they are."

"And what does that mean?"

Ellegaard paced with arms folded.

"It means if Linnea ran away, what did she run away from? Or maybe *who* did she run away from? And were her reasons legitimate enough that her good, kind friends are protecting her from something she needs protecting from? Or did Linnea just take off for shits and giggles, and her friends are assholes for playing along and costing her parents a load of dough and emotional havoc and the police precious resources? Who's the real problem here, Anne? Is it Linnea? Or is it you and Roger?"

"Shap!" said Ellegaard. His face reddened, making his blond eyebrows stand out like neon caterpillars. "That's enough."

"And how important is Roger's business meeting that he can't be reached about his missing daughter? Maybe you two like the attention of all this more than you realize. Or maybe it's exactly as much as you realize."

Ellegaard's phone dinged. He looked at the screen. Anne looked down at the shaky creature in her lap.

I said, "Is that email from St. Paul?"

Ellegaard looked at me, and Anne looked at him. My old friend and new business partner seemed resigned to this not going his way. He'd hoped the Engstrom case was over. He said, "The St. Paul police have reviewed the Starbucks security camera footage and weren't able to spot anyone matching Linnea's description. "But they said"—he read the email aloud—"'the Starbucks location is crowded with college students, many wearing hats, some wearing hoodies with the hoods up. Please review the attached footage and look for familiar movements or gestures or known friends/acquaintances that suggest Linnea's presence.'" Ellegaard looked to Anne. "It's your call, Anne. We can bow out now and you can deal directly with SPPD and Madison Police. Or we can review this footage with you, and then you can decide whether or not you'd like our firm to stay on the case."

Our firm he said, as opposed to us.

"Well," Anne said, removing her windowpanes and rubbing the gray eyes under her chestnut bangs, "I wish I didn't have to make any decisions without talking to Roger first. But I suppose I'd like to watch the surveillance video now if possible. You work the rest of the day, help me communicate with the police, then I'll discuss with Roger whether or not you should stay on."

After a few minutes of messing around with settings and devices, we streamed the video from Ellegaard's phone to my TV. The screen was split into four sections, each showing the angle of a fixed camera. We watched the entire hour and paid special attention to the twelve minutes Linnea's phone was logged into Starbucks' Wi-Fi as indicated by a running time code at the top of the screen. We saw faces clearly when students ordered and picked up coffee. Other than that, we saw high-angle shots of people sitting at tables, conversing, studying, surfing the Web on their phones and computers. During the hour-long clip, Anne saw nothing that suggested one of the patrons might be Linnea. She saw none of Linnea's friends, no familiar articles of clothing, no familiar hand gestures or postures or gaits, those little telltales that are almost impossible to hide.

When it was over, we went back to Linnea's supposed twelve-minute log-in time and watched again, focusing on anyone looking at their cell phone. That narrowed the potential Linneas by half, but even pausing the video several times, no one appeared to be her.

"That's disappointing," said Anne. She removed her oversize glasses again and set them on the coffee table. Her eyes were red and wet. Ellegaard grabbed a box of tissues off the end table and handed them to her. She dabbed her face and blew her nose. "I suppose this means we're back to where we started."

I said, "All this video proves is she wasn't in Starbucks or at least she wasn't in an area covered by their security cameras. Every coffee place I know has a Wi-Fi signal that extends beyond the physical location. Linnea could have been outside, next door, in an apartment above Starbucks if it's that kind of building. We need Madison PD to request surveillance video from neighboring businesses. Also from the parking lot or street if that video exists."

Ellegaard slouched like someone had let the air out of him. He closed his eyes and rubbed his forehead. His red face had faded to a dull pink. "Shap's right," he said. "I'll get our junior investigator, Annika, on the phone with SPPD and Madison. See if we can find more surveillance footage. Anne, why don't you try Roger again. We need to keep him in the loop."

Anne nodded, returned the picture windows to her

face, and picked up her phone. Ellegaard texted Annika then looked at me and shook his head. He never wanted me working on this case, now the entire company was. It's tough for a Boy Scout to run a company. Too many merit badges conflict with each other. If he wanted to earn one for the Linnea Engstrom case, it thwarted his effort on the BrainiAcme case. He couldn't earn both, not at the same time anyway. Ellegaard didn't have those problems wearing a gold shield for Edina PD. There, most everything was straightforward. He didn't celebrate victories—he expected them. Failure was the exception. He'd built up no resistance to it, now it was knocking him off his feet.

"No answer," said Anne. "Maybe he left his phone in the car. It happens sometimes."

"When his daughter is missing?"

"No, I suppose not."

"Do you know where he's meeting?" I said.

"He didn't say."

"Is there anyone you can check with? His assistant back in Warroad, maybe?"

She nodded then stood and meandered into the kitchen and made the call.

I approached Ellegaard, who seemed to be somewhere else. "Hey E, when you drove in, did you notice a Latino kid sitting on a white bucket against the building?"

"Yeah. You know him?"

"Never seen him before today."

"Want me to see if he's still there?"

"No, I'm going to head out in a minute. I'll take a look then."

"You should stay home and rest."

"Winnie Haas wants to talk to me without Ben around. She's working from home this morning. Said I'd meet her around 10:00. I had planned on tailing Ben, but his mom might have something important. I can drop you and Anne wherever you need to go on the way."

"You're okay to drive?"

"I'm fine. I'm not on any pain meds, and Micaela hired me a full-time nurse."

"Is her name Lauren?"

"Jameson."

"Is that a joke?"

"No. I have a nurse practitioner named Jameson."

Anne walked into our conversation. "Roger's assistant has no idea where he is. She wasn't aware he had a meeting this morning. The only thing Roger has on the books is something this afternoon with Honeywell. Honeywell wants to push it back half an hour. She tried to reach him about that, but couldn't."

Ellegaard looked at me and said, "Let's go." But his eyes said something else. We all got in the Volvo, and when I backed into the street, the Latino kid was still sitting on the white plastic bucket. I stopped the car. Ellegaard rolled down his window. "Can we help you with something?"

The kid kept his hands in his pockets and looked at us with his left eye, his right eye lost inside the jacket's hood. "You Nils Shapiro?" He had an accent from a Spanish-speaking country. Maybe Mexico. Maybe Guatemala. Probably not Spain.

"No," said Ellegaard. "Why?"

"I got a message for Nils Shapiro."

"I can get it to him," said Ellegaard.

"Got to give it to him myself."

"Why don't you take your hands out of your pockets?"

"Is that him driving the car?"

"I got friends in the Minneapolis Police Department."
Ellegaard held up his phone. "I make one call, you're going to have a rough day."

"I gotta give a message to Nils Shapiro."

"What's happening?" said Anne from the backseat.

"Lie down," I said.

"What?"

"Lie the fuck down."

11

"Oh my God." Anne unfastened her seat belt and dropped onto the backseat. "Oh my God," she repeated between a whisper and a squeal.

The kid stood up off the bucket. Ellegaard had his gun out before the kid's knees straightened.

"Dude, dude, dude!" said the kid. "What are you doing?"

I jumped out of the car, ran around the front, and said, "Hands! Now!" The kid yanked his hands out of his pockets. They held nothing. "Put 'em above your head!" He did. My left hand was in the sling. I reached into his jacket pockets with my right and removed his wallet, a smartphone, and half a Snickers. I dropped them to the sidewalk, spun him around, and patted him down, the empty left sleeve of my jacket half a step behind like the languid trunk on a child's elephant costume.

All that moving around hurled swords through my shoulder, but the adrenaline kept me from passing out.

"What the fuck, man?"

The kid had nothing else on him. "Who are you?"

"Ernesto Cuellar. That's the truth. Look in my wallet."

"Back on the bucket." He sat. I picked up his wallet and stood to the side so Ellegaard had a clean shot at him. Ernesto Cuellar carried a provisional Minnesota driver's license and lived on East Thirty-First Street near Powderhorn Park. He was sixteen years old. The bill compartment contained a few ones, a five, and Ulysses S. Grant's big head on a crisp fifty. I took out my phone, snapped a picture of his ID, returned it to the wallet, and handed it to him. "I'm Nils Shapiro. What's the message?"

"Can I have my Snickers and my phone?"

"You can have your Snickers."

He grabbed it and put it back in his pocket.

"I don't have all day, Ernesto. And you should probably get back to school. I'm sure it's killing you not to be there."

He looked up at me, his dark brown eyes full of fear. "Stop looking for Linnea Engstrom. She's okay and doesn't want to be found."

"Is that the message?" He nodded. "Who sent it?"

"I don't know."

"Not good enough. Who sent the message?"

"I don't know! Someone put an envelope in my locker. It had a fifty-dollar bill and a note that said your name and where you live and the message I should give you and after I gave it to you I would get another fifty."

"You know what, Ernesto? I think you're full of shit."

"It's the truth."

"It's bullshit."

"No, man! I promise! I'll show you. The note is in my shoe."

I looked over at Ellegaard. He shrugged.

"Show me. And that guy with a gun on you? He's a terrible shot. He might aim to wound, but that bullet could go anywhere. So the only thing that better come out of that shoe is a nasty-smelling piece of paper."

"Shut up. You think I'm stupid?" Ernesto removed his left boot and pulled out an envelope. He handed it to me.

Inside was a piece of plain white paper that backed up Ernesto's story in a sans serif font printed on an ink-jet printer. He could have made it himself to back up a lie, but ever since Ernesto's hands came out of his pockets, he looked more like an innocent scared kid and less like a threat. "I'm going to have to keep this."

"I don't care. I don't need it anymore."

"So whoever gave you this, how are they going to know you delivered the message so you get your fifty bucks?"

"I don't know."

"Unlock your phone for me."

"Dude, that's against the law."

"I don't think it is, but maybe we should call the police and ask them to come over and clarify what's legal and what's not. Just in case. What do you say?"

"I say this sucks and so do you." He grabbed his smartphone off the sidewalk, unlocked it, and handed it to me.

I said, "Lucky you. Now my fingerprints are all over your phone so the police can prove I asked you to unlock it."

"Shut up. You're not funny."

"Funnier than you, Ernesto." I looked at his text messages. His mom said she had to work late. A kid asked about a missed assignment at school. Another kid asked him why he wasn't in class. He followed Trevor Noah and Gabriel Iglesias on Twitter. His Facebook page showed pictures of him running cross-country for Southwest High

School—in my old neighborhood—and standing under a mathlete banner with half a dozen other kids. I saw no pictures of him kneeling by a dead deer with a bow resting at his side. No pictures of him competing in an archery competition. No pictures of him smoking a cigarette or drinking a beer. Kid was a straight-up nerd. "You go to Southwest?"

"What about it?"

"Kind of far from home, isn't it?"

"So what? Lot of kids go to schools not by their house."

"Do you go there because of the IB program?"

"Just give me my phone."

I punched in my number. My phone rang. I hung up and handed Ernesto his phone. "You have my number. Use it if you need it."

"Why would I need anything from you?"

"I'm a private investigator looking for Linnea Engstrom. She's only a year older than you. If you find out anything about Linnea and think she might be in danger or if you just want to do what's right, give me a call. Plus, there's a hell of a lot more than a hundred bucks in it for you."

Ernesto kept his eyes on his phone. "How much more?"

"Five times as much. I know you can do the math. And even if you don't find out anything about Linnea, it's good to know a private investigator who might be willing to do you a favor."

Ernesto shot me a quick glance, softer and inquisitive. Then he got off his bucket and walked away. I returned to the Volvo. Anne was still lying across the backseat. "You can get up now."

Anne popped up. She spoke with a sense of urgency,

the most I'd heard since I met her. "Does that boy know where Linnea is?"

"My guess is no. Whoever put that note in his locker did so because they know he's smart enough to not fuck up delivering a message."

"Oh," she said. "Oh, that's too bad."

I dropped them at the Saint Paul Hotel, where Ellegaard's car was still parked in the ramp. I told Ellegaard I'd meet him back at the office around noon and to call me if he heard anything more from Madison PD or Roger Engstrom. Then I drove east to Woodbury and the house on Crestmoor Bay. Heavy gray clouds threatened something wet.

I parked on the street and approached the columned facade. The front door was ajar an inch. Maybe Ben was late for school and ran out in a hurry. But it wasn't summer and the house was wired for security. Even in the isolated opulent suburb of Woodbury, an unattended open front door is unusual. I rang the bell and waited for Winnie Haas's voice. It didn't come. I rang the bell again and waited two full minutes. No answer.

I pulled a leather glove out of my jacket pocket, put it on my right hand, and opened the door. "Hello! Anyone home?" Silence. I stepped into the foyer and shut the door behind me. I walked back to the kitchen. It was spotless. And no Winnie Haas. Same with the great room, where Ellegaard and I had sat with Winnie and Ben last night. The glass of the glassed-in fireplace was cold and dark. I walked back to the foyer and paused. Cool air tripped down the stairs. I looked at the thermostat. Sixty-two degrees. It sure as hell wasn't sixty-two degrees upstairs.

I climbed the oak staircase, listening between steps. For

a running shower, a hairdryer, the sounds of sex, anything that would explain why Winnie Haas hadn't responded to the doorbell or my voice. I tried one more time. "Hello?" I ascended another step. "Winnie?" Nothing.

When I reached the top landing, the draft became a breeze. At the end of the hall, double doors stood open at unequal angles. I felt cold air on my face. Everything seemed wrong. I walked toward the double doors. The cold got colder.

I slipped through the master suite's double doors and saw Winnie Haas bent over on the bed, facedown, an arrow in her back. Red shaft. Yellow fletching. She wore jeans and a lavender sweater with a salad-plate-size circle of blood soaked through the cashmere, the arrow at its center like the circle had always been there, and the archer shot a dead-center bull's-eye. I walked toward her with small, light steps, as if life might return to Winnie Haas's dead body, and I didn't want to scare it away. I pulled off my right glove with my teeth and felt the back of her neck. She had cooled but wasn't cold. Close to room temperature, I guessed. I got on my phone to call the police but saw another text from Char Northagen and called her first.

I told Char I'd found a lukewarm body in Ramsey County with an arrow in its back and gave her the address. Then I called the Woodbury Police, St. Paul PD, and Ellegaard. Dozens of people would be there in minutes. I wasn't looking forward to the wait.

The breeze breathed some life into Winnie Haas's hair, and for the first time since entering the room, I noticed a pair of French doors open to a deck off the master bedroom. The right door jostled in the March wind. But the left door was wide open, pinned against the inside wall. The sun broke through the clouds, and I saw the blood.

Tiny droplets splattered on the left French door. The pattern looked unusual. It took me a moment to realize that's because the blood splattered from the bottom up. I walked around the foot of the bed toward the open doors.

First I saw the yellow fletching, just below the height of the bed. Then, wedging the door against the wall, Roger Engstrom lay faceup, his dead eyes open wide, a red arrow in his chest. Blood had sprayed from his mouth.

12

I needed to know one thing about Winnie Haas before the police arrived. I found it in the master bathroom's medicine cabinet. The label on the prescription pill bottle read oxycodone. The bottle was full, but the prescription had been issued eight months ago. I took a picture of the label then went downstairs, wondering why an old prescription would have that many pills in the bottle. Sirens interrupted my thoughts.

They came in cars and vans and trucks with tires squealing and lights flashing. Vehicles from Woodbury PD and the Ramsey County sheriff and Ramsey County medical examiner competed for parking with reporters and news producers and camera crews. They poured out of squad cars and unmarked cars and trucks and news vans with satellite dishes sticking thirty feet into the air to beam it all live. They filled the curb around the cul-de-sac, shrinking the asphalt circle and aligned themselves down Crestmoor Bay and around the corner out of sight.

Woodbury Police took charge. A uniform with an iPad

stood at the front door, the bouncer outside a club called
Double Murder. They set up base camp in the attached,
heated, triple garage. Police filled it with folding tables
and chairs. Half an hour after I discovered Winnie Haas's
body, she was hosting a party with cardboard cartons of
coffee and to-go cups on a concrete floor dusted with
sand and road salt.

St. Paul PD sent one officer as a liaison representing
their search for Linnea Engstrom. Officer Terrence Flynn,
the no-neck doughy uniform who Ellegaard and I encoun-
tered outside dead Haley Housh's cave, poured himself a
little coffee and a lot of half-and-half. It wasn't St. Paul's
investigation, and Officer Flynn seemed to be luxuriat-
ing in his bystander status. We made eye contact. He offered no smile then slipped into the throng.

The forensics people combed the house while Char
Northagen scraped under twenty fingernails and em-
ployed two rectal thermometers. She and I had something to discuss, but it would have to wait until the latex
gloves came off.

A Detective Waller from Woodbury PD questioned me
then had me walk her through my movements from the
point I got out of my car to when I found the bodies.
Detective Waller had large, round brown eyes. She stood
five six in a slight body. Her face was triathlon gaunt—
you could make out her skull under her skin. She wore a
navy-blue pantsuit with a silk cream blouse buttoned all
the way to the collar. She had yellow, shoulder-length hair
cut for her convenience more than anyone's pleasure. Jamie Waller's appearance made no statement. Everything
Detective Jamie Waller wanted you to know about her
could be seen in her big brown eyes that weren't all that
big—they just appeared that way in a face with so little
flesh.

Detective Waller asked me to check out the basement with her, so we headed downstairs where we found Ben Haas's quarters. They functioned like a separate apartment with a kitchen, living area, and a door that led to the back patio. Sculpted sage-green carpet. Painted tan walls trimmed out with white molding. Posters for Trampled by Turtles and Pete Seeger and The Avett Brothers. Framed architectural drawings hung on the wall next to a piece of broken-up Sheetrock taken from some other wall and signed with a gold Sharpie. The signature belonged to Minnesota-born, rock-and-roll legend Graham Itasca.

A plastic architectural model of a modern home sat on the dresser, probably a gift from Raynard Haas, hoping his flawless aesthetic taste would rub off on his son despite living in Winnie's cookie-cutter McMansion. The model showed every stud, beam, and joist. Meticulous work.

Recessed lights pocked the ceiling that was a full eight feet high. The basement didn't feel much like a basement at all. Light poured in through a wall of windows that looked out to the backyard and slough beyond.

Papers and books buried a desk. The kind of furniture manufactured in North Carolina and sold in expensive mall-adjacent stores where parents buy small children big furniture to grow into. Guitars and mandolins stood on stands and lay stored away in cases. Ben had a queen-size bed in the sleeping area. We found it unmade and disheveled, as if a writhing snake had slept in it.

"Let's take a look at the mechanical room," said Detective Waller.

I followed her into a room with walls of poured concrete, a washer, dryer, tank-less hot water heater, a manifold board of red and blue PEX plumbing tubes, a similar board of coax cable connectors, and a laundry chute that fed dirty clothes into a bin made of spaced wooden slats. The bin was empty. I said, "What are you looking for in the mechanical room?"

"I have no idea," said Detective Jamie Waller. "I just want to hear what do you think happened before you got here, and this seems like a good place to talk." I must have looked dubious. She continued, "Woodbury has a small police department. I'm the only experienced homicide investigator. I spent sixteen years as an MP in Iraq and Afghanistan investigating friendly-fire victims and suicides and outright troop-on-troop murder. I saw a lot of bodies and a lot of blood. The one thing I learned investigating all those deaths: it's no good going it alone."

"I'm not available for hire the moment."

"That's okay, because I can't hire you. Woodbury hired me in case we catch something like Sandy Hook or San Bernadino. They're not going to fork over extra for a private."

Detective Jamie Waller wanted a freebie. It didn't happen every day with cops. They didn't want to be in a private detective's debt. But once in a great while a cop couldn't avoid it, and you can't have enough police officers owing you favors.

"I'm not looking for a specific chain of events," she said. "I just want to pick your brain."

I looked around the room to buy a little time, then said, "All right. I think Winnie Haas knew something about Linnea Engstrom's whereabouts, most likely through her son, Ben, who was sleeping with Haley Housh."

"The girl who was found in the cave?"

"Yes. She's also from Warroad. And I believe Ben Haas has more of a connection to Linnea than he's admitted. I hope now he'll be more willing to talk. That is, assuming he had nothing to do with this mess. I received a text from Winnie late last night saying she wanted to talk to me without Ben present.

"Maybe whatever she had to tell me she wanted to share with Roger, as well. So she asked him to come over. He told his wife he was going to a business meeting. Why he didn't tell her the truth is something worth looking into. But it may be as simple as he didn't want to get her hopes up. Or the reason may be more complicated.

"Someone out there doesn't want Linnea found, maybe someone who shoots arrows. It could be Linnea herself. Or a friend of hers. Or a lover. Then again, maybe someone snatched her off the street, didn't expect this much heat, and is protecting himself. Whoever it is, he or she moves about town unencumbered by bow and arrows and, as far as we know, undetected. I don't know how that happens but it did in downtown St. Paul yesterday and again today here in Woodbury."

Waller bit the inside of her cheek and leaned against the utility sink. "So you got nothing."

"Less than nothing. But as soon as your crime scene unit is done upstairs, I'd get 'em down here to look for signs of Linnea. A hair in Ben's bed or in the lint trap of the dryer. I wouldn't be surprised if they found her fingerprint on the door that leads directly outside."

Waller looked dubious.

"Arrows don't leave shell casings, so I'd check the slough out back for trampled reeds or anything that might have fallen out of a pocket or quiver. The slough has a clean view of the master bedroom. It's possible the archer never entered the house but shot through the open French doors. The victims stumbled around a bit after they got shot then fell where I found them. And check the backyard under the edge of the master bedroom's

deck for any sign of someone jumping out or using a rope
to climb up. Then again, the archer may have been in the
house."

Waller sighed. "You're boring me. Besides, you told me
the front door was open when you arrived."

"You asked for my gut. Did you expect a name and
address?"

"I expected something that warrants your reputation."

"I'm looking for Linnea Engstrom, not who killed her
father and Winnie Haas."

"You're so full of shit, Shapiro. Linnea disappears then
her father's found murdered, and you don't think the two
cases are connected?" She had me there. "If we work together, you won't just be helping me, I'll be helping you.
And no one's so good they don't need help."

"It's not that I don't need help. It's just sometimes less
of a pain in the ass to go it alone."

"Are you looking for who shot you?"

"That's not my first priority."

"Seems odd."

"Now you're getting to know me."

"I am. And I'm not impressed."

"Listen. I'm not one of those crime scene savants who
can look at the position of a body and the dust on a ban-
ister and intuit the butler did it so he could steal the
family jewels and run off to Iowa with the maid. I inves-
tigate one step at a time. It involves talking to a lot of
people, not my favorite, hours of sitting around, sticking my neck out, putting miles on the car, and running
into dead ends. Once in a while it pays off. Most of the
time it doesn't. I don't know if you're trying to get this
double murder wrapped up before your spring vacation, but my helping you probably won't speed things
along. So if we work together, you'll need to adjust your

expectations. That is, coincidentally, the key to happiness. You may want to try it."

Waller stared at me, her jaw clenched. I could see the muscles strapped under her face and the horseshoe of teeth in her upper jaw. "I am a patient person, Mr. Shapiro. And I don't go on spring vacation. Like Saturday nights and New Year's Eve, it's for amateurs." She smiled at me, using only her brown eyes. Sixteen years in the army had taught Jamie Waller the value of making an alliance. She wanted a body next to her on the front line, not a friend.

I said, "All right, Detective. I'll update you daily."

"Twice daily, at least. And it'll flow both ways."

We shook hands as if it meant something then returned upstairs. Ellegaard stood in the kitchen. Anne Engstrom sat in a wooden chair. Her face had neither color nor expression. Her eyes looked dull behind their plate glass windows. Ellegaard said something to her about his needing to talk to me and we'd just be on the other side of the room if she needed us. He touched her shoulder, which she didn't seem to notice, then we stepped away.

"Anne just ID'd Roger's body," he said. "She has a sister in Wayzata. The sister is on her way to take Anne home. Where were you?"

"In the basement with Detective Waller from Woodbury PD. Ran me through it because I discovered the bodies."

"You want to fill me in on that?"

"In a minute. Any sign of Ben?"

"He's in an upstairs bedroom with a couple counselors from the high school. He has alibis for the whole morning. Poor kid had to make the ID. He's a mess. The dad's in Chicago visiting a job site. Woodbury Police got ahold of him. He's on his way to O'Hare now."

"I think Linnea's been here."

"Based on what?"

"Something's not right. I don't know what. Just something . . . Walk through this with me, will you?" I pulled a pair of latex gloves from a wire mesh cart labeled CSU—DO NOT TOUCH then led Ellegaard to the front door, which was closed. "When I got here, the front door was ajar an inch." I opened the door. Outside, a throng had gathered to look at whatever there was to see, adorned in their Patagonia and L.L. Bean and Turtle Fur. I shut the door.

"It's not our case, Shap."

"Yeah, I was just saying the same thing to Detective Waller. Our job is to find Linnea Engstrom."

"Is it? Our client is dead."

"You think Anne's going to give up looking for her daughter after what happened to Roger?"

"The woman's in shock. She can't make that decision right now."

"Just stay with me for a few minutes. Then you can get back to looking for whoever's stealing Post-it notes at BrainiAcme." Ellegaard was too polite to tell me to fuck off, so he just sighed. "I walked inside and called out to see if anyone was home. No answer. I walked through the foyer and into the kitchen, which was spotless."

"Are there dirty dishes in the dishwasher?" said Ellegaard, both proud and irritated with himself for thinking of the question.

I pulled open the dishwasher and saw three plates in the lower rack, each speckled with toast crumbs. Three knives smeared with bits of butter and red jam. Three coffee mugs in the upper rack along with three juice glasses. Winnie Haas didn't rinse the dishes before putting them in the dishwasher. I've never understood people who do.

That's what the damn machine is for. There'd be DNA aplenty to identify the breakfast eaters. I pulled on the door of a base cabinet with the handle at the top and two plastic bins slid out: one for garbage and one for recycling. The recycling bin contained an orange juice carton. The garbage was empty.

"Huh."

"I'll see if CSU has checked the garbage can outside," said Ellegaard.

"There should be paper napkins or paper towels on top. Unless . . ."

"Unless what?"

"Follow me." I led Ellegaard down into the basement mechanical room. I looked through the glass door of the front-loading washing machine. It was empty. Same with the dryer. "This is what's off—no dirty clothes. No laundry."

"It's probably in hampers upstairs or she did it last night or early this morning."

"Maybe. But if she had company this morning for breakfast and if she used cloth napkins, she wouldn't throw those in the second-floor hamper. Why not just throw them down the chute? And if she did laundry this morning, did she have time after breakfast to run the washer and dryer then fold everything and put it away?" I opened the door of the laundry chute bin, stuck my head in, and looked up. Nothing but black. "Stay here. I'm going to find the top and call down to you."

I went upstairs. On the main floor, I saw Detective Waller talking to two uniforms. "Time to share," I said. "Walk with me." She excused herself and followed me up to the second floor. I found the laundry chute in the main hall, opened it with my gloved hand, and looked into it. Nothing but black. "E," I said. No response. "E!" I said, louder. Still nothing.

"What are you doing?" said Waller.

I got out my phone and took off the latex so I could touch the screen. I called Ellegaard. "I can't see any light from up here and you can't hear me," I said. I turned on the phone's flashlight and pointed it down. I stuck my head in as far as it would go, which was enough to see a clump of dirty clothes topped with cloth napkins. I pulled my head out and turned to Waller. "Grab a few of your people and meet me in the mechanical room. Something's blocking the laundry chute."

13

The lowest-ranking Woodbury cop, round-faced and eager, stepped into a white jumpsuit seemingly made of the paper-like material houses wear under their siding. He crawled into the laundry bin and shined a spot up into the chute. "Looks to me like a brown paper bag," he said.

Waller said, "Check the chute door and around it for forensics, then retrieve that bag."

Another young woman cop with a blond ponytail entered the mechanical room and said, "Detective, he's ready now."

Ellegaard, Waller, and I climbed the stairs to the second level and entered a guest bedroom. It was furnished in simple-lined antiques made of bird's-eye maple. Ben Haas lay on a full-size bed, his eyes red and swollen. He had exhausted himself from crying and stared at the ceiling. His dead mother lay two rooms away.

The school counselors insisted on remaining present. One was a midforties woman with bangs and long, dry, light-sucking hair the color of bad coffee. A pair of drugstore reading glasses hung from a drugstore chain and rested on her teal, cowl-necked sweater that was thread-bare on the elbows and bursting with pills everywhere else. She looked the type to have a poster of Jungian archetypes on her office wall and a nightstand full of mouthpieces to combat her TMJ.

The other counselor was a pasty white man. Burgundy sweater vest over a red-checked shirt and camel-colored pants that I can best describe as slacks. His curly hair was the color of the sun and I couldn't tell if it was natural, lightened from a faded brown, or darkened from white to mask albinism, the latter possibility suggested by his sapphire blue eyes that no doubt soaked in a container of saline as he slept.

"Ben," said TMJ, "are you okay to answer a few questions right now?" He nodded. Then TMJ turned to us with an authority she didn't possess, "A few questions will be all right."

"Thank you," said Waller. TMJ nodded and almost succeeded in suppressing a smile, her cup of self-importance filled to the brim.

Then Sweater Vest said, "I'm going to ask that you please be sensitive to what Ben is experiencing and feeling right now. There will be plenty of time for more questions later."

"Of course," said Waller. Sweater Vest and TMJ looked at each other with shared satisfaction, then Waller said, "I'm sorry, Ben. I know how hard this is, but please try to answer the best you can." He lay there and stared at the ceiling. "Did you see Roger Engstrom at home this morning before you went to school?"

He shook his head.

"Was anyone else here at the house this morning that you know of?"

Again he shook his head.

"What time did you leave for school?"

He took a breath. "Six thirty. I had zero-hour jazz combo."

"Did you eat breakfast this morning?"

He nodded.

"What did you have?"

"Toast," he said. "And orange juice."

"Did your mother eat with you?"

He shook his head. The tears started again.

"Something's blocking the laundry chute. Do you know what it is?"

"No," he said. It came out as a whisper.

Waller said, "Ben, did your mom have a boyfriend?"

"No."

"Any past boyfriends?"

"Not that I know of."

"How does she get along with your dad?"

"Fine. I don't know how they ever ended up together. They're really different. But they get along okay, other than him making fun of this house."

Waller looked at me and raised her eyebrows and cocked her head to convey *your witness*.

"Ben," I said, "have you ever seen Roger Engstrom here at the house before?"

"No. I didn't even know my mom knew him."

"Did you know him?"

"No. Never met him."

"Last night we talked about how well you do or don't know Linnea Engstrom. If you want to clarify anything today, no one's going to hold it against you, and it may help us find who did this to your mom."

He kept his eyes on the ceiling. Tears leaked toward his ears. TMJ handed him a tissue from a box she clutched on her lap. She had designated herself the great bequeather of tissues. Ben wiped away the tears and waited for his breath to steady. "When Haley drove down on weekends, sometimes Linnea would ride with her. Haley would drop her off. I don't know where. And then pick her up on Sunday and they'd drive back to Warroad together."

"Did Haley know why Linnea came to the Cities?"

"No, and she didn't seem to care. I wasn't bullshitting last night. Haley never talked about Linnea. Or almost never. She'd only say stuff like Linnea drove for a few hours so Haley could take a nap."

"Weren't you curious about the nature of their friendship?" said Waller.

"No," said Ben. "Haley was so weird. Whatever she was doing when she wasn't with me, I didn't want to know about. I really didn't."

"So just to be clear," I said, "you've had no contact with Linnea?"

Ben shook his head. "I swear."

The round-faced jumpsuit-wearing police officer stepped into the room holding a wrinkled Kowalski's grocery bag rolled shut at the top.

Waller said, "Do you recognize this bag, Ben?"

He rolled onto his side and looked at it. "Looks like a regular grocery bag."

"That's enough for now," said Waller. "Thank you, Ben. And again, our deepest sympathy."

In the garage, Anne Engstrom's sister sat next to Anne on a plastic chair at a plastic table. She was about forty and wore rimless teardrop glasses over gray eyes. Unlike her sister, her lenses were small and sized more for a human face than for the Hubbell telescope. She wore her brown hair pulled back in a loose ponytail. Her skin was clear and smooth and pale. She carried an extra few ounces on her cheeks that weighed down her face into something dumpy and adorable. A brown crewneck sweater and faded Levi's completed her library-dweller look. Ellegaard said something to her and gave her his card. She nodded then put her arm around Anne. Detective Waller asked Anne if she'd seen the bag before. She shook her head no.

We stepped outside and into an overgrown police van that had taken the liberty of parking on the driveway. Reporters hurled questions at us. We ignored them like TV commercials and entered the van. Waller and I stood comfortably, but Ellegaard barely fit. The vehicle contained a rack of guns ranging from pistols to shotguns to assault rifles. On the opposite wall hung riot shields, Tasers, cans of teargas, and canister launchers. Quite a militarization for an outer-ring, wealthy suburb that was closer to rural Wisconsin than it was to St. Paul.

Detective Waller removed a wand from a charging base and waved it on all sides and underneath the bag. It contained no metal. She opened it.

"*Ufda*," she said. Then she held the bag open for Ellegaard and me to see.

"Sheesh," said Ellegaard. The bag was full of cash. Detective Waller dumped it onto a stainless steel table and, with gloved hands, counted the bundles.

"A hundred thousand dollars, give or take," said Jamie Waller. "This sure mucks up an already mucky pond."

"Sheesh," Ellegaard said again.

I stared at the bundles. "You can count how many pairs of underwear were stuck in the chute on top of the bag and we'll most likely know how many days the money was in there. Winnie didn't seem the type to let laundry pile up before tossing it down the chute. If the number is zero, someone stashed the money in there this morning."

Ellegaard said, "Before cleaning up breakfast."

"Yes."

"I questioned Anne Engstrom earlier," said Waller. "She was unaware Roger even knew Winnie Haas or that Winnie or Ben even existed. Whatever the relationship was, Roger hid it from his wife. He told her he had a business meeting this morning."

"Maybe it was business."

"Maybe," said Waller. "We'll see if anyone had sex with anyone else and check cell phones and email and social media to piece together their communication. God dammit. This money makes no sense."

"Now you're getting to know what it's like to work with Nils Shapiro," said Ellegaard. He was not smiling.

Waller looked at me. "You lied to me, Nils."

"Did I?"

"You said you aren't one of those savants who can take one look at a crime scene and figure out what happened."

"I have no idea what happened other than someone stuck Winnie Haas and Roger Engstrom with arrows."

"But you knew something was wrong because there was no dirty laundry in the bin."

"That's not how it happened, but if that's the story you want to tell yourself, go ahead."

"I'll need you to come down to the station and sign a statement."

"Maybe tomorrow."

"I need you to do it today."

"Today doesn't work for me."

"It's imperative."

"Listen, Detective. I know you have a job to do, but

I'm on day two of looking for a seventeen-year-old girl and so far all I got is a hole in my shoulder that starts in the front and goes out the back. You strong-arm me into giving you a statement now, you'll get a bunch of facts and nothing more."

Waller looked at Ellegaard who had braced himself by pressing his hands against the van's ceiling. He offered her no help. "Fine," she said. "Tomorrow morning at 8:00. Sharp. Take my card. Just in case."

I took it. "See you then, Detective."

Ellegaard and I returned to the house. He spent a few more minutes with Anne Engstrom, and I went upstairs to find Char Northagen measuring how far the arrow shafts protruded from each body. "Same arrows?" I said.

"We have to talk," said Char, keeping her eyes on her work. "Now."

14

Char Northagen bagged her instruments and corpses, working around the arrows, which she'd sheared off just above the bodies. She'd remove the rest at the morgue. Then we left the house on Crestmoor Bay, got in my car, and drove away.

"Nice Volvo wagon," she said. "I've always wanted a stay-at-home wife who'd drive the kids around in one of these."

"I thought there was a law all lesbians have to drive Subarus."

"There is," she said, "but it only applies to lesbians with dogs. Lesbians with kids can drive anything they want." Char adjusted the dashboard vent to give herself some air. "Shap, I finished the autopsy on Haley Housh."

"She didn't die of carbon monoxide poisoning?"

"She did. But she was also sexually active just before she died."

"Interesting."

"Whoever she had intercourse with used a condom. I found no sperm, but I did find traces of lubricant and spermicide associated with condoms. It also appeared to be consensual. No evidence of forced penetration."

"Have you found any DNA belonging to someone else?"

"Not yet. She probably showered afterward. I found little bacteria built up in the places it usually builds up."

"So she had sexual intercourse, but we have no idea who her partner was."

"That's the gist of it, yeah."

We crossed Valley Creek Road and parked in front of Caribou Coffee. "So that's what you wanted to talk to me about?"

"That's the preamble. For the rest I need coffee."

The Caribou Coffee looked like every other Caribou Coffee in town with its slate and wood floor and moss-green walls. Arts and Crafts–style lanterns hung from chains to create a cozy, cabin-like atmosphere, except behind the fake panes of mica, energy efficient bulbs generated a thin greenish light that was far from cozy. Char ordered a soy latte. I ordered an Americano.

The place was crowded with the usual weekday Minnesota suburban coffee shop activity: business casual informational interviews, insurance agents reviewing policies with clients, post-school-drop-off parents talking about whatever the hell they talk about, and the ever-present Alcoholics Anonymous sponsor/sponsoree meetings where the two recovering alcoholics, each with an open book before them, take turns reading aloud so everyone in the place can overhear words like *steps* and *amends* making the anonymous part not so anonymous, after all.

We spotted an open table in the corner and headed for

it. Char drew her share of stares and sucked a few decibels out of the room. Her six-foot-two frame stands out even in a land of giants like Minnesota with its Northern European gene pool, especially with her magazine cover face, giraffe neck, and mile-long legs.

We sat, and Char got right to it. "The arrows I just examined appear to be the same as the one that lodged in your shoulder. I won't know if the arrowheads will be an exact match until I remove them in the lab.

"But here's what's interesting: the UK developed a technique for recovering fingerprints from metal even if someone wiped them off. I won't bore you with all the science but the oil in fingerprints causes corrosion on metal almost instantaneously, even on stainless steel. So no matter how well the oil of the fingerprint is removed, an indelible image of the fingerprint is left behind. It takes some monkey business in the lab to reveal it, but when it's over, the fingerprint is crystal clear. There's a lab in Minneapolis that can do it. Yesterday, I sent them the shaft and arrowhead we took out of you. I got an email last night saying they found a print on the hosel of the arrowhead."

"Have you run it through IAFIS?"

"Yes, and, so far, there are no matches."

"But a print is a print."

"That it is. And here's the kick in the crotch. SPPD officially reprimanded me for ordering the lab work in Minneapolis and the IAFIS search. They said I overstepped my bounds as a medical examiner and should have left that work to forensics. I said forensics didn't think of it or, if they did, they didn't act on it. We had a bit of a shouting match late last night."

"Why do they care, if you're all working for the same team?"

"My guess it's because last month I filed suit against the St. Paul Police Department."

"For?"

"Sexual harassment. I don't mind a little ribbing here and there, but it crossed the line. And not just one time from one cop, but dozens of times from several cops. Gay marriage is the law of the land, and a lot of Joe six-packs have come around. Problem is, it's easier for some guys to accept a gay woman they don't find attractive. If they want to sleep with you, they think the reason you prefer women is because you've yet to spread your legs for a man like them.

"Then it gets ugly. Dick picks aplenty and dildos in desk drawers and lust letters. They're lewd at best and some are downright threatening. So for my sake and the sake of other women on the force and civilians who might get pulled over on a dark road, I felt I had to do something. It's just a few bad apples, but they shouldn't be carrying badges."

"I agree. But what's this have to do with the fingerprint on the arrowhead?"

"The day I filed suit, I called a reporter friend at the *Strib*. He's been documenting the whole thing and plans to write a series of articles about it. SPPD got wind of it and now it's a shit show flambé. I have to go before a review board, and regardless of the review board's decision, my days as a Ramsey County medical examiner are soon to be over. Ramsey County isn't all about St. Paul, but St. Paul's got enough pull that if they want me out, I'm out. After last night, they wanted to suspend me without pay, but the other two M.E.s had their hands full with that chain reaction multifatality in the fog on Interstate 94. This morning, when you called me directly about the Woodbury bodies, I ran right over before someone pulled me off the case."

"Sorry you're going through all that," I said, still not understanding the connection.

Char looked down at her latte then continued. "Anyway, the reason all this matters is because now I'm on my way out so I got nothing to lose."

"Ah. Now I get it. What'd you do?"

"I called Warroad Police at 2:00 A.M. and spoke to an Officer Stensrud. I may have misrepresented my position in Ramsey County law enforcement, but I'm sure he didn't question it because of the number that showed up on his caller ID. I used a flirty voice and my real name. He probably googled me while we were talking and saw a mess of pictures from my beach volleyball days."

"Good thing. You're a horrific sight now."

She smiled then continued. "Anyway, he got real chatty real fast. So I asked if he could do me a favor and lift a few prints off the lockers of your hockey players, Luca Lüdorf and Graham Peters. I know we took prints on Luca and Graham, but SPPD locked me out of the database."

"How did you even know about them?"

"Before SPPD locked me out of the system, I read reports on the case. Kind of took a special interest in it after I saved your life outside the cave." She smiled a cocky little smile and may have even winked.

"This cop in Warroad, he didn't get fingerprints for you, did he?"

"Yes, he did. Officer Tony Stensrud is bored out of his mind because eighty percent of Warroad is down here for the hockey tournament and the other twenty percent is infirm. Even Marvin Windows closed up shop for a few days. The school's empty. So he waltzed in and got the prints."

Char raised her eyebrows then took a sip of her latte. "And?"

She set her latte down and took a breath. "And none of the hockey players' fingerprints match what we found on the arrowhead."

"Look at you. You're all aflutter. I'm just going to sit back and enjoy the rest of the story because I know you got something, otherwise we wouldn't be here."

"No we wouldn't. Because I asked Stensrud to get me someone else's prints. And guess what?"

I glanced to my right and caught a pair of eyes on us. A puffy man about fifty with a cheap haircut and no-wrinkle pants, no-wrinkle shirt, and no-wrinkle tie, each a different shade of green. He was clean-shaven and overly pink in the face. Whatever he was drinking had a softball of whipped cream on top ribboned with choco-late and caramel. That's a cop perk. He had plainclothes written all over him.

"Keep your eyes on me," I said under the din of the insurance agents and recovering alcoholics. "Don't look away and keep your voice down. We got company. A cop to your left, about nine o'clock. I'm getting up to grab a napkin. After I've taken a step away, stop me and ask me to get a stir stick or something. You'll get a look at him."

We performed our little skit then I returned with the napkins and stir stick.

"He's Woodbury PD," said Char just loud enough for me to hear. "Probably has buddies in St. Paul." Char reached into her purse and took out a pen then grabbed the napkin I'd just fetched. She scribbled something on it and slid it toward me. It read: *The fingerprint on the arrowhead belongs to Warroad hockey coach Gary Kozjek.*

I stood, took the napkin, shoved it in my pocket, and walked away.

"Shap?"

I continued past the Woodbury plainclothes and through the glass door to outside. It was probably forty degrees but it felt like seventy-five. The sun bounced off the white sidewalk. It hurt my eyes and I liked it. I walked through the parking lot toward a crop of new two-stories facing a park of dormant grass. In the far corner of the lot, a minimountain of plowed snow slumped like a drunk. I heard birds tweet, and in the blue sky overhead, a cursive V of Canada geese honked their way north. In the master-planned suburbascape, a few blades of grass leaned toward green, brave early adopters who were willing to pay the price for the March blizzard that was sure to come.

I had to think. I walked fast, my legs working like bellows to stoke the part of my mind I can't access. I forgot that whoever shot me might try again. I passed a pregnant woman wearing a man's T-shirt, her milk-white arms reflecting the sunlight. She walked a pair of blue-eyed silver labs who took their time trying to sniff the brown grass back to life. I continued around the block, which for no apparent reason, was shaped like a peanut. Ten minutes later, I walked back into Caribou Coffee. The inside felt dark and wrong. I passed the plainclothes as he broke a piece off a cookie the size of a manhole cover. Char Northagen was where I'd left her. I sat in my chair and felt a drop of sweat run down my spine. I pushed into the chair back to kill it.

Char said, "You always get up and walk away in the middle of a conversation?"

I almost whispered: "Gary Kozjek told me he hunts bow season."

"Yeah, I nosed around," said Char. "Got an ex at the DNR. Kozjek has a bow-hunting license. He registered a doe in September."

"But," I said, "something's wrong with the fingerprint."

"What do you mean?"

"Here," I said and passed Char a straw. She took it. Then I wadded up a napkin and handed that to her. "The straw is the arrow shaft. The wadded-up napkin is the arrowhead. Show me how you screw the arrowhead onto the shaft."

Char held the wadded napkin between her left thumb and forefinger then used her right hand to screw the straw into the napkin.

"Stop. Look how you're holding the arrowhead. You need two fingers to do that, at least, but they only found one on the arrowhead. It can't be done with one."

"Maybe it's the only clean print."

"They would have told you if they'd found a partial. Faking one fingerprint is easy. There are several ways to do it. Low-tech and hi-tech. But faking a room full of fingerprints the way a person really uses their hands, on tables and light switches and computers and phones— that's hard—that's art. Same is true in this situation. But a monkey can fake one fingerprint."

Char let the idea bounce around in her head then said, "But if someone went to the trouble of faking Kozy's fingerprint, why would they wipe it off?"

"No idea. Maybe they changed their mind. Or maybe they knew the one would look so obviously faked they assumed the police would use the new technology. And if they found the fingerprint with new technology, it would legitimize the print."

"I don't know, Shap. It's weird. How could they assume I'd know about this new method of finding wiped-off prints?"

"Because if it's new everyone knows about it. It's the definition of the word *news*. I bet if you google how to wipe fingerprints off metal, something comes up about the new tech, and new is all anyone cares about. The Web was built for it. It's not like *Pudd'nhead Wilson* where the townsfolk are a decade behind."

"What's *Pudd'nhead Wilson*?"

"Something old. Which is why you don't know about it."

Char pulled the plastic lid off her latte then stirred it with the wooden stick. She looked at me. I didn't respond. Char's mouth tightened and her forehead wrinkled. "Except . . ." She shook her head. "Except there was about an hour between when the Engstroms hired you and you got shot. So how would the archer have found out they hired you, had time to fake a fingerprint, then know you'd be outside that cave and when?"

"How could anybody know?" I said. "And what's the motive?"

"I can think of one," said Char. "Kozy was involved inappropriately with Linnea. He's trying to cover it up. And as far as the fingerprint goes, maybe he wore gloves most of the time but accidentally touched it once."

"That's a real possibility. Now you're starting to think more like an investigator than an M.E. Maybe you should use your medical degree and deductive reasoning skills on living people."

"Maybe I should. Maybe I will. We'll see . . ." Char glanced over at the Woodbury cop.

"Does SPPD know about Kozjek's print being on that arrowhead?"

"I don't think so. You're the only person I've told. Why?"

"You can't withhold the information from them. Not legally. Not ethically. No matter how difficult they're being. But we can tell Woodbury first. Let them send this morning's arrows to the Minneapolis lab. See if they turn up the same thing."

"You going to invite the Woodbury cop with the whipped cream on his chin to join us?"

"I'm not sure yet. Do you know a Detective Jamie Waller with Woodbury?"

"I've met her a few times. Seems like a good cop."

"She's awfully interested in working with me. Any idea if that's personal or professional?"

"Are you asking me if she's straight? What's wrong, Shap, your gaydar on the fritz?"

"My gaydar works only on dudes. With women, their lack of personal interest in me could be because they're gay or because of a hundred other reasons."

"Oh, I bet it's more than a hundred." Char smiled then said, "Waller's straight as far as I know. You interested?"

"Nope. Just trying to figure out her game." I took out my phone and Waller's card and reached her at the crime scene. I told her Char and I were at Caribou and had some information for her.

Char said, "You didn't tell Waller about her colleague being here."

"No, I think we should let that awkward scene play out naturally."

15

We only had a few minutes before Waller arrived, so I got to it. "We're just going to give Waller the basics," I said. "Gary Kozjek's fingerprint was found on the hosel of the arrowhead you pushed out of my shoulder."

"Okay," said Char, "that's what I was thinking we'd say. How is that just the basics?"

"We don't tell her we think the fingerprint could have been faked. And we offer no speculation or suggestions on what she should do next."

"Why not tell her it could be a fake?"

"We want Woodbury and Saint Paul PD to have a suspect."

"Because?"

"Because a double murder in Woodbury is the biggest thing to hit this town since it lost the horse racing track to Shakopee thirty years ago. Especially since both victims are rich and white and one of them was a high-level executive at 3M. There's tremendous pressure on the police to make an arrest. Nothing would make them happier than having a suspect. So let them come to their own conclusions and go after Kozjek if they want. When St. Paul gets wind of it, they'll join the hunt."

"So you're giving them Kozjek to get them out of your hair."

"Seventeen-year-old girls disappear all the time. But the people looking for them don't get shot by arrows. Something's wrong here, and I need time to feel my way into it. With the police on Kozjek, I'll get it. And if Kozjek ends up being the shooter, all the better."

Char understood. She took a sip of coffee then said, "Where was the archer when he shot you? Did anyone see anything?"

"I didn't. SPPD questioned Ellegaard and the officers outside the cave. No one saw anything. They say they're investigating, but I haven't heard a word."

Waller entered. She spotted us in the corner and headed toward us, passing her colleague, who she recognized but walked by as if she didn't.

She pulled a free chair away from a nearby table and joined us. We said our hellos then I told Waller about Gary Kozjek's fingerprint on the arrowhead. Waller jumped where I thought she would by instructing Char to send this morning's arrowheads to Woodbury CSU. Then she looked at me with her skeleton face and said, "Why did you tell me and not St. Paul?"

"I thought we were helping each other out, Detective."

"You are so full of shit. What do you want?"

I looked at Char. Her eyes widened, as if I expected her to answer. I said, "You're good at your job, Detective."

"Don't fucking flatter me. Just tell me."

"The colleague of yours sitting over there who used a coupon on his haircut—why's he on us?"

"He's not on you."

"Yes, he is. And we want to know if it's Woodbury business or a favor for St. Paul."

"Pretty sure it's not Woodbury. What's going on with St. Paul?"

Char told Waller about her impending lawsuit and how SPPD locked her out of the database and that she probably wouldn't be working for Ramsey County much longer.

Waller shook her head and said, "Fuckheads. They're everywhere."

"So who is this guy?"

"McNamara," said Waller. "But that's as much as I'm saying. I don't shit on my own."

"Why wasn't McNamara at the crime scene this morning? A double murder in Woodbury. I would have figured the whole force would be there."

Waller paused, started to say something, then stopped. The fingers of her right hand drummed the table. "I don't know. I'll get into it. Thanks for the information. Dr. Northagen, I expect those arrowheads this afternoon." Waller got up and walked away.

I dropped Char at Crestmoor Bay then drove 94 back to Minneapolis and parked in my reserved space in the City Center ramp. Minneapolis has its share of beautiful buildings. City Center is not one of them. It's a forty-seven-story rectangle sided with brown granite, but the rock is crushed so, unless you're standing right next to the building, it looks like brown dirt and something nineteenth-century Pueblos would access via ladders.

I rode the elevator to the thirty-second floor and followed the sign to Stone Arch Investigations as if I didn't know the way. Leah Stanley sat behind the reception desk. "Look who's back from the dead."

"Nice to see you, too, Leah."

"Got a load of messages for you. Stacked them on your desk."

"Is it in your job description to read 'em to me?"

"It is not."

"Hey, Nils! Welcome back!" said Annika, carrying a cup of coffee out of our tiny kitchen.

"Annika will probably read them to you," said Leah. "She's nicer than I am."

"A wolverine is nicer than you, Leah."

The door opened behind me. Robert Stanley walked in. Leah's father was a retired Minneapolis cop pushing sixty with medium brown skin and freckled cheeks. He wore a rag wool sweater, jeans, and neon yellow running shoes, though his belly looked like it hadn't been carried on any marathons lately.

Robert lived up north in Blackduck, on the northern edge of the Chippewa National Forest. He fished and hunted and only stepped foot in the Cities for newborn babies, funerals, and graduations.

I said, "Robert Stanley. What's the occasion?"

He shook my hand and said, "God damn niece had a baby. And during the last week of ice fishing. Shame." Robert exchanged hellos with Annika then walked around the reception desk to hug his daughter. "Hey, baby."

"Hi, Daddy."

"They treating you okay here?"

"They are not."

Most of the old guard Minneapolis cops aren't fans of Ellegaard and me because we didn't return to the force after the layoff. But Robert Stanley never seemed to care. He didn't understand why cops got mad at us. We didn't lay us off. The mayor did. When Leah wanted to work for a year before going to law school, Robert called and asked if we needed any help at our newly formed Stone

Arch Investigations. We met Leah and hired her on the spot. She was not grateful.

Robert Stanley said, "Hey Shapiro, if you guys are ever short of personnel, I could use some detective fringe work. I'm getting a little rusty and wouldn't mind sharpening up my skills."

"Good to know. We were just saying the other day we could use a rusty old cop around here."

Robert Stanley laughed. "Goddammit, Shapiro. I got four daughters and always wished I'd had a son. Until I met you." Robert Stanley hugged me hard and lifted me off my feet. "Thanks again for giving the baby girl a position in your illustrious firm. Keeps her out of my house."

"You shut up, Daddy." Leah gathered her purse to go to lunch with her father when I noticed the blinds were up in Ellegaard's glass-walled office. He sat at his desk across from a skinny guy with short-cropped hair so I said, "Who's the skinny guy?"

"Earl Davis. The CEO of BrainiAcme."

"Dammit."

But it was too late. Ellegaard was on his feet and waving me into his office.

I said to Leah, "Thanks for the warning."

"You are the laziest man I have ever met."

"You haven't met enough men."

Annika smiled. Her eye didn't droop when she smiled.

I walked into Ellegaard's office. He introduced me to Earl Davis. Earl stood. We shook hands. He had a firm grip meant to convey his straightforwardness or maybe he just had something to prove.

We talked about the details of Earl Davis's case. BrainiAcme is a boutique ad agency. A certain Fortune 100 company hired it to create viral YouTube videos. But six weeks in, Davis felt the job was a shell. What the certain Fortune 100 Company really wanted was to hire away his best talent and take them in-house. I was supposed to follow around his employees to see if they were having any off-the-book meetings with the Fortune 100 Company. But fortunately, Linnea Engstrom disappeared, and I got shot by an arrow and almost bled to death. So the exciting business of tailing ad agency creatives would have to wait.

I fed him a load about how excited I was to work on the BrainiAcme case. He said he understood the importance of my search for Linnea Engstrom.

"I have a seventeen-year-old daughter. I can't imagine. Do you think she ran away?"

"I can't discuss it," I said. "You understand."

"Of course. If she did, you can hardly blame her. Roger Engstrom is a piece of work."

My eyes asked Ellegaard's if this guy knew Roger was dead. Ellegaard's eyes said no. "Yeah?" I said. "You know Roger?"

"Anyone who works in tech in this town knows Roger Engstrom. That guy's bounced around since the early nineties. Always talks his way into a CEO job then sends the company into a nosedive but manages to jump ship just before it crashes. I'm a New Yorker. I don't get it. This town is too polite. No one wants to talk shit about anyone else. So Roger kept getting gigs. But after what he did at app-Etite his reputation caught up with him."

"Is that a food company?"

"No. App development. They had a load of VC money and he fucked it up. Put it all into a series of games no one liked. That's why he moved up to Warroad. He finally achieved clown status in the Cities. Guess he found a new sucker up there."

16

I sat shirtless on my stainless steel kitchen counter as Jameson White cut off his morning's work with scissors.

"What are those scissors called," I said, "the kind with the flat piece for cutting off bandages?"

"Bandage scissors," he said.

"I guess sometimes the answer is just that simple."

"Sometimes it is." He balled up the gauze pads and wrap and tape and threw them into a plastic bag. He inspected the wounds in front and back for over a full minute then said, "No sign of infection. How's the pain?"

"I've had a good distraction, so I haven't fainted yet. It feels like I'm getting stabbed when I move suddenly or get bounced around in the car. Other than that, it's a constant throbbing ache."

"Oh, brother. There's a few conditions that fall into the constant-throbbing-ache category, aren't there? I sometimes wonder if the good Lord gave us those so when we're on our deathbed, we think, *Well at least I don't have to deal with that shit anymore. This dyin' ain't so bad*." Jameson White cleaned the area with alcohol then applied an ointment. It stung. "You have a high tolerance for pain, my friend."

"Chalk that up to a general insensitivity."

"Ha!" He cut open a new package of gauze pads and a new roll of wrap. "So those distractions that are helping with the pain, are they personal or professional?"

"Both, but the professional have pushed out the personal, so I guess work gets most of the credit."

"Tough case, huh?" He taped the pads over the wounds then said, "Gonna have to lift your left arm a bit to wrap this. You may feel it."

He did what he'd threatened, and I felt it. I closed my eyes and breathed through the sausage making in my shoulder. I said, "Yeah, this case has some moving pieces. Most, on their own, make sense. A teenage girl disappears. Another teenager girl is sexually adventurous and winds up dead. A husband tells his wife he has a business meeting but instead meets another woman at her house. A businessman moves away because he's burned all his bridges in town. But there are a few things I just can't get my head around, like who makes a bow and arrow their weapon of choice?"

"Someone who doesn't like guns," said Jameson. "Or maybe someone who's fine with guns but doesn't want to make any noise."

"Then why not just use a knife or a cord around the neck?"

"You think whoever shot you could have walked right up to you and strangled or stabbed you? They either aren't strong enough or brave enough or just want to be stealthy. Arrows can't fly as far as bullets but they can fly pretty damn far. I've never shot one before, but I saw it on the Olympics in Brazil. I don't know how far away the target was but it looked like about a football field. That ain't nothing. Probably better range than a pistol. And no noise. I bet if you shot at someone and missed, they might not even know it."

"You've put some thought into this."

"What else am I going to do while waiting for your call? I got taken off the market for two full weeks. Now I'm like all pretty things, sitting on a shelf waiting to be used. Plus, I have treated more gunshot wounds than I can remember, but you're the first person who got shot by an arrow. I looked at those arrowheads on the internet. That's some nasty shit. Like four-sided razor blades. At high speed, they go through you like you're made of Jell-O or something and cause way more bleeding than a bullet."

The service door opened. I didn't need to look to know it was Lauren. It was the way she pulled open the heavy door, first a foot or so before wedging herself inside and giving the thing one last nudge with her shoulder. She slid past and the metal slab closed hard, the pneumatic cylinder at its top in need of replacement. Then her keys jingled the way they do as her boots scuffed up the cement stairs from the loading dock to the old factory floor. "Hello," she said.

"Jameson, this is Lauren." I said it quickly, almost before Lauren finished her "Hello" so Jameson didn't have time to ask if she were Micaela. "Lauren, Jameson White."

She walked over, and I caught a whiff of hospital mixed with something faint and flowery she always smelled of. Jameson turned, smiled, and shook her hand. They exchanged nice-to-meet-yous then Lauren said, "I mentioned to Micaela that Nils might be more receptive to treatment if he got it from someone other than me."

Lauren's emerald eyes swung toward me to start a conversation I would have to end. Then she looked back toward Jameson. "Micaela offered to hire someone full-time for a little while, and I thought it was a good idea. Looks like it's working out."

Jameson said, "You're the one who wrapped him up last night, right? You did a nice job."

"Thank you. I'm a bit out of practice. Wounds aren't my specialty. I was hoping it would get him through the night."

"No, no, don't be modest, girl. You're good."

"Not that good," said Lauren, her eyes on my freshly dressed wound but her mind somewhere else.

"Well that wraps it up, ha-ha. I will see you at the end of the evening, Mr. Shapiro. Don't even think of skipping it. We got that hole in your shoulder on the mend." Jameson White put his Windex-blue jacket over his gray cotton sweatshirt then lowered himself down the loading dock stairs, carrying his nurse's bag like an old lady carries a purse, by the handles as it banged off his knees.

I slid off the counter, grabbed my corduroy shirt with my right hand and started to work the left sleeve over my damaged wing.

"Not like that," said Lauren. She stepped toward me. "Like this." She took over and we said nothing until my shirt was on and buttoned. Then she said, "Are you headed back out?"

"I have to be at the Xcel Center at 7:00 for the Warroad semifinal."

"Are you free for an early dinner?"

I hadn't eaten lunch and was hungry, so we walked to Bar La Grassa on Washington and arrived just as they were opening the doors at 5:00.

We took a semicircular booth in the dining room and

sat under a large black-and-white print of Waylon Jennings and Johnny Cash. The dining room was quiet, but the bar in the front room had filled. The noise of people who worked in offices no longer being in offices drifted our way.

I knew what this dinner was about, so when Lauren asked how my day went, I said the case took a turn and left it at that. If I told her I had discovered Winnie Haas's and Roger Engstrom's bodies with arrows in them, we might have avoided the unavoidable. After Lauren gave me a perfunctory version of her day, she said, "I'm sorry to do this now, but we need to talk about things."

A waitress with red hair, not natural but cardinal red, appeared and asked if we wanted to start with drinks. Lauren ordered an Able Black Wolf Stout, and I ordered the same. The waitress smiled and disappeared.

Lauren said, "I'm not going to put this on you by asking where you are in this relationship. But I want to tell you where I am." She slid out the napkin from beneath her silverware and put it on her lap then said, "I am . . . I've been . . . —Oh, fuck it. I am putting it on you. You're the problem, Nils."

I sunk back into the leather booth. Lauren did not ask the question she wanted answered. A man/boy with 1890s whiskers came over, lit the candle on our table, and left. I said, "I love you. But I feel like we're not moving forward."

She nodded and thought then said, "Does that mean you want to end it?"

"I don't know."

"What kind of chicken shit answer is that?"

"If two people love each other, they can make a relationship work. Or, if two people are not in love with each other but their relationship functions in a way they both value, they can make that work. In either case, both people's expectations are met. So no one is disappointed. But if one person is in one place and the other person is in a different place, well, that's when things get difficult."

Lauren said, "How clinical of you. Kind of boiled it down to the nuts and bolts there. I trust you've conducted enough experiments and collected enough data for a thorough analysis."

"Okay. You want to tell me what that was about?"

"I'm a human being, Nils, not a fucking case." I failed to see the difference, but succeeded in not telling her so.

Cardinal Head returned, set two mugs of beer on the table, and asked if we were ready to order. Lauren said she was fine with whatever I wanted. I took that figuratively and literally and ordered small plates of gnocchi, roasted butternut squash, grilled leaks, and bruschetta with soft eggs and lobster. The waitress praised my choices and left.

I sipped my beer and turned my body toward Lauren, leaning my right shoulder into the dark leather. She did not turn to meet me. She bit her lower lip and reached for the votive on the table then turned it between her thumb and finger. The flame danced. I could see the clear lens of her left eye, the iris underneath reflecting green even in the dim light. More people slipped into the dining room. The restaurant had grown louder but our booth remained quiet.

Lauren said, "We're not in the same place, Nils."

"It's felt that way for a while. I've hoped it would pass. And maybe it will. But I feel your frustration every day."

"What you feel is not my frustration but my disappointment. I am *so* disappointed in you, Nils. We were on this great road together then you just veered off and left me by myself." Lauren took a sip of her beer. Then another. "I can't keep doing this if you're where you are. Because then, what are we even doing? Just hanging out? Hoping something changes? That doesn't work. Not for me anyway."

The conversation continued but got soft, like wet tissue without form and barely holding together. 1890s Whiskers brought the food. We said nothing while he set the plates on our table. He was slow and chitchatty and, by the time he left, we'd forgotten who last said what and what needed to be said next.

We ate without commenting on the dishes or anything else. Then I said, "I'm sorry I can't be where you want me to be."

She reached for her beer, stopped, and said, "And I'm sorry for keeping you from getting there." She turned and looked at me for the first time since we sat down and said, "I have to go." She slid out her side of the booth and walked away, her jacket clutched in one fist.

I had finished my beer, but Lauren had barely touched hers. I lifted her pint but stopped. She'd left a lip print on the glass just below the rim. My eyes glossed over, and the candles in the dining room twinkled like stars.

17

I drove to St. Paul, spent twenty-five dollars to park in a small lot to avoid getting trapped in a ramp, and paid double face value for a ticket from an individual who does not go to the dentist every six months. Inside the Xcel Center, I bought a coffee then made my way to the standing area at the top of the arena to gaze at the Warroad student section below me. The Xcel Center is a hockey arena with symphony hall acoustics and living room comfort. It's intimate and inviting, and fans watch the icy oval of speed and violence as if they're looking into another world.

Both teams had taken the ice for warm-ups. The higher seeded Warroad Warriors, wearing black jerseys with white and gold insignia, circled the close end of the ice. Wayzata, wearing white jerseys with blue and yellow, circled the far end. High above the glass, I heard sharp blades gouge ice as they propelled skaters over the gray sheet, leaving behind trails of dusty snow.

I used binoculars to watch Graham Peters and Luca Lüdorf skate with their teammates. Left crossovers clockwise then right crossovers counterclockwise then the same but skating backward, then the goalie drifted into the net for warm-up shots. Coach Kozjek, black windbreaker over a white shirt and gold necktie, stood behind the boards, arms folded. His assistant coaches clustered at the opposite end of the bench, leaving the hockey god with his thoughts.

The students of four teams filled the four corners of the arena. Warroad below me. Wayzata in the opposite corner. Duluth East in black and red to my right. Elk River in the same colors to my left. Parents, lovers of the game, college and NHL scouts, filled the seats between. All had come to see the best high school hockey in the United States. And often, that's what it was.

I aimed the binoculars on the Warroad students. The band sat right behind the glass and the rest of the students behind them, a mass of black and gold, painted faces, shiny beads, and big hats. I didn't know what or who I was looking for, but it wasn't Linnea Engstrom. She couldn't hide here. Her father had yet to be officially identified as one of the Woodbury murder victims, but word had leaked out. Even if the entire student body had conspired to keep Linnea's presence a secret, a teacher, a parent, someone would spot her and report it. All four sets of fans buzzed, but Warroad was more subdued. Despite standing directly above them, they were the quietest of the four towns. If Linnea Engstrom were here, Warroad's buzz would top them all.

I spotted Anne Engstrom's sister sitting high in the Wayzata section. She seemed to be alone. I wasn't sure why I'd come to the game other than to observe most of

Warroad's citizens in one time and place. But when I saw Anne's sister, I lowered the binoculars and headed to the opposite corner of the arena.

She sat in the top row. I stood behind her and said, "Excuse me."

She turned around. She'd changed into a royal blue sweater and carried a black jacket over her right arm. Her ponytail, rimless teardrop eyeglasses, faded Levi's, and adorable cheeks remained.

"My name is Nils Shapiro. I—"

"I know who you are." She stood. "Mel Rosenthal. I'm Anne Engstrom's sister."

"Do you have a moment?"

"I guess, yeah." Her seat was in the middle of the row. Fans blocked her exit on both sides. I offered her a hand. She took it, climbed up and over her seat. I'd seen her sitting down at Crestmoor Bay and hadn't realized she was so short, five foot one at most.

We walked to the escalator, descended to the club level, and found a hightop in the bar at the Jack Daniel's Old No. 7 Club. Cherrywood, slate, and stone that came together in a suburban chain restaurant kind of way, comfortable and pleasant—the kind of place that won't fuck up a burger or chicken wings. Fans from Elk River and Duluth East filled the dining room while awaiting the start of the second game.

I ordered another coffee and hoped it'd be better than the concession stand cup that had gone down like brown water. Mel Rosenthal ordered a glass of Old Vine Zin. She was at the X because her daughter, Ivy, played trumpet in the Wayzata band. Mel hadn't told Ivy about Uncle Roger yet. It didn't seem right if Linnea didn't know. She said Anne was staying with their parents, who lived in the first alphabet of St. Louis Park just west of Cedar Lake.

"Sleeping in her old room. It's terribly sad. All of this is terribly sad."

I said, "Are you close with Linnea?" Mel Rosenthal blinked a few times and pushed her empty coaster around. "Is this hard to talk about?"

"Kind of," she said. "It's difficult to explain . . . well, let's just say, it's not an appropriate time to speak ill of anyone." She looked up at me with the grayest of gray eyes.

"I'm sorry to tell you this, but it is the time. It's an important time. The few days after a kid disappears are crucial."

Mel Rosenthal nodded then said, "Okay." She swallowed. "Linnea and I had been quite close the last few years. She would call or text me every day. I guess she reached an age where the differences between her and her parents inspired her to seek out a more like-minded adult. In some ways, I guess, Linnea outgrew her parents."

"In what ways?"

Mel Rosenthal winced. "I suppose a nice way of putting it is Linnea's emotional intelligence exceeds her parents'. She's a sensitive kid. Always has been. Roger and Anne tried to deal with it by buying her stuff. When she was little, she saw a dog get hit by a car, so they bought her a pet rabbit to distract her. She'd see something on the news and get depressed—they'd buy her an iPad. It worked when Linnea was young, but when she hit her teens, it stopped working."

"Did she rebel?"

"You could call it that. It's normal for a kid to individuate from her parents at that age. But this was more than the norm. Anne and Roger weren't cut out to be parents. And to their credit, they never intended to be. Linnea wasn't planned, and Anne had her tubes tied during her C-section to make sure there'd be no more surprises."

"So Linnea turned to you."

"We had coinciding misfortunes. Linnea outgrew her parents, and I lost my husband."

"I'm sorry."

"Thank you. His name was Howard. He was a lovely man. Twenty years older than me. Handsome and successful and kind. So very kind. One day he went out for a jog on a warm March morning. He slipped on a patch of ice hidden under a puddle and hit his head on the curb. They couldn't stop his brain from swelling, and he died six weeks later."

The drinks came. I didn't take my eyes off Mel as the waitress set them on the table. Mel pressed her fingers on the base of her wineglass. She kept her fingernails short and wore no polish. She stared into her wine and said, "He died that May, and Anne and Linnea moved in for a few months." She lifted the glass and took a sip. Her eyes did not contain even a hint of blue, even next to her royal blue sweater. Eyes sad and warm and honest. "Anne wanted to be there for me. She meant well, but Linnea was our real support. During the summer, she and I grew quite close. To be brutally honest, even closer than I am with my own daughter. For a while there anyway. Linnea confided in me about school and friends and boys. She told me about her dreams."

Mel smiled and was quiet for a minute then said, "I should have established stronger boundaries. Guess I didn't try all that hard because Linnea is like Howard. All heart. Always taking in stray dogs and cats, squirrels that fell out of trees, abandoned baby raccoons, a crow with a broken wing.

"Last year, a wounded doe wandered into the Engstroms' backyard up in Warroad during hunting season. It had been shot in the hind leg and was terrified, but the deer let Linnea give it food and water and salt. Linnea led it into the garage and bought some bails of straw from the feed store to make it a bed until the vet could get there. The vet cost Roger twenty-eight hundred dollars. I remember the amount because Roger mentioned it every chance he got then made some stupid joke about not even getting any venison out of the deal."

I had questions for Mel Rosenthal, but she was on a roll. I wasn't about to stop her. Maybe she'd answer some I hadn't thought to ask.

"Linnea was the same with people," Mel said. "She befriended oddballs, artists, a kid with a speech impediment, foreign exchange students, LGBT kids, Guy Storstrand, the star of the Roseau team who was a couple grades ahead of Linnea."

"Isn't Roseau Warroad's arch rival?"

"Yep. Drove people in Warroad nuts. Especially since Guy is from Warroad and went over to Roseau to skate for the enemy. He plays for the Montreal Canadiens now."

"How did Roger and Anne feel about their daughter hanging out with a guy two years older?"

"To be honest, Roger and Anne weren't paying that much attention. Roger was preoccupied with business, and Anne was preoccupied with Roger. Linnea said she and Guy were just friends, but I think she wanted it to be more."

"So how does a hockey star qualify as a stray?"

"Guy has Tourette's. Hockey is the one place he felt on equal footing with everyone else. Until he met Linnea. She didn't give a damn that he ticks or that he's a big hockey star. My guess is he appreciated that."

"Is she still in contact with him?"

"I don't know. Linnea and I had a falling-out last Christmas." She looked down and said nothing for what felt like too long then said, "The game is starting. Do you want to go out to the seats?"

"I'd rather hear what happened between you and Linnea."

Mel said nothing happened. They had grown close, communicated three, four times a day, but she started to feel like she was cheating on her own daughter and robbing Anne of the chance to have a better relationship with Linnea. When Mel explained that to her niece, Linnea didn't take it well. Mel tried to negotiate some lesser version of what they had, but Linnea wouldn't have it. One day Linnea just cut Mel off. Stopped responding to Mel's texts. Didn't answer her calls. Mel talked to Anne a few times a week and knew Linnea was okay, but that was it.

I said, "You've never told Anne about you and Linnea?"

"No. Like I said, I felt like I was betraying Anne. I didn't want to hurt her and I felt guilty. But I thought you should know—maybe it'll help find her." Mel Rosenthal picked up her wineglass, but it was empty.

"Do you think Linnea ran away?"

Anne nodded. "I fear she found a new surrogate parent who got her into something bad."

I said, "Do you want to get out to the game or is it okay if I ask a few more questions?"

"There are seventy-five TVs in this bar. I won't miss anything. I don't even care about hockey. I'm just here to support Ivy."

"Do you think Luca Lüdorf's a stray? Does dating him fit Linnea's pattern?"

"I'm not sure. I don't know him. They started dating a few months ago. I've asked Anne about Luca. I've read about him online. That's Minnesota for you—no shortage of information about high school hockey players, especially those going on to play at the next level. Other than his hockey skills, he seems to be an average kid. Polite. Well liked. And according to Anne, he's crazy about Linnea. Sends her flowers. Buys her gifts. Does all that boy-in-love stuff."

"Have you told the police everything you've told me?"

"All of it," she said. "Every bit."

The arena erupted. The horn sounded. I looked up at a TV and saw the Wayzata Trojans celebrating in front of the Warroad net, sticks up in the air, helmets pressed together. The band played the fight song.

"Not my sport," Mel said, "but Ivy's loving this." Mel looked at the TV as the camera panned the Wayzata band. If she saw Ivy, she didn't say so. She just smiled, and her eyes shined.

"Nice start for Wayzata," I said.

"It's strange we're playing Warroad, isn't it?"

"Two elite programs. Not that strange. Do you get up to Warroad much?"

Mel said, "A couple times a year."

"I get the sense Roger and maybe even Anne aren't so welcome in Warroad."

Mel shook her head. "No one who knew Roger liked him. Except Anne. After all these years, I have no idea why she loved him so much. It's like in those stupid sitcoms starring an unattractive, loudmouth husband who's always causing trouble, but his beautiful wife loves him, so the audience is supposed to think he must be okay. Only with Roger, no one other than Anne thought he was okay."

"I only met him once. Why did people dislike him so much?"

"He was withholding. Never said what he was thinking. Only what he thought he should say. Something about the man was a lie. Actually, Howard used to say, everything about Roger was a lie. He was always trying to get Howard to invest in some new thing or another. And he'd make his pitch just as his current business was crashing into the ground. Howard never bit. But Roger would always find another sucker and pull together some kind of deal. That's why they moved to Warroad."

"You think people didn't like Roger because his bullshit didn't work in a place like Warroad?"

"I'm sure it did. What I heard was Roger hired away some key people from Marvin Windows. Doubled their salary. Gave them stock options. And it created a ripple through Marvin, which has a reputation for being a happy and healthy company. It's hard to attract good workers up there. A town of under two thousand people that's six miles south of the Canadian border. It's not for everyone."

"Do you know who funded Roger's business in Warroad?"

"NorthTech? No idea."

"Does Anne know?"

"I'm sure she does. Not that it mattered to her. Anne believed in Roger. She was his biggest fan. Sometimes two wrong people are somehow right for each other."

I thought *ain't that the fucking truth* but said, "What's wrong with Anne?"

"I shouldn't have said that."

"But you did."

Mel smiled a sad smile. "I love my sister, but she wants

whatever she doesn't have. And what she has, she doesn't want." Mel cocked her head and looked like she might cry. "Maybe that's why she loved Roger so much—she never really had him."

I said, "Did Anne have Linnea?"

"When Linnea was younger. Absolutely."

"And that made Anne an absent parent?"

"I think so. Unfortunately." Mel Rosenthal picked up her empty wineglass a second time. I flagged the waitress, ordered Mel another Old Vine Zin and a Grain Belt Nordeast for myself. Mel thanked me and said one more was her limit.

"Has Linnea made any attempt to contact you or Ivy?"

"Seriously?"

"It's a fair question."

"I know it's a fair question. The police have asked it ten times. You think I'd withhold that information? Especially now that Roger's dead? My sister's grieving. Nothing would give her more comfort right now than finding Linnea."

The arena erupted a second time. I looked at the TV. Wayzata had scored another goal. The heavily favored Warroad Warriors were trailing 2–0 just ten minutes into the game.

Mel said, "I'm sorry. I didn't mean that. I'm a little raw right now."

I wanted to let Mel off the hook. Tell her it was okay she snapped at me for asking a reasonable question. But, as Mel said, she was a little raw. And Mel's rawness had yielded me a freighter of information. "Any chance Linnea would contact Ivy?"

"I don't think so. Ivy's such a . . ." She stopped herself then said, "Goody Two-shoes."

"What was that pause? What were you going to say?"

Mel almost smiled then said, "I almost said Ivy's such a straight arrow."

"Ha!" We laughed, as we should have. Humor is like death. Eventually, it wins.

18

Mel said she'd call if she remembered any more specifics or if Linnea contacted either her or Ivy. She returned to the Wayzata section, and I found my seat twenty rows above the opposite blue line. The Zamboni made its final pass, leaving the ice wet and gray and clean. Then two workers opened swinging doors, and the ice resurfacing machine disappeared under the seats. The workers shoveled up the residual snow near the door then pulled the goals back onto the ice and slid them to their spots.

I got a text from Annika telling me to check my email. She'd forwarded a report from Madison PD. The only nearby business open at the time Linnea Engstrom logged into Starbucks' Wi-Fi was a tanning salon. It had a security camera, but the footage showed no one resembling Linnea Engstrom. There were offices above Starbucks, but they were closed last night. Linnea Engstrom remained as invisible in Wisconsin as she did in Minnesota.

The players returned to the ice with scattered applause

and cheers. The second period wouldn't start for seven minutes. Fans still crowded the concession stands and bars and bathrooms and souvenirs shops. Warroad finished the first period down 2–0. Maybe Wayzata's goalie was hot, or maybe Warroad hadn't found their groove. Coach Kozjek stood alone on the bench, looking at the far end of the ice where his team skated warm-ups. I put the binoculars on him and saw a reddened, tense expression. He'd lose eleven starting seniors after the season, including Graham Peters and Luca Lüdorf. He wouldn't get another shot at the state championship for at least two years. Maybe he felt the pressure. Maybe his stress came from somewhere else.

Kozy kept his hands in his jacket pockets and spit on the floor. If people get reincarnated as inanimate objects, the last thing you'd want to come back as is the rubber flooring under a hockey bench. As if cold hard steel skate blades aren't bad enough, you're under a constant barrage of spit, sweat, blood, and snot rockets.

Parents of the Warroad players and students sat behind the bench. Haley Housh's family had gone back to Warroad, but I looked for them anyway. I saw no familiar faces, except two.

St. Paul PD Officer Terrence Flynn sat directly behind the bench wearing plainclothes. He held a plastic souvenir cup. Not a beer. That meant nothing, of course. Maybe he didn't drink. Maybe he preferred soda. Then again, maybe he was on duty. Nor did it mean anything that Officer Julia Mason, the orange-haired cop with big gums, sat one row behind Flynn and a few seats to Flynn's left. She wore her hair down in front of her shoulders. That, too, meant nothing. But when Julia Mason lifted her hand to her mouth and spoke, and Terrence

Flynn nodded then spoke into his hand, the two had blown their cover. I scanned the stadium and saw other cops both in and out of uniform, including my new friend, Detective Waller from Woodbury, and her colleague with the discount haircut. Woodbury had apparently decided Kozy was their man for the murders on Crestmoor Bay. St. Paul Police concurred. They had chased the shiny object and were in position to take him in for questioning after the game.

The second period didn't go any better for Warroad. The great Luca Lüdorf was off his game, missing passes, fanning on a wrist shot, losing races to the puck. Linnea's disappearance had taken its toll on Luca. Wayzata kept the puck in Warroad's end. Warroad's goalie made a few stellar saves, but with four minutes left in the period, Wayzata scored their third goal. I left my seat to use the bathroom before the period ended to avoid the long line of full bladders. When I returned, nothing happened. I saw no one. I spoke to no one. The Zamboni resurfaced the ice. I sat and waited for the third period and wondered when and where the police would take Kozjek.

During the break, Warroad found its soul. They returned to the ice with yells and grunts audible far above the glass. Luca Lüdorf approached the center-ice face-off with his chest out and bumped the Wayzata player getting in position. Down 3–0, it appeared Kozjek's strategy was to intimidate Wayzata through ferocity.

Hockey can be a display of speed and agility and grace, a dance on ice, like electrons whipping around a nucleus to make one atom of glorious motion, the way the Europeans play the game. But hockey can be far from that in the American and Canadian game, where speed submits to mass and grace is destroyed before it can form.

That's the game Warroad played in the third period. Some of it was within the rules and some of it wasn't. Warroad served two, two-minute minors, but killed both penalties without yielding a fourth goal.

The score changed eight minutes into the third period when Graham Peters checked a Wayzata winger off the puck near the Warroad net, a hard but clean hit that dropped the Wayzata player to the ice headfirst. Graham picked up the puck and flicked a board pass to Luca who had started toward the Wayzata end. Luca had a clean breakaway, the closest defender trailed by ten feet. Luca approached the net at full speed, faked with his wrist then backhanded the puck over the goalie's left shoulder and into the back of the net.

Warroad trailed Wayzata 3–1.

The Wayzata player still lay on the ice. Ten minutes later, emergency medical personnel slid a wooden board under his back, taped down his body and head, then carried him away. The entire arena applauded, but the Wayzata Trojans felt a cold called fear. Warroad was out for pain.

The next few minutes featured elbows and shoves and one-handed cross-checks. The refs pulled players apart, blew quick whistles, but couldn't get the game under control. They called a prophylactic penalty on Warroad when a Wayzata winger slipped during routine jostling for the puck. Kozjek and his assistants screamed foul. A ref skated over to Kozjek and appeared to administer a warning. Graham Peters showed his dislike for the call with a risky move to intercept a cross-rink pass. The risk paid off. He broke toward the Wayzata goal unde-fended. But Graham couldn't match Luca's speed, and the defender was catching up. So Graham unleashed a wounded duck outside the blue line. It landed a foot in

front of the goalie and bounced between his legs. Warroad trailed 3–2.

There were over six minutes left in the game, plenty
of time for Warroad to score a tying goal. The Warroad
band blared its fight song sloppy and energetic. The Warroad fans refused to sit. Choreographed chants pounded
the Wayzata fans across the arena. Warroad won the en-
suing face-off. Graham dumped the puck into the Wayzata end. Luca raced a Wayzata defenseman into the
corner. Luca won the race, but the Wayzata player made
no attempt to stop. He skated full force into Luca, sending him into the boards face-first.

The penalty is called boarding. It's a five-minute ma-
jor, but the referees didn't call it. Wayzata picked up the
loose puck and skated toward the Warroad end.

An avalanche of boos tumbled toward the ice. Coach
Kozjek reached over the boards and banged with his fist
as play went on. Luca Lüdorf got back on his feet. He
flew toward the Warroad end, feet spread, carving the ice
with each stride. Luca dropped his stick at center ice. His
gloves fell a second later. He hit the Wayzata cross-
checker full speed and tackled him to the ice. Before the
refs or anyone else could stop Luca, he ripped off the
Wayzata player's helmet and threw four hard lefts into
the kid's face. Blood burst from what used to be his nose,
staining his white Wayzata jersey, Luca's fist, and the
snowy ice. It took all three refs to pull Luca off the kid.
The benches cleared.

The referees lost control. Players fought in twos and
threes and fours. Coaches from both benches slid onto
the ice in street shoes, shouting at and shoving each
other. A few fans had climbed the glass and hung ready
to flip over and onto the ice. It takes a lot for stoic Minnesotans to lose their shit. But when they do, watch out.

Most have little experience yielding to their passions. They don't know how to manage that level of emotion. They have a child's meltdown in a grown-up's body.

Security personnel armed with walkie-talkies and yellow jackets jumped onto the ice joining several dozen uniforms from St. Paul PD and the Ramsey County Sheriff's Deputies. They spread themselves along the boards. The drunkest and dumbest of fans dropped onto the ice. Six or seven, I counted. Police wrestled the trespassers to the ice and bound their hands with cable ties.

When it was over, Luca Lüdorf had been ejected along with Coach Kozjek. They walked into the tunnel to a mix of cheers and boos. Officers Terrence Flynn and Julia Mason walked onto the ice, badges around their necks. They gathered half a dozen uniforms and followed Kozy into the tunnel. In the locker room, they'd ask Kozjek to come in for questioning. If he refused, they'd arrest him on the spot. Either way, news would break late tonight or tomorrow morning, depending on how publicity hungry the police were feeling.

Maintenance personnel scooped away the bloody, broken ice and replaced it with wet snow, packing and scraping as they went, as if they were spackling a damaged wall. It'd only take a few minutes for the refrigeration coils in the floor to freeze the repair job into hard ice.

Detective Jamie Waller had disappeared from her seat. I texted her something about not being good at sharing and I was taking my toys and going home. She didn't respond. But I did receive a text from Mel Rosenthal.

Mel: *It's Mel. Are you still here?*
Me: *I am. Need another drink?*
Mel: *I do. Downtown Minneapolis to get away from*

> *this mess? I should stay until the game ends, but*
> *then?*

Me: *Yes. Wherever you'd like.*

Mel: *The Bachelor Farmer.*

Me: *See you there.*

I tried to convince myself meeting Mel Rosenthal was for work. I failed. I pictured taking Mel home to a bed Lauren had slept in last night. It would smell more like Lauren than me. I had slept on the couch. The night probably wouldn't go that way—we'd just met—she didn't seem the type, and that had never been my style. But you never know.

The players skated tentatively. They'd seen violence unleashed, felt its potential in themselves, and it frightened them. They wanted no more trouble and seemed willing to go through the motions so the clock could tick away. Warroad lost 3–2.

19

I parked my car at the coat factory and walked over to meet Mel Rosenthal at the Bachelor Farmer. The top two floors are a restaurant that serves foodie-grade Norwegian fare. It's good but specific—I doubt they get a lot of requests to franchise. The basement is a bar, accessed in back through a gray steel door set in yellow brick. The room is small, long, and narrow with a bar of white marble over a plywood base. Scandinavian chic.

We found two spots at the end of the bar near some twentysomethings wearing too many layers and winterlike hats made of something light so they could display the fashion without getting sweaty heads. Mel ordered a martini and I ordered a Redbreast, neat. The two cocktails cost more than thirty bucks, yet people still have the gall to call Minneapolis Minnie-no-place.

Ivy wouldn't be coming home tonight, Mel said. The entire trumpet section of the marching band was sleeping in a mansion on Lake Minnetonka in a neighborhood you call home if your name is Pillsbury or Cargill. We talked about Linnea and Roger and Anne, then our conversation transitioned to personal.

Mel hadn't dated anyone since Howard died a few years ago. She'd been on dates, but nothing had come of them. Nothing wrong with the guys—okay that was a lie, she said—plenty was wrong with most of them—but she wasn't ready. Ivy would be leaving for college next fall and then, Mel said, is when she thought she might make more of an effort.

"You had her young," I said.

"When I was twenty-three," said Mel. "Howard didn't want more children. He has two from his first marriage, and I was indifferent. But it happened, and I'm glad it did. Do you have children?"

"No," I said. "I was married and we lost one at four months."

"Oh, that's terrible. I'm sorry."

"Yeah, thank you. It wasn't fun. My wife didn't want to try again after that. It's not the reason our marriage ended, but it gave it a little push."

She sipped her martini as I calculated she was forty-one, give or take a year.

"I apologize," I said. "I don't know why I told you that. I just met you."

"No need to apologize. It's good you can talk about it."

I pictured Lauren walking away from the dinner table and felt a wave of grief. A dying relationship is like an Alzheimer's patient. When it finally succumbs, it's less tragic because a big part of what you loved is already gone. It can even feel like a relief. But the finality still stings. The loss is just as noticeable. I'd had no intention of asking Mel out for a drink. But when she asked me, I didn't say no.

Somehow I felt less guilty because Mel was a widow.

Jesus Christ, I was having a drink with a widow. It felt so grown-up for no good reason. There are plenty of young widows. Too many. And yet, it made me feel like I had to be responsible, that Mel was extra vulnerable, as if she weren't capable of protecting herself and thus the job fell to me. That was bullshit, of course. Mel was perfectly capable of protecting herself and maybe that's the last thing she wanted to do. Maybe she wanted a quick lay to see if she cared or maybe she knew she didn't and wanted one anyway.

I was feeling quite proud of myself for giving her the freedom to do what she wanted when she leaned over and kissed me. It was a small, polite kiss, and I responded with gratitude.

"I wasn't planning on that," she said, "hope it was okay."

"You're lovely."

She smiled and looked down for what felt like a long time. Then she said, "Thank you for saying that."

We finished our drinks and each ordered another. A group of designer types entered sporting attention-getting haircuts like the kind you see in magazines and think, *no one would actually ever look like that on purpose*. They were loud and drunk and pushed themselves to the back where they'd bump into us and apologize but not mean it.

We endured it for a while then Mel said, "Know anywhere around here we can go to sober up before driving?"

We walked to the coat factory and drank water and made out. I told her I'd just had surgery on my shoulder but not why, in fear it would kill the mood. Adjusting position for my injury led to some laughs, and we somehow understood it wouldn't go too far. After a while we ran out of steam. I left the couch and dropped a couple of purple Nespresso pods into the machine and made us each a hot cup. We sipped coffee and talked like two people who were happy to have met each other. I walked Mel to her car. We kissed good night and ended with a long hug. I watched Mel Rosenthal drive away, walked back to the coat factory, and fell asleep in the sheets that smelled like Lauren.

20

I lay in bed reviewing my stumbles with women when my phone buzzed. The screen's faint glow did nothing to lighten the never-dark coat factory. Too many windows and city lights. I had propped myself into a comfortable position and was afraid I'd never re-create it, so I left the phone where it was. In the last forty hours, I'd taken an arrow to the shoulder, nearly bled out, undergone surgery, and looked for a missing girl but instead found three cold bodies and one warm one. The text could wait.

I needed sleep to end a day of awkward good-byes. *So long, Roger Engstrom. You were the easiest good-bye of the day. It was a pleasure, Winnie Haas. I wish I'd had a chance to know you better. Later, Ellegaard. I walked out of your office feeling your disappointment in my choice of cases. All right then, Lauren. I didn't even say good-bye to you. You were halfway out the booth when you said, "I have to go." Sweet dreams, Mel Rosenthal. I wonder if I'll see you again.*

I left my phone on my nightstand and did what detectives do. I told myself stories about who sent the text and analyzed which felt most plausible. Lauren didn't want our last conversation to end the way it did, so she texted to make a plan for a proper good-bye. Mel Rosenthal hadn't felt anything for anyone since Howard died. She felt a little something for me and wanted to say one last good night. Maybe a thank-you. Or perhaps an apology because she's not ready and shouldn't have let the evening go where it went. Ellegaard wanted to meet first thing in the morning to dissuade me from continuing on the Engstrom case. Jamie Waller returned the snarky text I'd sent at the Xcel Center. Jameson White chastised me for missing my final wound cleaning and redressing of the day. They all felt plausible, but I didn't have to play detective. The answer lay on my nightstand. It buzzed a second time to remind me.

I inched myself up into a sitting position and reached for my phone with my right hand.

Dude if you have $500 I have info about Linnea Engstrom.

I'd forgotten about that awkward good-bye. Ernesto Cuellar walked away from the white bucket, hands in his pockets. I returned the text with my right thumb.

When and where?

Do u have the cash?

I do. Let's meet in public. No offense.

That's cool.

Dunn Brothers on 50th and Xerxes at 7. Give you enough time to get to school?

Yeah dude.

I sent one more text before attempting to get comfortable. I asked Jameson White for an 8:30 A.M. wound dressing. He responded saying he thought less of me for missing tonight's wound dressing, but he'd be there. I set my alarm.

At 6:00 A.M. I checked my phone and saw no emails, voice mails, or texts about Gary Kozjek's arrest. I checked the St. Paul *Pioneer Press* website. Nothing there, either. I showered with my shoulder in a bag, then tried to contact Linnea's friend Guy Storstrand, who played for the Montreal Canadiens. I left messages with the Canadiens' front office, on Twitter, and on Facebook. I didn't expect a reply and didn't get one.

I kept a thousand dollars in cash taped inside the body of a ceramic lamp. One day the internet would go down for a while and take the ATMs with it, and I didn't want to run out of peanut butter funds. I took five hundred, put it in a gas bill envelope, and drove out of the coat factory.

Dunn Brothers on Xerxes hadn't changed in the year since I'd moved out of the neighborhood. Same baristas. Same "hello how you doin's" as if I'd never moved away. Ernesto Cuellar waited for me at a table near the front window. He wore jeans, a white Southwest Lakers hoodie, and the same scared expression I'd seen the day before. He said, "Do you have the money?"

"Can I interest you in a beverage?"

"I'd take a hot chocolate."

"Whipped cream?"

"Yeah, man."

I got our drinks and a few muffins. "So what do you know, Ernesto?"

"First the money."

I removed the gas bill envelope from my jacket pocket and handed it to him. He took it, lowered it below the table, and counted the money. To anyone else he looked like he was bowing his head in prayer, thanking God for the hot chocolate and muffins before him. He raised his head, satisfied that the money was all there.

Then he took a sip of hot chocolate and said, "After you were such a dick yesterday I went back to school and rigged a camera in my locker so it looked out a hole where the number plate used to be screwed on. Whoever gave me the note must have been watching me or something, 'cause he knew I delivered his message. So when he paid the second fifty like he promised, the camera got a good look at his face."

"You're not just book smart, are you, Ernesto?"

Ernesto tried not to smile, failed, and covered it by taking another sip of hot chocolate. "The kid on my camera is named Joaquin Maeda." Ernesto swiped his finger through the whipped cream and stuck it in his mouth.

"That's all I get for five hundred?"

"No, man. Joaquin lives in my neighborhood. He's the only other kid there who goes to Southwest. Sometimes we ride to school together on the city bus or one of our moms drives us. I know him okay."

"Is he a good student like you?"

"Kinda. He's good at writing and poetry. He's in a hip-hop band. But he sucks at math and science, so I help him out sometimes. Guys he hangs with in the neighborhood are pretty rough, though."

"Gang rough?"

Ernesto just looked at me then said, "What's this bright green muffin? Lime or something?"

"Pistachio."

"Like the nut? No way." He took a pinch from the top, put it in his mouth, and made a *not bad* face. "Joaquin didn't want me to know it was him who wrote the note telling you to back off. I think that's kinda weird. So I figured he knows that girl you're looking for. I checked

his Twitter and stuff. Linnea follows Joaquin on Instagram. Then I cross-referenced who follows Joaquin and
Linnea Engstrom and found Miguel Maeda. He's Joaquin's cousin and lives in Mexico."

"When are you going to stop impressing me, Ernesto?"

"I can't help it." Suppressed smile. "And I googled you.
You're that dude who solved the Edina murder last year.
That's kinda cool."

"So you thought you'd show me your detective skills."

"It's just logic and shit."

"I'll take that as a compliment. But you've only earned
about two-fifty of that five hundred so far."

"I ain't done, man. Here's the superweird thing. Joaquin posts a bunch of pictures of Call of Duty on Instagram."

"He posts screenshots of him playing a video game?"

"No. That's what's weird. He posts just the cover of
the DVD. Sometimes it's World War II or Black Ops III
or Black Ops II or Modern Warfare. And just the covers,
nothing else. So I figure, it has to be some kind of code,
you know. I downloaded the posts and zoomed in on 'em
and then I found it. In the Y of Call of Duty, there's these
little bullet holes. Sometimes there's three or four or five.
Sometimes more. Sometimes less."

"And there aren't normally bullet holes in the Y?"

"There aren't normally bullet holes anywhere."

"Wow. You really wanted that five hundred."

"It's a lot of money. I need it. I'm building this dope
computer."

"So what do you think those bullet holes are?"

"Three holes, play the game at 3:00. Five holes, play
the game at 5:00."

"So Joaquin's Instagram followers who know the code,
they know what time to play? Like in a private lobby?"

"Yeah, man. I think that's what it is."

"Why are they using a code to communicate when they're playing a video game?"

"Dude, it ain't about the game. Yeah, they play it, but everyone on the team has a microphone. I bet what they're really doing is just talking."

"And the NSA can't listen in."

"I don't know what they're talking about. I'm not in the lobby. You have to know what it's called to join and you need to be invited. Can't get in if you're not. But since he's the one who put a hundred bucks and the note in my locker telling you to back off Linnea, it could be about her."

A group of Southwest kids in purple-and-white letter jackets sat down at a table near the locomotive-shaped coffee roaster. They carried full backpacks and spoke with loud voices. A girl said hello to Ernesto, and he said hello back.

"Are you worried about them seeing you with me?"

"Nah, man. I'll just tell him you're interviewing me for the summer jobs program or you're a mentor or something. No one cares." He downed the remainder of his hot chocolate then wiped his lips with his sleeve.

"So your friend, Joaquin, can talk with whoever he invites to his private lobby without cell phones or email or Facebook. And the government will never know about it."

"More like without Reddit or Snapchat, but yeah." Ernesto finished the pistachio muffin then peeled the paper cup off the banana one. "Oh, sorry, man. You want this one?"

"No. It's all for you."

"Thanks, dude."

"You want another hot chocolate? Something else to eat?"

"I'd take another hot chocolate."

I went to the counter and bought Ernesto a second hot chocolate and a chocolate croissant as backup. My phone dinged.

Jamie Waller: *Expecting you in Woodbury at 8*
Me: *I don't travel on one-way streets.*
Jamie Waller: *Bring coffee. The station's stinks.*
Me: *Where's Gary Kozjek?*
Jamie Waller: *See you at 8*

I didn't respond.

I waited for the hot chocolate and bounced around some ideas. Joaquin Maeda knew where Linnea Engstrom was. I just had to get him to tell me. That might be easy or it might be impossible. I had to learn more before I made my approach. When I returned to the table, I said, "Do you know Joaquin's Call of Duty screen name?"

"I know the one he uses when I play with him. But he's probably got another for private lobbies."

"Any way to get it?"

"I'd have to get on his machine."

"Console or PC?"

"Xbox."

"Is it possible for you to get on his Xbox?"

"No, man. I don't go to his house. I just see him around."

"Can you hack into it if you're playing online together?"

"I don't do that kind of stuff."

"But could you?"

"Maybe. But I won't. It's not cool. Dude's my friend. If I thought he would hurt that girl, I'd do whatever. But I don't think he would."

"You think Linnea Engstrom is on those chats?"

"Maybe. And I bet it involves his cousin, Miguel. Joaquin, he's kind of emo. Can't keep his mouth shut. He has to get it out or he'll explode or something. He wrote this verse about his cousin Miguel being locked out of the country. And Miguel knows Linnea online. And he was here last year. I met him a couple times."

"Why isn't Miguel allowed in the country?"

"He was here as an exchange student then got in trouble for something and got deported and the government won't let him back in."

"Do you know what he got in trouble for?"

"No, but I could probably find out."

"How much is that going to cost me?"

"How much you got?" Ernesto Cuellar stopped trying to hide his smile.

"How can someone from Minnesota get into a private game lobby with someone in Mexico? Don't they have to be on the same regional server?"

"You're shittin' me, right?"

"I use the internet. I have no idea how it works."

"VPN, dude. You can make it look like you're anywhere." The table of Southwest High kids emptied behind me. "Hey, I should get to school. I'll text you if I find out anything else that's worth some money. Thanks for the hot chocolate and stuff."

Ernesto Cuellar got up and disappeared into the pile of kids. My favorite barista, sporting pink and yellow hair, dropped a napkin on my table. It said *Margaret Glaspy*.

21

I texted Jameson White that I needed more time. He said he had all day and so did the bacteria in my shoulder, so I should quit dillydallying and get shit done. Half an hour later, I sat across from Minneapolis PD Inspector Gabriella Núñez in her first precinct office. She'd let her black hair grow since I'd last seen her, which thickened the French braid behind her head. Her big, round black eyes had no creases around them. She had just turned thirty-nine but looked twenty-nine, probably because she'd never married, had no kids, and her parents and siblings lived in San Diego. She ran ten miles every morning regardless of what Minnesota's weather had to say and ate a hamburger and fries for every lunch.

Gabriella Núñez kept her office as clean and neat as her life. Simple furniture with straight lines. Nothing on her desk but a computer terminal and phone. A dozen pictures and accolades hung on the walls. OCD, if pointed in the right direction, can be a good thing.

"Nice digs," I said. "One of us has come a long way."

"I had lunch with Ellegaard last month. I saw your offices. City Center. Administrative assistant. Junior investigator. You're doing okay." She stood. "I want to show you something." She went to the wall and liberated a framed photograph from its hook and handed it to me. Thirty-two Minneapolis Police cadets taking their oath. Black pants. Blue shirts. White gloves. Ellegaard stood in the back row. Gabriella and I stood in the front row. I looked twelve years old.

Gabriella smiled. She didn't smile often, but when she did, you had to squint. She said, "Seen that lately?"

"No. Mine's in a box somewhere."

"You and Ellie should hang one in the reception area of your office." I handed it back to her, she returned it to its hook then straightened it. "You ever wonder what would have happened if the mayor hadn't laid us off right after we graduated?"

"I know what would have happened. You'd have bossed me around the next seventeen years."

"Yeah, I would have." She sat behind her desk. "So what's so urgent?"

"I have reason to believe there's a Minneapolis kid who's in contact with Linnea Engstrom. He lives by Powderhorn Park." I didn't need to catch her up on the case or why I was in a sling. She'd heard what happened. Word spreads fast in the biggest small town in the world.

"Why do you think the kid knows where she is?"

I told her about my run-in with Ernesto Cuellar yesterday and our friendly breakfast this morning.

"Do you think this Joaquin Maeda is holding Linnea against her will?"

"No. But I'd still like to find her."

"Do you think Linnea's in danger?"

"No idea. Her father was murdered yesterday. Same

kind of arrow that stuck me. All I know is Joaquin's message to me was to stop looking for Linnea and that she was okay."

"So how can I help?"

"You can tell me what Miguel Maeda did to get himself deported."

Gabriella wasn't smiling now. She shook her head then logged on to her workstation. The keyboard clicked. The blue-white screen danced in her dark eyes. She exhaled something unpleasant, then said, "Tagging."

"What?"

"Miguel Maeda was arrested for tagging. It fell under Gang Task Force, and if you're not a citizen, that's an automatic ticket home."

"For tagging?"

"He was caught with known gang members. There's no leeway in that situation."

"What about his cousin Joaquin Maeda? Does he have a record?"

Gabriella's fingers drummed the keyboard. "He's been picked up a few times. A couple of curfew violations and a loitering. One shoplifting charge, but it was dropped. Not bad for a kid in that neighborhood."

"Can you send a uniform to press Joaquin? See if he knows where Linnea is?"

Gabriella looked at me hard. "Listen, Shap. We've worked our asses off building police goodwill in that neighborhood. All the problems we have in North Minneapolis, we don't want to start that with the Latinos."

"You won't even press a kid?"

Gabriella Núñez gave me a *did you seriously just ask me that* stare. She would be the next chief of police, not because she played the game well, but because she was that good of a cop. It was not my opinion but common knowledge. She said, "If we press Joaquin Maeda he'll know something's up and go deep underground. That'll make your job a hell of a lot harder if not impossible. St. Paul PD will press him if you ask them to, but I wouldn't."

She was right, of course.

"I know you'll do whatever you want, Shap. But don't make trouble in a neighborhood that doesn't want it. Kids like Ernesto Cuellar, he's an example of all the good that can happen when families and school and police and community programs and churches work together. So whatever you do, leave it as you found it. Pack out what you packed in."

She saw I understood then leaned forward and almost whispered, "There's a reason you're not a cop, Nils. Do what you do best. You'll get your answers. Just be careful and keep your mouth shut. You lose your license and you'll take Ellie with you."

Joaquin Maeda wasn't the only one sending coded messages. Gabriella Núñez just told me to break the rules. If I got caught, she wouldn't help me. I could live with that. I would not involve Ellegaard. I would not even tell Ellegaard. He couldn't have a Stone Arch Investigations principal going rogue. Leaning hard on Ernesto Cuellar was my last idea, but I let it go. The kid had a future. No matter how slim the risk, involving him could jeopardize that future. I wouldn't even ask Ernesto for Joaquin's address.

I was on my own. It felt like old times.

Jameson White met me at the coat factory. He cleaned my wound and counted my antibiotics and lectured me about not missing any more appointments with him. Micaela had taken him off the market for two weeks. I was his sole responsibility, and he wasn't the kind of guy who let shit slide. I promised we'd return to three changes a day and shook his giant hand when he left.

I created a fake Instagram account under the name of Selena Espinoza using a young woman's likeness I screen-grabbed from a website that made me click a box confirming I was eighteen or over. Then the fictitious Selena Espinoza followed Joaquin Maeda on Instagram. That morning, he'd posted a Call of Duty WWII cover with four tiny bullet holes in the Y.

I went to Best Buy and bought a new voice-activated digital recorder. It was smaller than a pack of gum and its battery lasted longer than a going-out-of-business sale at a Persian rug store. It wasn't hard to find Joaquin Maeda's address online. The only challenge would be getting into the house during broad daylight with little time to plan. Joaquin should be in school, but I had no idea about parents, grandparents, siblings, or dogs.

I stopped at Settergren's Hardware in Linden Hills, said hello to my favorite Münsterländers, who greeted me with wagging tails and leaning bodies while I listened to the storeowner tell me people and tulips were confused by the warm weather. Both were out in their yards despite the March blizzard that was sure to come. He wasn't putting away the shovels anytime soon.

I walked out of the hardware store and looked each way down Forty-Third Street. I was an easy target if an archer wanted to make me one. If the police had any idea who that archer was, I would have disappeared until they caught the person. Even if Gary Kozjek was the shooter, I had no idea if he'd been taken into custody. But without knowing who might be hunting me, my options were to hide or to live my life. It wasn't a hard choice.

I returned to the coat factory and changed into a pair

of navy Dickies work pants with a matching blue shirt featuring an embroidered patch over the left pocket. The patch, in a cursive script, read DAVE. I topped it off with my navy baseball cap and a pair of wire-framed dummy eyeglasses. I whipped up a few brochures and business cards on my MacBook then headed back out.

Joaquin Maeda lived on Tenth Avenue South in a sage-green, two-story home so narrow it only had one window on each floor facing the street. The front yard was dormant brown and not made of grass but of mowed-down weeds. It measured about ten by ten feet square. A few broken concrete steps, stained with rust from the rebar inside, led up to a weathered aluminum storm. I pressed the doorbell and heard a ring from 1930. A dog barked, and a woman between fifty and seventy answered the door. She wore a floral print dress of pastel flowers on a beige field over her heavy, shapeless body. Her gray hair was pulled back tight. She peered at me over half-moon readers.

"Yes?" she said in a heavy Spanish accent.

"Good morning. My name is Dave Peterson. I work for Minneapolis Radon Control. We specialize in radon detection and mitigation." I tried to sound as if I'd memorized a sales pitch. "As I'm sure you know, radon is a problem in many Minneapolis basements, which can act like a vacuum and suck radon gas from the surrounding soil into the house through cracks in the foundation," I held up the brochure. She opened the storm door and took it. The dog barked again. She looked over the brochure and the business card.

"What do you want?"

"I would like to place this radon detection kit in your basement." I showed her the kit I'd purchased at Sette-gren's Hardware. "You don't have to do anything. I'll set up the kit in your basement. It has to sit there for several hours, then I'll pick it up later this evening."

"How much?"

"There is no expense to the homeowner."

"Free?"

"Yes. Detection is free. If we find radon, we work with the city and your insurance company to pay for mitigation, which involves installing a pump under your foundation to relieve the pressure so gas no longer enters the home. I'm sure you're well aware of how long-term exposure to radon increases risk of lung cancer. I just spoke to the Gomez family next door and put a kit in their basement."

Everything I said was true except my name wasn't Dave Peterson, I didn't work for Minneapolis Radon Control—that company doesn't exist—nor would any insurance company or city be paying for mitigation if the kit detected the radioactive gas. The woman looked at the brochure, then looked at me. I have a face people trust. The Gomezes next door trusted it. So do TSA agents and the Costco employees who compare your receipt to the contents of your cart. They never even look under my hay-bale-size package of paper towels. They just make a checkmark on my receipt and let me go. They all trust a boyish-looking white guy with no tattoos or piercings who serves a big pile of polite garnished with a smile. Having one arm in a sling didn't hurt either.

"Okay," said the woman. She opened the door, and I stepped into a tiny foyer.

The Maeda house was neat and clean and comfortable-looking. As the exterior suggested, it was only one room thick. There was a coat closet to my right and the living room straight ahead and what I assumed was the kitchen behind that. Maybe a family room, as well. It occurred to me that the Maeda household might not be like every other house I knew with teenagers. The video game console might not be in the basement. It might be in the back den or in Joaquin's bedroom, wherever that was. I had to improvise a contingency plan.

I shook her hand. "Dave Peterson. Nice to meet you."

"Chrissia Maeda."

"A pleasure to meet you, Chrissia. Would you like to come downstairs and watch me set up the kit?"

"It's okay. No thank you."

"Depending on the layout downstairs, I may leave a few tiny test buttons upstairs. I'll let you know if that's the case."

"Okay."

"This will only take five minutes. I'll be right up."

"Okay." She smiled.

I found the basement stairs off the kitchen and descended the narrow, steep staircase. It was a typical Minneapolis old home basement. Nine-by-nine-inch linoleum tiles, ancient and backed with asbestos but harmless as long as they stayed glued to the cement floor. Cinder block walls painted yellow. A low open ceiling, not more than seven feet high with exposed floor joists riddled with corrugated conduit. And payday, a ratty afghan-covered couch facing a sixty-inch flat-screen on an IKEA TV bench holding an Xbox, game controllers, and a Bluetooth headset, all charging and ready for action.

I set the kit on the TV bench—it would create a nice diversion—then removed the recorder from my pocket, covered its LED lights with electrical tape, turned it on, and looked for a place to hide it. The braces in the floor joists overhead were wide enough. I turned on the recorder, placed it atop a brace, sat on the couch, and said, "Hey, Mickey. I'm in a house on Tenth Street. I'll be over as soon as I can." I retrieved the recorder and listened. My voice sounded clear. I rehid the recorder in the ceiling, went back upstairs, and told Chrissia Maeda everything was set and I'd be back after dinner.

22

I got in the car and tuned the radio to WCCO in time to catch the top-of-the-hour headlines. No mention of Gary Kozjek. Something wasn't right.

Leah Stanley called and said a man was waiting for me at the office. I had nothing to do, so I stopped by. I saw him from the corridor through the glass door. Raynard Haas sat in the reception area wearing black pants tucked into knee-high black boots and a black jacket festooned with buckles and zippers. His round, cobalt-blue plastic frames glowed under the fluorescent overheads. A thick portfolio rested on the floor. I wondered why he didn't leave it in the car. Maybe he thought his work was too precious to be left alone. I entered, and he said, "Thank you, Mr. Shapiro, for coming in to see me."

"What can I do for you, Mr. Haas?"

"I'm worried about Ben."

"My office?"

"Please."

I hadn't been in my actual office in weeks. Someone kept it clean and someone else had stolen my Nerfoop, probably Ellegaard trying to spit-shine our corporate image. I sat behind my desk. The chair was too low. My desk came up to my chest. I tried to adjust it, but it wouldn't budge. I suspected Leah Stanley of swapping chairs. Raynard Haas sat in the chair across from me, but he was so short we looked at each other eye to eye.

I said, "I would imagine Ben's going through a bit of hell right now."

"Yes," said Raynard. "How could he not be? His mother was killed."

"And you think there's some way I can help?"

"That's my hope. Whatever Ben says about Haley Housh, I think her death hit him pretty hard. He'd convinced himself he didn't love her, that their relationship was just physical. But he's a sensitive kid. I think he felt it more than he'd like to admit."

"Okay . . ."

"Then adding his mother's death on top of that . . . I'm worried about Ben's ability to cope. He may have to take some time away from school, which could jeopardize his acceptance to Stanford."

"I doubt that, considering the circumstances. But even so, would that be the worst thing in the world?"

"No, of course not. The worst thing in the world has already happened. Ben lost his mother. They were very close."

He picked up the Kevin Garnett bobblehead from my desk and turned it in his white, soft hands—his nails and cuticles were flawless. I pictured Raynard Haas in a nail salon, his feet soaking in a tub while he regaled the manicurist with the dramatic events of his week. "I'm feeling a bit helpless when it comes to comforting Ben. I guess

I'm just hoping to hear you have some leads in the case. I could relay that to him, and maybe he'd feel like there's some logic in the world, after all. That maybe something is being done to right the wrongs."

"Which case are you talking about?"

He looked at me, puzzled, as if I'd just asked the most stupid question in the history of Mankind. "The double murder in my ex-wife's house."

"I'm sorry, Mr. Haas. I'm not working on that case. You'd have to talk to Woodbury Police."

"But it's tied to the Linnea Engstrom case. Her father was killed. Didn't the Engstroms hire you to help find her?"

"I am looking for Linnea Engstrom, but I don't know if her disappearance is connected to the murders on Crestmoor Bay. And I'm sorry, but whatever I've learned about that I'm not able to share."

"Huh," he said. "I just assumed . . ." He trailed off and rubbed his bald head. "You know, I'm a guy from a small town in Northern Wisconsin. I know a little bit about architecture and design, but I guess I'm still naive when it comes to how the world works."

"I wouldn't be too hard on yourself. Unless you'd worked with a private investigator, you wouldn't know how much we value discretion."

"I suppose."

"You really think catching the person who killed Winnie would help Ben's emotional state?"

"Honestly, I don't know. I'm just a dad trying to help his kid. Grasping at straws, really."

"Where'd you grow up in Northern Wisconsin?"

"Hurley."

"I know it well."

"No one knows Hurley."

"Liberty Bell Chalet has the best pizza in the world."

He smiled. "There's no close second. Just don't ever say that to anyone from New York."

"My family's right across the border in Bessemer."

"Yupers." He smiled. "They're good people."

"I wish I could help you, Raynard. But even if I do find Linnea Engstrom, I don't know what good that'll do Ben."

"You're probably right. I'm sorry to have bothered you. I don't know why I thought you'd be working on Winnie's and Roger Engstrom's murders. And I sure do hope you're close to finding Linnea. That family doesn't need another tragedy." I said nothing. It got too quiet for too long. "Right, right," said Raynard. "You can't say anything. Didn't mean to pry."

"Tell Ben to call me if he thinks of anything else regarding Linnea. Or Haley. No matter how small, it could be useful."

"I will. Thanks for making time for me."

Raynard stood. I shook his hand. He turned and walked out of my office, lifting his giant portfolio so it didn't drag on the floor.

I stepped out of my office. Leah Stanley said, "I'm thinking of getting electric-blue glasses like that guy's. How do you think I'd look in those?"

"Your personality would overpower them. You need something more bold. By the way, did Ellegaard take my Nerfoop?

"I don't know. I haven't seen anything."

"You work in a private detective firm. You're supposed to notice when things get stolen around here."

"All I notice is you never go in your office. Now leave me alone. I'm busy."

"I marked my office chair."

She didn't blink. "Tell someone who cares."

"If you're sitting in it—"

"Then what?"

I smiled. Leah did not. I said, "Man, law school is a total waste of your talents. You should be an assassin."

Then she smiled and said, "You know, you really should hire my dad."

"I thought he only came down to the Cities for funerals, babies, and graduations."

"He'd add part-time work to the list. He's a good detective."

"The best. Ellegaard and I learned a lot from him."

"So hire him."

"Next time we need help around here, I'd love to. Where's Annika?"

"BrainiAcme."

"Really?" I looked into Ellegaard's office. He was on the phone with the door shut. I went in anyway. He was saying something about an initial consultation and our fee structure and sent the call out to Leah to get a meeting on the calendar. Then he hung up and looked at me.

The Boy Scout in Anders Ellegaard was gone. He'd lost the twinkle, the eagerness, the satisfaction of doing a job the right way, the way he'd been taught, the way that would earn him the merit badge. The path, for Ellegaard, was everything. That's why he lasted so long at the boring Edina PD. There, staying on the path was natural and rewarding. If I hadn't shaken something loose in him during the Somerville case, he would have retired as Edina PD.

When he looked at me with those beleaguered eyes, I wished, for his sake, I hadn't come back into his life. I said, "I hear Annika is at BrainiAcme."

"They understand why you can't be there right now,

but I had to put someone on the case. She'll do a good job."

"She'll do great."

"Have a seat."

I sat. "I'll know more about Linnea Engstrom tonight."

He sighed, like a man watching bad news on TV. "We're working for free. We won't get any more money out of Anne Engstrom. I doubt she has it, and she's not responding to calls or emails."

"I'm pretty sure Linnea's alive and okay. If we get that information to Anne, we'll hear from her."

"You know, Shap. You'll do what you're going to do, regardless."

"Regardless of what?"

"Of what's best for this firm. Regardless of what's best for our clients. And to tell you the truth, regardless of what's best for you."

He was right. He and I were both about the path. Maybe that's why we loved and respected each other the way we did. The problem was our paths were different. It made for an impossible situation. Neither of us wanted to dissuade the other from what he was doing. But neither of us wanted to join the other, either.

I kicked back in the chair and put my feet on Elle-gaard's desk. "Was starting Stone Arch Investigations a mistake?"

"I won't tell you to stop looking for a seventeen-year-old girl, Nils. If one of my daughters were missing, you'd be the first person I'd call. A mistake was made putting this firm together, and the mistake was all mine."

"It wasn't a mistake. We've succeeded so far."

"Barely. We've done good work on some routine jobs. Jobs that pay well and let us office here and make a good impression and keep Leah and Annika on the payroll. That thing we have in common that drives us—"

"What is that thing?"

"I guess you'd call it an overinflated sense of right and wrong, as if the world's a fair place or at least should be. I think that's what lights a fire under both of us. You've directed yours at the world. I've directed mine at our company." Ellegaard picked up a pen and leaned back in his chair. It was the click kind of pen and he clicked it. He shook his head, but I didn't know about what.

"Are we in trouble, here?"

"A little, yeah. We got about sixty days' operating expenses. Ninety if you and I go without salary for a month. BrainiAcme is paying a fraction for Annika of what they would've paid for you. I'm not saying that to make you feel bad. I'm just saying we got a trickle coming in. It's my fault."

"It's not your fault."

"I was a cop all those years protecting the high-living citizens of Edina. Guess deep down I wanted to be one. But we don't need this upscale office. We don't need to be downtown. We should have officed in Northeast or Armatage in something cheap or have not even rented offices at all. You never did and you did okay."

"Bullshit I did okay. Listen, I'm all for finding cheaper offices, but let's do what we can to keep Leah and Annika. And let's make the company work. I can go without salary for a month. I used to go without it a hell of a lot longer than that. I'll wrap up Linnea Engstrom and we'll take a boring job. We'll be like movie stars, Ellie. We'll make a superhero movie, then a horror movie, an international spy movie, then after our bank account runneth over, we'll make a good movie."

Ellegaard smiled. "Sounds all right to me. Our lease here is almost up."

"Good. I hate this fucking place. Let's find a shitty little dump in Northeast. Leah's getting too comfortable here, anyway. Plus, she swiped my chair. And did you steal my Nerfoop?

Ellegaard opened a desk drawer and tossed me the hoop. "I was giving Earl Davis a tour. Tried to make the place look respectable."

"And the ball." Ellegaard handed me the ball, and I got up to leave.

"You need help on Linnea?"

"Not now. Like I said earlier, I'll know more in a few hours."

"Let me know."

"I will, buddy. I will."

23

Jameson White changed my wound dressing mid-afternoon. Char Northagen called and said her sources turned up nothing on Gary Kozjek. I suggested she make a flirtatious call to her cop friend, Stensrud, in Warroad to see if he'd heard anything. She made the call. He hadn't. My SPPD contacts didn't return my calls. Nor did Jamie Waller. I guessed we were having a tiff. Ellegaard hadn't heard anything. The world had gone silent regarding Gary Kozjek.

Mel Rosenthal texted to see if I was free later. I said I had to work until 9:00 but should be free after that. We made a plan. I took a nap then changed my Lauren-smelling sheets. I wanted to call to see if she was okay but restrained myself—there were too many ways that could make matters worse. I ate a peanut butter and jelly sandwich for dinner, changed back into my faux navy-blue work clothes and dummy eyeglasses, then returned to Tenth Street shortly after 7:00.

Chrissia Maeda answered the door wearing the same

floral print dress but under a sand-colored cardigan. She said her grandson was in the basement, but I could go down to retrieve the radon test kit. I thanked her, told her I'd send the kit to the lab and call when the results came back, then descended the narrow basement steps.

Joaquin Maeda sat on the afghan-covered couch next to a half-eaten frozen pizza, his face in a worn paperback of *One Hundred Years of Solitude*. He wore jeans and 1970s Nike Waffle Trainers, yellow with a blue swoosh, probably reproductions but I couldn't tell, and a purple Southwest High School sweatshirt. His brown unkempt hair fell over his ears. He had heavy eyelids, a week's worth of stubble, and an asymmetrical but not unpleasant-looking nose. He looked up and said, "You the radon test dude?"

"I am. Sorry to bother you. This will just take a minute."

"No worries. Is it done?"

"Should be. Just have to take a quick look and retrieve the electronic sensor to make sure there wasn't any IR interference." Ernesto Cuellar told me Joaquin Maeda wasn't good at science. I was counting on that being true.

"What do you mean?"

"Sometimes wireless devices in the home throw off the test." Complete bullshit. "You know, TV remote, video game controllers, cell phones."

"No shit?"

"Yeah. That's why I left a monitoring device."

"You mean the test near the TV?" He held the book open. I hoped he'd keep it open. That's where I wanted his attention. He closed the book.

"No. That's for radon. The electronic interference monitoring device is in the ceiling."

Joaquin looked up. "I don't see it." Then he looked at me. "Why the ceiling?"

"Because the device detects interference from down here and also from the floor above."

"Why not just put it next to the radon test? That's where the interference is most important, right?"

Maybe he was better at science then Ernesto thought. "Because," I said, "if the device is next to the test, it will interfere with the test. That's why I put it in the same room but not too close." I reached up into the low ceiling and, five feet from Joaquin's face, retrieved the digital voice recorder. I looked at its LCD screen and said, "A little IR interference but not bad. Nothing that would make a difference."

Joaquin didn't question the device's authenticity. "My video game controller is Bluetooth. Does that mess with the test?"

"Nope. Just infrared." I put the recorder in my pocket then gathered the test kit. "Hope this comes back negative. Wouldn't want to mess up your gaming space."

"I don't play that much. Mostly read down here. If I do it upstairs, someone's always on me to do something like take out the garbage. When I'm down here, they forget about me."

Then my slow brain clicked in. I don't know why I didn't make the connection earlier. Maybe it was getting shot by an arrow and knowing the shooter was still out there. Maybe it was a side effect of the general anesthesia I underwent during surgery. Maybe it was the stress of Lauren having dinner with Micaela and the aftershocks that followed. Maybe it was the stress of Ernesto sitting on the white bucket, hands in pockets, face in hood. Whatever caused my lapse, I hadn't even asked the question until I answered it.

Yes, I had wondered how whoever stuck the arrow in my shoulder knew I was looking for Linnea Engstrom less than an hour after Roger and Anne hired me. But I'd never wondered how Joaquin Maeda knew I was on the case. "Stop looking for Linnea Engstrom," Joaquin Maeda's note said. Who told Joaquin I was looking for Linnea? There could only be one person: Linnea Engstrom.

Linnea Engstrom knew I was looking for her. She told the archer. She told Joaquin Maeda. But who told her? Who knew Roger and Anne had hired me? Roger did. Anne did. And Mel Rosenthal did. One of those people was, or at least had been, in contact with Linnea.

Joaquin saw the gears turning in my head. "You all right, man?"

"Yeah. Just remembered something I have to do."

I left the Maeda house and got in the Volvo. I wanted to listen to the recorder right there, but if Joaquin suspected my deceit, he could make one call, and I'd never get out of that neighborhood. I drove straight back to the coat factory. When the loading dock door closed behind me, I listened to the chitchat in Joaquin Maeda's private lobby.

I heard three distinct voices. One belonged to Joaquin Maeda. The second, which I heard through the TV, belonged to a male with a strong Spanish accent. The third belonged to a young woman. They spoke over machine guns, explosions, computer-generated commanders urging them to victory, and the screams of fallen warriors.

Young Woman: *Did you buy the GPS?*

Spanish Accent: *Yes. I've been using it to make sure it works.*

Joaquin: *Do you have the right map?*

Spanish Accent: *Yes. It is downloaded.*

Young Woman: *How long is the battery life?*

Spanish Accent: *It says sixteen hours. But I have not tested it.*

Young Woman: *Sixteen hours isn't enough. It's not even close.*

Spanish Accent: *I got the one that uses double A batteries. I have ten extras.*

Joaquin: *That's plenty. Has everyone checked the weather?*

Young Woman: *Yes. Looks great from here.*

Spanish Accent: *And from here.*

Joaquin: *Same GPS coordinates and time?*

Spanish Accent: *Yes.*

Young Woman: *Yep.*

Joaquin: *No further contact then for a while. If there's an emergency, post the pic, okay?*

Young Woman: *Got it.*

Spanish Accent: *Sí.*

Joaquin: *Good luck, you guys.*

That was the end. I got out of my car, climbed the loading steps, changed out of my faux work clothes, ditched the dummy glasses, then bagged my shoulder and let my mind swirl in the white noise of a long, hot shower. If I was correct, the young woman's voice belonged to Linnea Engstrom. I would confirm that with Mel. The Spanish accent belonged to Miguel Maeda. I could confirm that with Ernesto Cuellar, though I hoped I wouldn't have to bring him into this any more than I already had. Miguel would sneak across the U.S./Mexican border, with Linnea waiting on the other side. Where and when I had no idea.

I finished my shower and texted Jameson White. Deodorant, brushed teeth, boxers, and jeans. I left my shirt off but slipped into my Blundstones just before the big paw of Jameson White knocked on my service door.

I sat on the stainless steel counter. Jameson wore yellow sweatpants and a gigantic UCLA sweatshirt in baby blue. He cut his handiwork away with bandage scissors and said, "Whoa. Clean and showered and fresh. Someone must have a date tonight."

"I think I do."

"You think you do? You don't know?"

"I suspect it's a date. But it might not be. Half the fun will be finding out. She may show up while you're still here. Look at how she's dressed and acts. If you think she thinks it's a date, cough once. If you think it's not a date, cough twice."

"Are you serious?"

"No."

"Good," said Jameson. He finished taping my shoulder and discarded the trimmings in the trash. "What time tomorrow? I won't expect anything early."

"What do you think of a trip south?"

"You inviting me?"

"Yep. Maybe El Paso or San Diego or Tucson. I need you to keep an eye on my shoulder."

"Let me clear it with Micaela. Gotta keep the boss happy. But a trip south sounds great to me. Minnesota's all brown and melty and ugly this time of year. No leaves on the trees, and you know more snow is coming. Gotta fly first-class though. I'm too big to sit in coach."

There was a light rap on the service door. I slipped on a dusty blue cashmere V-neck. Jameson helped me into my sling. I descended the loading dock steps and opened the door. Mel Rosenthal stood sans ponytail, hair down and resting on her shoulders. She wore a midlength trench coat belted at the waist and, I assumed, a dress underneath. Her bare legs stuck out of the coat and ended in a pair of patent leather flats. She carried a bottle of Dom Perignon. She wore diamond studs on her ears, at least a karat each, and the same frameless teardrop eyeglasses over eyeliner and mascara. She smelled of gardenia, and her lips shined.

"Ha!" said Jameson from above the loading dock stairs. "It is definitely a date!"

"We should have used the code."

"Come on, man. That's beyond code." He laughed.

Mel Rosenthal blushed and stepped inside. "Mel," I said, "I'd like you to meet my nurse."

"Nurse *practitioner*," said Jameson.

We walked up the stairs. Jameson took her hand with the gentle touch of a watchmaker. Mel thanked him for taking such good care of me and asked if he wanted to join us for a glass of champagne. He appreciated the offer but declined, saying he was on call.

"On call my ass," I said.

"To God's ears," said Jameson. "Looks like you might get hurt tonight." He laughed his big loud laugh and had to catch his breath then said good-bye and exited with his bright blue jacket over his arm.

Mel removed her coat. She wore a simple black dress underneath. And why not? She had so much to mourn: dead Howard, two years of celibacy, a devastated sister, her brother in-law, and a once-sweet relationship with her missing niece.

I shot the champagne cork across the room then we kissed our way through the bottle. A few coherent facts escaped. Mel had put Ivy on a plane to Boston that day. Howard's eightysomething-year-old parents insisted on taking her to see the few colleges she'd applied to but hadn't yet visited. I explained how Jameson White came into my life. Mel updated me on Anne, who was still at their parents' house in St. Louis Park, Ativaned up to her chestnut bangs while planning Roger's funeral. Roger's parents had flown in from Aspen and so had a brother from San Francisco and a sister from Los Angeles. Roger had come from big money and had tried desperately to earn his way back into it. He never succeeded.

It was a night of blurred lines, from those painted around Mel's eyes, smeared with tears, to the boundaries I smudged with disparate motives. I wanted Mel's spirit, her body, and to destroy her defense and coping shields. The first two she gave generously. I'm not big on couch sex—it's like shower sex, a nice idea fraught with logistical challenges and physical hazards. But that's where it first happened. My damaged shoulder let her undress both of us. I felt her clumsily with my untrained right hand. I'm southpaw all the way. Operating as a righty forced me into adolescent territory. I switched tactics and explored Mel with kisses instead. Clothing and couch cushions dispersed from ground zero.

Mel Rosenthal was the opposite of her sister, Anne: understated with no cry for attention. Not with dyed, chopped hair nor vintage store clothing nor little fucking dog. My lips found soft, pale skin. She gasped with each of my discoveries. A narrow waist and hips that were both round and slim at the same time. Thighs that felt preserved by time. She came hard with a violent seizure-like wave through her entire body. It lasted a long time. A downpour of tears followed.

I let her cry. She'd hoarded so much pain and desire. It was nested inside her and would take years to clear it out. A few minutes later I lay on my back, and she took me into her. She came again, almost immediately, even more violently. Her head fell to my good shoulder and she shook and cried herself dry.

She said, "Oh God, I'm so embarrassed."

"If I hadn't had sex in two years, I would have come when you introduced yourself at the Xcel Center."

She laughed and said, "I'm spent. Your turn."

"Let's go in the bedroom."

We did. I apologized for never learning how to do one-handed push-ups and, if she didn't mind, I'd have to roll onto my back again. She said "Just like Jack Kennedy" and, despite saying she was done, came a third time, and I joined her. I would have liked to take credit for her three-hit night, but celibacy had pumped her primer for two years. The only thing I did was give her a warm body and safe place. She rolled onto her back and stared at the factory ceiling high above the bedroom walls.

I hated to do what I was about to do, but it was the only way to get an honest reaction. She hadn't caught her breath yet. She was as vulnerable as she could be. I reached over to the nightstand and grabbed the digital recorder. "I have something I want you to hear. I recorded it today."

I pressed play. The voices talked about a GPS device and weather forecasts. Mel Rosenthal lit up. "That's Linnea! She's okay! You recorded this today?!"

"Yes. This afternoon."

"Oh, thank God. Do you know where she is?"

"I don't. But someone tipped off Linnea after she disappeared."

"What do you mean *tipped off*?"

"Someone is or has been in contact with her. They told her I was on the case, and she told the kid who told me to stop looking for her."

Mel pulled the sheet up to her shoulders then rolled onto her side. "Do you think I've been in contact with her? I told you last night—"

"No. I don't think it's you." I kissed her. She looked confused. "I just had to make sure. Because it was either you or Anne or Roger."

"Anne wouldn't—"

"Anne couldn't. It was Roger. He hired me to find Linnea, but I think the biggest reason he hired me was to find a hundred thousand dollars that went missing with Linnea."

"What are you talking about?"

I told Mel about the paper bag in Winnie Haas's laundry chute.

"And you think Linnea stole Roger's hundred thousand dollars?"

"I think Linnea knew Roger was up to something illegal. I don't know how, but that hundred grand was part of something that helped fund NorthTech. Linnea found out about it and took the money. Maybe for herself or just to spite Roger or in some Robin Hood kind of way."

"Then how did it end up at Winnie Haas's house?"

"It's just a hunch, but I think Winnie Haas replaced you."

"But Ben Haas—"

"He's either a good liar or he doesn't know."

"But how could Linnea and Winnie Haas become so close?"

"If you'd seen Ben with his mother you'd get it. They talked like parents and kids don't usually talk. About sex. About boundaries. About love. Any kid who had a crap relationship with her parents would fantasize about having Winnie for a mom. You could tell her anything. She listened, didn't judge, but was in charge. Still the mom.

It's got to be comforting to have a parent who is your friend but also your guide, someone who sets the rules based on an intimate knowledge of you, not some arbitrary bullshit she got from Dr. Phil or a mommy blog."

"I try to be that kind of mom for Ivy."

"And I bet you succeed. Do you know who the boy with the Spanish accent is?"

"No."

"Did you know Linnea came to the Cities with Haley Housh some weekends?"

"Yes. Anne told me she visited a couple times."

"More than a couple. My guess is Linnea befriended the boy with the accent. His name is Miguel Maeda. Linnea took him in like another stray. Then he got deported for tagging. I know. Don't ask. Now she's run off to help sneak him back into the country. Does she have any friends or relatives who live in the Southwest?"

"None that I know of."

I cupped my right hand under Mel's head. She pressed its full weight into my palm. I said, "I'm sorry I had to play you that tape when I did. I really am. I just . . ." I didn't want to say what I intended to say.

"What?"

Mel's gray eyes glowed soft and kind. "I like you a whole lot so I had to eliminate any possibility you're in contact with Linnea. Just the possibility of it would ruin things. It's like standing in a picturesque trout stream with fish rising but you forgot your fishing license. The slight chance of the game warden showing up wrecks the experience."

"Really?" She smiled. "You're comparing me to a day of fishing?"

"A great day of fishing on a pristine stream. The best day ever."

She kissed my bandaged shoulder then lay her head on my chest and said, "Want to have an uncomfortable conversation?"

"I thought we just did."

"I need to be up front about something."

"Please."

"I don't mean to put any pressure on this. I have no expectations. I promise. I don't have an empty space in my heart that needs to be filled. I'm not looking for you to solve anything."

"Okay . . ."

"But if this would turn into anything more than tonight. Or more than a few nights. You have to understand I may never get over Howard. I may always be in love with him."

I let that sit a moment, stroked Mel's soft, straight hair, then said, "Perfect."

"I'm sorry, Nils, it's just that—"

"No. I'm not being sarcastic. If this turns into a relationship, I'm okay with you still being in love with Howard."

"Really?"

"It's the best possible situation."

"Okay, you're weird."

"I was dating someone for a year until yesterday."

"What?"

"She broke up with me just before I went to the hockey game. And you know why? Because she'd realized I'm not over my ex-wife. I don't want to be in love with my ex-wife. I don't want to see her or even talk to her. I can't get her out of me though. She's like a piece of shrapnel that's lodged in my heart. Can't cut it out. Got to live with it."

"That's sad. But you don't sound sad when you say it."

"I'm not."

"Do you think there's a chance you'll get back to-gether?"

"Nope. Almost none. Which is okay. She's just there. Probably like Howard's lodged in your heart. What can we do?"

Mel said nothing. A car drove by the loading dock. The headlights swept through the coat factory and lit up the ceiling above the bedroom walls. Mel found my hand and said, "Well, one thing we can do is have sex."

"Yes. That we can do."

24

We fell asleep before midnight. Mel woke a couple hours later and wanted to leave. I walked her to her car while she explained she wasn't ready for a sleepover. That was all right with me. I needed actual sleep, and new bed partners aren't conducive for that. Sometimes I wonder if the sleep deprivation that accompanies new relationships fertilizes romance. Sleep deprivation makes people more responsive to cults. Why not love?

I woke at 7:10 and texted Jameson White for a bandage change. I left another message for Guy Storstrand at the Canadiens' office in Montreal. I checked the Canadiens' schedule. The team from Montreal was on a road trip. Monday, they played here in St. Paul against the Minnesota Wild. Last night they played the Blackhawks in Chicago.

It couldn't be a coincidence. Guy Storstrand was in the Twin Cities the night before Linnea disappeared. Then her cell phone logged into a Starbucks Wi-Fi signal on Wednesday night in Madison, Wisconsin, which is en route to Chicago, where Guy Storstrand played the next night. I checked the schedule again. In twelve hours, the Montreal Canadiens would be in Winnipeg to play the Jets. Winnipeg, Manitoba, a seven-hour drive from the Twin Cities. Less than three hours from Warroad.

I had figured Linnea angled southwest after Chicago to meet Miguel. Those border crossings aren't easy. Not as easy as they used to be anyway. But Miguel was free to travel to Canada. He had no criminal record in the United States. He'd just been caught tagging with known gang members. It wouldn't show up on Canadian records. And crossing from Canada into the Unites States, especially into Minnesota, during winter, isn't nearly as difficult as crossing the Mexican border.

Again I considered forcing information out of Joaquin Maeda. He had to know the time and place Miguel planned to meet Linnea near the border. But something told me not to and did so loudly. Gabriella Núñez was right. Any conversation with Joaquin would drive Linnea and Miguel underground forever.

I drank a third cup of coffee under the breathy roar of the gas heater. I stepped outside. The pavement was dry. No water. No ice. Another warm March day. Too warm. March feigned with its left. The big roundhouse right had to be coming.

I couldn't stop thinking about Guy Storstrand in Winnipeg, Manitoba. Mel Rosenthal's tales of Linnea had knit me a tapestry. I had hung it on the wall and couldn't take my eyes off it. She had knit the same one for the St. Paul PD. They'd probably put it in storage. If they didn't loathe my existence I would have shared my thoughts with them. But they did so I didn't.

Jameson White arrived before 8:00. He removed his Windex-blue jacket to reveal faded denim overalls over a white thermal Henley. I offered him coffee and he accepted. He cleaned and redressed my shoulder, counted my antibiotics to make sure I hadn't missed any, and took my temperature.

"Lookin' good, Mr. Shapiro. Lookin' good."

Jameson helped me on with my shirt, and I said, "How long did Micaela hire you for? I can't remember."

"Eleven more days and then I'm back to the grind."

"You still up for that trip?"

He put the unused gauze pads into his bag and said, "San Diego sounds perfect. Tucson not bad. But I don't know about El Paso. That spicy food does a number on me."

"How about a place where there's no spicy food?"

"Where's that?"

"Winnipeg."

"Canada?" He said it like I just asked him if he wanted a root canal.

"You don't like Canada?"

"Not in March, I don't. What happened to the warm places?"

"Plans changed. Plus, it's not a vacation."

"No shit it's not. Winnipeg. You never take me anywhere nice."

"I will someday. I promise."

"So would I just be your nurse practitioner or do you need help doing detective work?"

"I'll probably need a little help."

"Well, you're the patient. Whatever's best for you. Micaela said to go wherever you go. She'll cover the expenses. Gotta keep the boss happy."

"Good. Pack a bag and meet me back here in an hour. And just out of curiosity, what the hell's with the overalls?"

"They're comfortable."

"Fair enough."

"Canada," said Jameson. "In March. Won't see no rob-ins up there. Spring isn't even knockin' on the door."

"You spend much time north of the border?"

"Fifteen years in the CFL."

"As a player or trainer?"

"I'm six foot seven, three hundred and ten pounds. What kind of detective are you?"

"The kind that doesn't assume a giant black man played football before going to nursing school."

"That's political correct bullshit is what that is. Of course I played football."

"Where'd you play your college ball?"

"*U-C-L-A.* In sunny Southern California. How I ended up in these frigid places, Lord only knows. Maybe He's keeping me cold so I stay fresh past my expiration date." He laughed his infectious laugh.

Jameson put on his Windex-blue jacket and left. I'd missed a call from Char Northagen so I returned it. She had heard nothing about Gary Kozjek's arrest. But last night, her boss called to tell her she's been suspended with pay. She looked for a flight to Hawaii, but it was crazy expensive at the last minute during spring break. I said it was a crazy coincidence this happened now be-cause I knew a hidden gem of a place to visit that was a whole lot more affordable.

I went into the bedroom to pack. Jeans and T-shirts and underwear and socks. Two fleece quarter zips. Mit-tens and gloves, a cashmere scarf, a wool hat lined with fleece. A down sweater, a down jacket, and a Gore-Tex shell that could go over some or all of it. A heavy pair of Sorels and a light pair and a pair of running shoes I had no intention of running in.

I received a text from Micaela. She was standing outside the service door.

The year I'd neither seen nor communicated with Micaela wasn't enough time to shake her. Lauren wasn't enough to shake her. And I knew Mel Rosenthal wouldn't be enough either. I loved Micaela in my bones. Fighting it had worn me down to what an optimist calls acceptance, a fair-minded person calls resignation, and I call surrender.

She climbed the loading dock stairs in olive-green corduroys tucked into knee-high brown suede boots, a cream cashmere V-neck under a baby-blue Marmot shell, and her strawberry blond hair pulled back tight. A few strands had escaped the clamping device and floated free, anchored only by their roots. They danced in the currents of forced air heat like tentacles of a sea anemone. Her face had remained pale and soft like the underside of a forearm.

This was her first visit since I'd moved. She looked around then said, "I love this place. What kind of factory was it?"

"Coats. They just made coats."

"And your kitchen works great. And the light . . . Really nice, Nils."

"Thank you. And thanks for Jameson. I don't know what I would have done without him." My face must have given something away.

She said, "What?"

"Nothing."

She looked at me knowing it was *something*, but let it go then said, "I know we're not supposed to see or talk to each other," her voice grew tired and on edge, "but Jameson said you asked him to go on a trip with you."

"Jameson is telling the truth."

"Yesterday it was the Southwest, but he just phoned to say you switched it to Winnipeg. Is there something important in Winnipeg?"

"It's Winnipeg. In March. That's like Minneapolis in February. You only visit if it's important."

She drifted away and looked around. She turned on the tap over the kitchen sink, as if she thought it might not be operational and I'd just installed it for looks. "I don't think you should go," she said.

"All right. Why not?"

"I don't have a good feeling about it. I've had some bad dreams lately, and I'm worried about you."

"That makes sense. I got shot by an arrow. I almost bled to death."

"The dreams started before that happened."

"You've had bad dreams as long as I've known you. Plane crashes and tornadoes and car accidents. Remember that time you didn't want me to go fly-fishing because you dreamed I drowned in the Yellowstone River? I went. Nothing happened. And that one where your mom died on your birthday? She's alive and well. None of those dreams have come true. Ever. I'll be fine."

"It doesn't feel right to me, Nils, that's all I'm saying. I had to tell you that." Her fear was real. I felt her love. It was her goddamn love that tethered me.

I said, "Did you dream I'd get shot by an arrow?"

She hesitated then said, "No, I didn't. Just forget it. I said what I had to say." She walked over to the bookshelf and browsed the titles. "So do you own this place or rent?"

"You know what all those dreams mean, right?"

"I don't need to know what they mean." She placed a finger on the spine of *The Given Day*. "Or at least I don't need to hear what you think they mean."

"Well, if you ever change your mind let me know. I could save you thousands in therapy bills. Pay you back for sending me Jameson White."

"You never have to pay me back for that. It's my pleasure."

"Did you give him permission to go to Winnipeg?"

"Of course. That's the whole point of hiring Jameson. So treatment goes where you go."

She looked at me but said nothing more. I wanted to tell her I was still in love with her, but her response would do more damage than the arrow. So instead I said, "Did you have any bad dreams about Lauren and me breaking up?"

Her face fell. "Oh, Nils. I'm sorry. I like her. I really do."

"That's what Ellegaard said."

"What happened?"

"I rent."

"What?"

"You asked me if I own or rent this place. I rent. With the option to buy when the building permits come through."

The button on the Nespresso machine glowed like it was breathing, in-out, in-out. I pushed it, and it blinked to warm up.

"Okay. You don't want to tell me what happened with Lauren." I said nothing. "It's okay, Nils. It's none of my business. Really."

We asked how each other's families were and how work was going, obligatory discourse that neither of us cared for. She said she had to get going, and I walked her down the loading dock stairs. Then she said, "So are we going back to no communication again?"

"No. It's all right. That's over. We can communicate now."

"Are you sure? You seemed pretty adamant about it last year."

"I was. But that's passed."

Micaela smiled something sweet and nodded. "All right. Have a safe trip." She pushed open the heavy service door and walked out.

25

I called Mel and told her where I was headed and why and that I'd like to see her when I got back. An hour later, I embarked on a journey with two giants. With good weather and coordinated bathroom breaks, we'd make it to Winnipeg in plenty of time to chat with Guy Storstrand.

Char road shotgun. Jameson sat with his back on the rear passenger-side door and his legs across the backseat. I'd complained a hundred times about my new Volvo being too big. Now it was barely big enough. We'd only driven fifteen minutes north when my dear friend, Woodbury PD detective Jamie Waller, phoned. I took the call on Bluetooth.

I said, "Hey, stranger. Whatup?"

"Where is he?"

"Where is whom?"

"Quit fucking around, Shapiro. Is it why you didn't show yesterday?"

"I didn't show because you didn't answer my texts at

the Warroad game. Your nonresponse ended our agreement to cooperate. Read the fine print of our contract."

"Don't be an asshole. Our agreement to cooperate has nothing to do with you giving an official statement about the double murder on Crestmoor Bay."

"I walked through the whole thing with you at the crime scene. Your insistence on me coming down to the station is harassment plain and simple."

I looked at Jameson in the review mirror. He nodded his approval.

"Are you with him?"

"It depends who *him* is?"

There was a long pause. Char mouthed "Kozjek?"

"You still there, Detective?"

"If you're with him, you'll do time in Stillwater. I'll make it my life's mission."

"Still no idea what or who you're talking about."

"I need you in the station right now."

"Sorry. Out of town." Technically, that was true. We'd just crossed into Maple Grove, a suburb of box stores with big signs facing the freeway to prove it. "What's this about?" Another long pause. "Don't tell me you lost Kozjek." No answer. "I saw you at the X Thursday night sitting next to Bad Haircut. Half of SPPD was there. You got to be kidding me, Detective. When Kozjek got ejected from the game, an army followed him into the tunnel. How the hell did you lose him?" Waller hung up.

Char said, "Kozjek ran?"

"Sounds like it. And lost two dozen police officers in the bowels of the Xcel Center."

"Is that possible?"

"He played five seasons for the Wild. He knows the locker rooms and facilities down there well enough."

We brought Jameson up to speed. He said, "Char, you

should call that Warroad cop who's got the hots for you. See what he'll tell you. Bet he knows what's going on."

Char dialed Officer Tony Stensrud as I explained to Jameson that no one says "got the hots" anymore. Stensrud took her call and confirmed that Coach Kozjek went AWOL after being ejected from the game. Stensrud wouldn't say more.

We made our first stop in Fargo at Doolittles Woodfire Grill, where we ordered lunch to go. Jameson redressed my shoulder in the men's room while we waited for the food. We got back on Interstate 94 for a few minutes then kicked north on Highway 29, leaving the banks of the Red River then reuniting with it an hour later in Grand Forks. We stopped again in Pembina, ND, for a bathroom break in case we got hung up at the border. We didn't. Ten minutes later, we entered Canada.

Char and Jameson tapped their sports world connections, and we learned the Montreal Canadiens stay at The Fairmont. We arrived just after 4:00 and sent Char to the front desk, where she informed the clerk she had an urgent message for Guy Storstrand from Linnea Engstrom.

While the clerk called up to Guy's room, Jameson and I sat in comfy lobby chairs like a couple of husbands waiting for our wives to try on clothes. Those men, God bless them, have lost the game of life. Where do the losers in the game of life go? The comfy chairs outside women's dressing rooms.

Char took a seat in the lounge. A few minutes later, Guy Storstrand joined her. She stood and shook his hand, then the two sat. Jameson and I walked over and joined them.

I said, "Hi, Guy. Glad you could join us."

"Hey, what is this?" said Guy Storstrand. The hockey player in him stood. He had a sandy blond mop that fell to his shoulders and Sir Walter Raleigh facial hair. If he weren't a broad-shouldered six-foot-three hockey player you might mistake him for an overgrown minstrel or tights-wearing juggler. He had soft Norwegian periwinkle eyes. They looked feminine contrasted with all that muscle and bone.

"My name is Nils Shapiro. I'm a private investigator." His expression changed to a curious *what the hell*? "Roger and Anne Engstrom hired me to find Linnea. I'm sure you've heard she disappeared in St. Paul Tuesday night."

Guy Storstrand hesitated then *cough, cough, cough* followed by an exaggerated blink of the eyes then *cough, cough, cough*. The sufferer of Tourette's looked at Jameson and said, "Who is this, your bodyguard?"

"No. My nurse."

"Nurse practitioner," said Jameson. He extended his hand to Guy, who took it. "Jameson White. Played fifteen years for the Montreal Alouettes. Next time I'm back I'll take you for a corned beef at Schwartz's."

Jameson laughed his big laugh. Guy smiled and sat back down.

I said, "I'm concerned about Linnea's safety and hope you have some information on where Linnea might be."

Cough, cough, cough. Blink. "What makes you concerned for her safety?"

"Well, for one, she's missing. And her father was murdered Thursday."

"What?" *Cough, cough, cough*. Blink. "What are you talking about?"

Char and I explained what happened at Crestmoor Bay. Guy's coughs and blinks fired more frequently. I said, "I think Roger was into something he shouldn't have been. I'm worried Linnea got herself mixed up in it."

Guy placed a hand on his stubbly cheek and said, "Mixed up in what way?"

"She took a hundred thousand dollars in cash from Roger. I don't know if he brought the money down to St. Paul or if he picked it up in the Cities to bring back north. My guess is the night Linnea disappeared, she hid out at Winnie Hass's house in Woodbury. Next morning, she heard her father come over and stashed the money in Winnie Haas's laundry chute then ran.

"She planned to go back for it but couldn't after the murders—the place was crawling with police. I'm concerned the money didn't belong to Roger and whoever it does belong to thinks Linnea still has it. They want it back and could be looking for Linnea. I'd like to find her first."

"Jesus," said Guy. *Cough, cough, cough.* Blink. Throat clear. *Cough, cough, cough.* Blink. "Do you really think she's in danger?"

"In a couple of ways." Guy shut his eyes and shook his head. "Did you see her in St. Paul when you were in town to play the Wild?"

"Yeah."

"Did she tell you she was going to run away?" He nodded. "Do you know where she went?"

Throat clear. "I don't know if I should talk to you anymore without a lawyer."

"I'm not a cop, Guy. I don't care if you helped a friend. I'm just trying to find her."

He looked at Jameson in his matching sweats and the supermodel-like Char Northagen and knew we couldn't be cops. "Okay. I saw Linnea in St. Paul. She told me her friend Miguel was in Canada. He needed some outdoor stuff. She gave me a list and four thousand dollars in cash."

"Do you know why Miguel wanted the outdoor equipment?"

"No, but he was here in Winnipeg yesterday. By himself. I had the day off, so we met at Tim Hortons then went shopping." *Cough, cough, cough.* Blink.

Char said, "What did you buy?"

"Winter outdoor stuff. Clothing and camping equipment and food. Dropped thirty-five hundred Canadian at Wholesale Sports. I gave Miguel the change, and he took the pack all loaded up."

Jameson said, "Did Linnea say what Miguel wanted all that stuff for?"

Cough, cough, cough. Blink. *Throat clear. Throat clear.* "No."

Char said, "Got any guesses?"

"Yeah." *Throat clear.* "Miguel will try to sneak across the border into the States. Linnea will meet him when he does. You really think someone else is after her?" Blink.

I said, "Someone's missing a hundred grand or the goods or services it was supposed to pay for."

Guy wrinkled his forehead and scratched his Shakespearian goatee. *Cough, cough, cough.* "Hey, I should go. I have to get to the arena."

"One last question," I said.

"Sure."

"I'm having a hard time getting a sense of Linnea. Sometimes she seems like a heroine who rescues people and animals, and sometimes she seems like a selfish, entitled shit."

Guy smiled. "Yep. That's Linnea."

26

Outside Winnipeg we caught Highway 12 South and continued into Steinbach, where Jameson cleaned and changed my shoulder in the Volvo while parked outside the A&W. Then we jogged southeast toward the border, bouncing along the two-lane highway of cracked asphalt. Windbreaks of tall pines protected the barns and farmhouses studding the flat, dormant land. The low gray cloud ceiling seemed just out of reach. The Volvo's dash read thirty-eight degrees. We smelled soft earth and cattle through the car's open vents.

I asked Jameson and Char if they'd rather catch a flight back to the Twin Cities, but neither did. Keeping me healthy was Jameson's job, he said. And Char was in no rush to get home. She'd been suspended with pay. She could get paid anywhere. Besides, she said, she might be of help with Officer Stensrud.

Jameson said, "You sure you still want to find this girl? She's the reason you got shot with an arrow. Her dad's dead. He's not going to pay you. Her mom probably won't either. And the food on this trip has been less than spectacular. And it sure as hell ain't going to get any better in Warroad."

I answered with a smile as we crossed the border where Canada's Highway 12 turns into Minnesota State Highway 313. Northern Minnesota looked no different from southern Canada. Five miles later we passed a small airport and the Warroad Estates Golf Course. A mile after that, Highway 313 T'd into Highway 11. The intersection had it all: the Marvin Windows Visitor Center, Lake Country Chevrolet, and Dairy Queen. Welcome to Warroad. Population: Not a Whole Fucking Lot.

Char had turned off her phone in Canada. No sense paying roaming charges when you're about to be off the payroll. She turned it back on. It dinged and donged with emails, texts, and voice mails.

She said, "Just got a report on Winnie Haas. No evidence of sexual activity. And she tested positive for W-18."

I said, "What the hell is W-18?"

"Some bad shit," said Jameson. "Synthetic opioid. Originally out of Canada. Hundred times more powerful than fentanyl. And fentanyl's a hundred times more powerful than morphine."

"It's tough to detect in toxicology tests," said Char, "but you asked me to look for oxy, so we looked for all opioids."

I said, "Where would a suburbanite get her hands on W-18?"

"I don't know. It's just starting to blow up."

"God damn pain pills," said Jameson. "Getting people addicted. Messing 'em up bad."

Char looked at her phone and said, "This is weird. Winnie snorted the W-18. But they found no excipient."

"What the hell is excipient?"

"It's the inactive ingredients in pills. The stuff that binds them together and gives the pill enough bulk."

"Shit," said Jameson. "She got it pure. It's a miracle she didn't OD."

I said, "That explains why Winnie had a pill bottle full of oxycodone. No need for that if she had W-18."

We turned left, passed a Super 8 motel, and pulled into The Patch Motel and the attached Izzy's Lounge & Grill. The single-story structure sat on a hunk of asphalt behind an expansive brown lawn. Even this far north, the only remaining snow existed in dirty, plow-made piles in parking lots.

Inside Izzy's we sat in vinyl upholstered swivel chairs surrounding a square, fake wood grain Formica table. Izzy's was half full, the mood subdued because of Warroad's recent loss or just because that's the way it is in Izzy's. Three men leaned on pool cues near a pool table as a fourth bent over the felt, surveying his shot. A fire danced in a gas fireplace and strips of blond wood ran on the ceiling.

The place was a shrine to Warroad's champions on ice. Both for hockey and fishing. Large photographs commemorated championship teams and trophy fish next to framed jerseys and mounted pike. Models of float planes hung from monofilament. Two Christian Brothers hockey sticks were mounted in an X paying homage to Warroad's once thriving hockey stick factory. The bar featured tap handles of beer you could buy anywhere: Coors, Bud Light, Sam Adams, along with Minnesota brews Surly and Bent Paddle.

No one took our order, so I walked up to the bar and ordered three bottles of Moosehead. The fortysomething woman bartender, a home-dyed blonde with green eye shadow and a pleasant face, hobbled to the glass-doored fridge and retrieved the bottles. She opened them and asked if I was in town for Marvin.

"No, just visiting. A lot of people come up for Marvin?"

"Every day," she said. "Mostly contractors and design-and-build folks come up to see what's new and place custom orders. All sorts from all over."

"Never a dull moment around here, then."

"I wouldn't say that." She did not smile.

"Sorry about the loss to Wayzata."

"Thanks. It hurts, that's for sure. But you count your blessings and move on."

I returned to the table with the Mooseheads. We had to leave the lounge to order food from a concession stand–like window in another part of the building. I don't know why. They brought the food to us fifteen minutes later.

After we ate, I left my tall companions, walked through the lobby, and approached The Patch Motel's front desk. A heavy-set woman in her sixties stood behind the desk watching TV on her laptop. She had a jet-black perm, ten-year-old eyeglasses, and plenty of vacancies.

I said, "Three rooms, please," and gave her my credit card.

She said, "Are you with Marvin?"

"No, but I must look like a contractor. You're the second person to ask me tonight."

"Oh, you don't look like anything in particular. It's just there's almost no other reason to visit Warroad. Unless you're a fisherman or hockey scout, but it's the wrong time of year to be one of them. I asked because Marvin visitors get a discount. You should have said you were with Marvin."

"What about NorthTech visitors?"

Her smile disappeared. "You visiting NorthTech?"

"Nope. Just driving through on my way back to Minneapolis. Read about NorthTech in a trade magazine. For some reason it stuck in my head they're in Warroad."

"We'll see about that."

"They're not doing well?"

She peered over the top of her glasses and said, "You hear about that murder down in the Twin Towns?"

"No. I haven't been paying much attention to the news lately."

"Two people got killed with arrows."

"What?" I said, forcing an incredulous expression onto my face.

"Yep. One of 'em was Roger Engstrom, the man who founded NorthTech." She gave me the details of the murder, most of which were wrong. My favorite was both bodies were found naked. She then went on about NorthTech being a fishy company with rumors of money troubles and no clear successor to Roger.

"Any other places you'd recommend in town for a guy to grab a beer later?"

"Well, don't tell anyone I mentioned it, but my favorite is Craig's Bar and Grill. That's a real fun place. It's Saturday night. They'll have live music going 'til 2:00."

"Thanks. I'll check it out."

"Oh, and if you have any single dollar bills, bring 'em along. People like to stick 'em on the ceiling."

27

A little after 8:00 P.M. we dumped our luggage in our rooms, Jameson changed my bandage, then I left my tall traveling companions to entertain themselves and headed to Craig's Bar & Grill. I parked on Lake Street and walked toward an old brick building. I could hear the Warroad River, full of snowmelt, flow behind me. The building lay under so many coats of paint it looked rubberized. The current color appeared gray in the streetlight. The front consisted of a steel door between a pair of square windows that reminded me of Anne Engstrom's eyeglasses. The building looked old and weathered. The windows looked new. Nice to live in a company town where the company makes windows. Neon beer signs filled the right window. A neon CRAIG'S BAR & GRILL lit up the left.

I couldn't hear the band until I stood a foot from the building. Marvin makes a good window. I opened and entered a bar like a million other bars in small, midwestern towns. Year-round Christmas lights and neon signs, trophy deer, pheasant, ducks, and fish on the walls. Photographs from all over the world featuring regulars wearing their Craig's Bar & Grill T-shirt or windbreaker. I breathed in eighty years of spilled beer and sloe gin fizzes. All the bleach in the world couldn't make it go away nor would you want it to.

Craig's Bar & Grill was comfortable but not all that friendly. In a town of two thousand people, you felt the eyes not recognize you. Not that they had anything against anyone. I was just a stranger who'd walked into a place they frequented so often it felt like their living room. The heavy drinkers sat at the bar with their drinks and coins they'd stacked into dollar-worth columns. You didn't run a tab at a place like Craig's. You paid as you went, and the more you went the drunker you got, so better have those coins precounted to make paying easy.

The band might have been local or might have come from Duluth or Grand Rapids or some other tiny cold city. Drums, two guitars, and a bass, squished onto a tiny stage, all twentysomething guys except for the twentysomething woman on bass. They wore thrift shop clothes. The rhythm guitar player parked his head under a fedora. The lead guitar wore a winter hat, Day-Glo, deer hunter orange. The woman bass player wore a T-shirt with ripped-off sleeves. She showed a sliver of side-boob, and no one, I'm sure, complained about that. All four of them failed to play David Bowie's "The Man Who Sold the World."

I looked up. Dollar bills crowded the ceiling like a leafy canopy. Some had dropped their quarters. Others had not.

"It takes some practice to stick 'em up there good," said a voice. I looked to my left and saw Mike and Connie Housh sitting on the same side of a green vinyl booth, a couple bottles of Bud Light on the table. Mike's corn silk blond bangs had been freshly chopped an inch above his eyebrows, giving him a juvenile air. Connie wore a more subtle shade of blue eye shadow, or maybe it just looked subtle in the bar light.

Connie said, "We heard about what happened outside the cave. Some people are saying you almost died. Kind of surprised to see you walk right in here like nothing happened." She took a swig of Bud Light and got that sad look people get when realizing their bottle is nearly empty.

"You mind if I grab a beer and join you?"

Mike said, "Go ahead. Just passing the time before we bury our daughter tomorrow."

I couldn't tell if he was being honest or sarcastic. "A couple fresh ones?"

Connie lifted her beer bottle and said, "Yeah. That'd be nice."

I went to the bar and returned with a Moose Drool and two cold Bud Lights. I sat across from the Houshes' sunken faces.

I said, "This place have food?"

"No," said Craig, "but the pizza place down the street delivers."

"So Craig's Bar and Grill is really just Craig's Bar?"

"Yep."

"Would you like a pizza?"

"Well," said Connie, "we figured we'd just drink our dinner tonight. It's not the right thing to do, I know, but it takes the edge off. Trying to get through the hours, you know."

I ordered a pizza from the number on a cardboard table tent then filled in the Houshes on what I'd been up to since I'd seen them Wednesday morning. Mike said he felt pretty bad for the Haas woman, but Roger getting it seemed fair. Connie asked if I thought the same person who shot me, shot Winnie and Roger. I said that was likely.

"This world," said Connie. "I just don't know. Maybe it's always seemed like it's falling apart. I just don't know. Maybe Haley was lucky." She forced a hopeful smile toward Mike. He didn't return it. Connie's faded into nothing. The band finished "Losing My Religion." The singer said something about the mild spring as a segue into "Good Vibrations." They were out of tune from note one.

"You know anything about what happened to our Haley?" said Mike.

"A little. I don't know where she went after the game or how she ended up in that cave. I have a feeling when I find Linnea I'll learn more." Mike and Connie shared sour expressions. "Did you know they drove down to the Cities together on weekends?"

"Of course we did," said Connie. "Haley had an internship on Saturdays at the public radio station down there. They put her up in a hotel and everything."

I let Connie hear her own words as the band's atonal harmonies filled the space.

Mike said, "Are you saying she didn't have an internship?"

"To the best of my knowledge she didn't."

Connie said, "Then what was she doing?"

"I'm working on that. I do know Haley and Linnea split up once they got down there. It was more of a carpooling situation than anything else. Haley spent most of her time with Ben Haas. She stayed at his house. It seems Linnea had a boyfriend or maybe just a friend down there, too. But Linnea and Haley were more connected than people thought. Even if it was just for the drive. That's six hours each way. Tough to spend that much time with someone in a confined space and not get to know each other pretty well."

Mike said, "You really think if you find Linnea you'll learn more about Haley?"

"There's a good chance."

Mike rotated his beer bottle on the table. He looked up long enough for me to see the beer had done its job—his blue eyes couldn't focus on any one thing. Then he looked back down at his bottle and said, "Half the town will be at Haley's funeral tomorrow. They've sent a lot of hot dish and cookies and cakes to the house. Don Lindgren, he's my foreman at Marvin, he told me to take as much time as I need, all paid, of course. That's what Warroad people do. Support each other.

"Everyone says they're so sorry and that they're praying for me and Connie and the kids and Haley. They say it's a shame, and that Haley was such a pretty girl. But you know what I haven't heard? Not one person has said Haley was nice. Was kind. Was good. Nobody says her death was a tragedy. Or even that she'll be missed. Terrible thing it is, to lose a child, they say. But I haven't heard one nice thing about Haley other than she was a pretty girl."

My phone buzzed in my pocket, but I didn't look at it.

Mike took another swig of beer. "You raise 'em right. You send 'em to church. Make sure they do their homework. Teach 'em how to fish and skate when they're two. Get 'em up in the deer stand when they're eight. Show 'em all that's good in life. But I'll tell you this: kids are who they are the moment they're born. We had four of 'em. Now we got three. And you know what people say about the other three? They're such nice kids. Good people. Hope my little so-and-so grows up to be like your Robbie or Cate or Mike Jr. Not with Haley, though. She

was born with a road map and that's the route she followed and it led her straight into that cave."

Connie put her arm around Mike and pulled him into
her. The band finished "Good Vibrations" then went
straight into "Pump It Up." There is nothing worse than
terrible musicians with good taste in music.

The door opened. A girl in a red windbreaker and
trucker's hat entered carrying pizza in an insulated sleeve.
I gave her a twenty and told her to keep it. The Houshes
looked at the pizza as if it were the first food they'd seen
in days. It wasn't, of course. Their fridge and countertops
were full, thanks to the town that takes care of its own.
They reached for their first slice. I glanced at the text on
my phone.

> Mel Rosenthal: *Came up to Warroad to get some
> things for Anne. Don't know if you're here yet, but
> I found something you should see.*
> Me: *Text me the address. Be there in 10.*

The band butchered Radiohead's "Creep," and I left
the Houshes with their pizza and two new Bud Lights
and an assurance from the bartender that they'd get a ride
home. I stood on the sidewalk and texted Char Northagen: *Check with your ex at the DNR. Does Mike Housh
have a bow-hunting license?*

Google Maps said Mel Rosenthal was 1.2 miles away,
just south of the river and west of Highway 11. I got in
the Volvo, started the engine, and for the second time in
a week, noticed a breeze where a breeze shouldn't have
been. I turned to look at where the rear passenger window used to be, but my head stopped when hitting something hard and cold.

"Just fucking drive."

28

Coach Gary Kozjek pressed a pistol against my temple. I closed my eyes then opened them. "I'm not comfortable driving right now."

"You want a bullet in your head?"

"Do I really have a choice?"

"Shut up and drive."

I didn't want to die, but I wasn't going to make it easy for him.

"Sorry, Coach. The last thing I'm going to do is take us to a remote location. Not that downtown Warroad is hopping, but if you're going shoot me, you'll have do it here. And you do not want me to drive, because if I do I'm going to take this car up to a hundred miles an hour 'til a cop chases us or I kill us both."

"You fucking asshole. Don't make this uglier than it has to be."

"I'm opening my door and getting out of the car. That'll be your chance to—" Pain shot through my left shoulder. It took my breath. And my sight.

＊　＊　＊

I woke on a floor that smelled of pine and dirt. My eyes opened to candlelight. I lay on my back, my hands bound before me looking at an open-raftered ceiling of rough-hewn beams. I wriggled my wrists. The hair pulled. Tape. I tried my legs, but they were bound at the ankles. I tried to sit up but fell onto my back.

"Jesus Christ, Shapiro, I barely touched you." I heard footsteps then felt his hands under my arms.

"No, no! Just the right shoulder." Gary Kozjek got on his knees and pushed me up onto my feet. I struggled to find my balance. Kozy braced me while grabbing a chair and swinging it behind my legs.

He said, "Sit."

I sat. I was in a small, rustic log cabin. Paper bags filled with groceries from Doug's Supermarket filled a simple, wooden dining table. Nothing but black outside the windows. Kozjek walked to the table and faced me.

I said, "What happened?"

"You said you were going to get out of the car, so I grabbed your left shoulder. Forgot about your injury. Must have hurt like hell. You passed out."

"You didn't pistol-whip me?"

"I didn't have to."

"Guess I'll put that back on my bucket list."

"Don't worry. There's still time." He reached behind his back and removed the gun from his belt. It was a black Glock, but that's all I could tell. He looked at it in the faint light then set it on the table. The cabin was so goddamn quiet the gun landed with a thud.

"Where are we?"

"Some asshole's hunting cabin just south of the border, not far from the bay."

"Did you have to use hockey tape? It's going to rip all the hair off my wrists. Good chance I'll faint again."

Kozy leaned on the table. Not even a hint of a smile. "It's not coming off anytime soon."

"That's disappointing."

He leaned down and put his face near mine. His scars gleamed in the candlelight. "Why do the cops want me?"

"You know the answer, otherwise you wouldn't have run."

"I don't know the answer," he said, walking back toward the table. "But I saw 'em during the game. I could hear their fucking walkie-talkies behind the bench. I'm not an idiot. Two girls from Warroad disappear. One shows up dead. The other's still missing. They must think I had something to do with it."

"Did you have anything to do with it?"

"Fuck you."

"Then why'd you run?"

He lifted the gun from the table and let it rest on its side in the palm of his hand, as if he were trying to guess its weight. "Can you get 'em off my ass?"

"Depends. You like to shoot people with arrows?"

He looked up. The candle revealed deep creases across his forehead. "I was coaching the state tournament. I didn't have time to take a shit much less shoot anyone."

"That's not what the cops think."

"You're going to help prove I didn't do it."

"I can help you put together a timeline of your whereabouts. You should have solid alibis."

He looked out the window at the black night. "Yeah, well I got a problem there." He just stared out the window. After a long hunk of quiet he said, "I didn't have anything to do with Haley Housh's death, but that doesn't mean I didn't have anything to do with Haley

Housh." He fogged the black window with his breath, lifted his finger toward the condensation but thought better of it, and lowered his hand. "For two hundred bucks, I got an hour with Haley to do whatever I wanted. Two hundred bucks is nothing. Nineteen years in the NHL and now I'm living in a town where a few hundred thousand dollars buys a big, beautiful house."

"So you've got no alibi for right after the game."

"I did. But she's dead. If I tell that to the police, I'll never coach again. Doesn't matter how big of a star I am in Warroad. They wouldn't tolerate that."

"Better to lose your job than go to jail."

"You know, it's just a habit I can't break. Sex on the road." He walked away from the window, leaned on the table and faced me. "Nineteen years in the NHL. Never got married. Every town I played in, there'd be women hanging around after the game. When I was young, they were young. When I got a little older, they were young. When I was the oldest skater on the ice, they were still young. Never had to give that up.

"Haley started working me when she was seventeen. I told her to get lost. But I couldn't get her out of my head. She came back to me after turning eighteen. I said if the time and place ever presented itself, I might take her up on her offer. It happened a few months ago when her family went duck hunting. Haley stayed behind and, well, it just took once and I couldn't stop."

"When was that?"

"Let's see." He looked up, as if the answer was written on the ceiling. "I think it was October."

"You sure about that?"

"Halloween decorations were up, so pretty sure."

"Where did you and Haley rendezvous after the game on Tuesday?"

"I had a second hotel room at The Wabasha. I paid for it myself. If anyone found out about it, I'd tell them I couldn't sleep in my suite because assistants used it to scout video late at night, which was pretty much true. The room was on a floor Haley and I could both access via the stairs. It was a little risky, but that was part of the fun. Haley left the game early and headed back to the room when no one else was around. I met her in there about 10:00."

"And where'd she go after that?"

"I don't know. Maybe she had another job."

"There were others?"

"Oh, yeah. Paying customers. And just boyfriends. Graham was one of them. Then she had that boy in Woodbury."

"Ben Haas?"

"Yeah. That's the one. She was worried he'd find out what she was doing because he was possessive."

"Graham Peters said something like that, too. But when I asked Ben about it, he said their relationship was just about sex."

"Well, one of 'em was lying. Or maybe it was Haley." Kozy ran his fingers through his short, thinning hair. "So the police obviously know I was sleeping with Haley."

"Actually, I don't think they do."

"Then why the hell are they after me?"

"They found your fingerprint on the arrowhead that struck my shoulder."

"You got to be shitting me!" Kozjek's face looked just like it had when Luca Lüdorf got boarded by the Way-zata player and the refs didn't call a penalty. Intense out-rage. Nothing fake about it. Only problem was I couldn't tell who he was mad at—me, someone else, or himself. "That's bullshit! The fingerprint's impossible!"

"No, it's not. You could have thought you were being careful but accidentally touched it once. Or it could have been faked. Do you know anyone who'd want to set you up?"

"No. Not everyone loves me, but I don't know anyone who hates me enough to frame me for murder."

"Anyone know you were sleeping with Haley? Anyone in her family? Maybe Ben Haas?"

Kozy hesitated then said, "I don't think so, although you never know. She wouldn't have been the first woman to brag about sleeping with me." He walked over to a small pack in the corner and pulled out a beer. "Want one?"

"Yes, please." Gary Kozjek twisted the cap off a beer I hadn't heard of and handed it to my taped hands. I had to hold it like a chipmunk. "Mind cutting this tape off?"

"Yeah, I do mind. I got a few more questions for you. You used to be a cop, right?"

"If you knew that, why'd you act like you didn't know me when we first met in St. Paul?"

"I didn't want you nosing around, so I was trying to make you feel uncomfortable." He picked up a beer for himself and opened it. "What I want to know is, how much trouble can I get in?"

"A lot if you kill or killed anyone. But first offense paying for sex, not much. It's the public shaming that'll cause the most damage."

"How do I prove I didn't kill anyone?"

The long, high-pitched howl of a wolf penetrated the cabin. I hadn't been this far north since the state had made it illegal to kill wolves except in defense of human life. There were over 2,500 of them roaming Northern Minnesota. I thought of Linnea and Miguel trying to evade border patrol in the wilderness. Maybe they'd succeed. But evading a circling pack of wolves was a different challenge.

"You can't prove you're innocent. You're the last known person to see Haley alive. And as far as the arrow murders go, even if you have an alibi, you could have hired someone to do it. That's what the D.A. will argue, anyway."

"Fuck."

"You know that old saying, you can't prove a negative? Let me find Linnea Engstrom. Let me find whoever shot me and killed Roger Engstrom and Winnie Haas. That's your only chance." Kozy took a long swig of beer and looked at me with cold eyes. "If you're innocent, Kozy, but don't let me go, you'll be an innocent man making yourself guilty."

He set down the beer and picked up the gun. He ejected the magazine, looked at it, then reinserted it. "I didn't do it. How could my fingerprint end up on that arrowhead?"

"If I were going to fake a fingerprint, I'd find one on a clean, glass surface like that beer bottle. I'd photograph it with a high-resolution camera and print it in silicone on a 3-D printer. I'd press the silicone fingerprint on my nose or scalp to pick up some oil then press it on wherever I wanted it to appear. Just like a rubber stamp. It's hardly a new idea. A ten-year-old could do it."

He went to the corner and retrieved another beer from his pack. "How much do you charge?"

29

Kozy cut the tape from my wrists, drove me into town, and dropped me in Lakeview Park. I walked the remaining few blocks to my car. Broken glass covered the curb near what used to be my rear passenger window. It was 11:42 P.M. and thirty-six degrees. I texted Mel Rosenthal that I ran into trouble but could still come over if she wanted me to. She did, and I headed to McKenzie Street.

The Engstroms lived in a long rambler with architectural windows. The siding consisted of an odd pattern of brick and stucco. The place looked like it had been built in the 1970s though it could have been new. I would've guessed Anne Engstrom, with her need for attention, would've lived in something more striking, like an old Victorian. Maybe the house was the best Warroad had to offer. Or maybe it was what the Engstroms could afford.

When I got out of the Volvo, Mel Rosenthal waited for me in the front door wearing flannel pajamas and bare feet and holding a glass of red. I walked in. She said hello, but not warmly, then led me into the living room. She waited for me to sit on the couch then chose a chair on the other side of the coffee table. The room looked as if Anne had ordered the furniture and decor by exactly how Pottery Barn showed it in the catalog, down to the fuzzy throw pillows and huge vase full of dead sticks.

I told Mel what had just happened with Gary Kozjek.

She stood, walked around the coffee table, sat down, and kissed me. "I thought you ran into trouble with a woman. Which is fine. It's not like we're dating. It just threw me, that's all. I'm sorry about the cold reception. I guess I don't know what the hell we're doing." She smiled and said, "Are you okay?"

"My wrists got balded when Kozy ripped off the hockey tape, but other than that, I'm fine. What is it you wanted to show me?"

Mel led me into Linnea's room. There was a twin bed and matching dresser and desk all in naturally finished oak. Posters of Dessa and Alicia Keys, Regina Spektor, and St. Vincent. A whole wall dedicated to Kendrick Lamar. Not a stuffed animal in sight. Maybe the police took them to x-ray.

Mel said, "Back when Linnea and I talked every day, she'd tell me about things she'd written in her journal. I assumed she took the journal to St. Paul or, if not, that the Warroad police found it when they searched her room. They found her MacBook, which wasn't password protected. It was a rule of Anne and Roger's—they wanted access to her email and social media. They thought that's what good parents do. But the MacBook didn't have a journal on it.

"Anne's not smart about those things. If you don't give a kid privacy, she'll just go underground. That's what I did when I was Linnea's age. So I did a little snooping around, in case there was a journal and Linnea didn't take it with her. And I found this."

Mel handed me a box made of walnut. It was the size of a few, stacked reams of paper. I lifted the top and saw jewelry on black velvet. Rings and earrings rested in tiny slits and holes. Underneath were two drawers. I opened the first one. Necklaces and bracelets, also on black velvet. I opened the bottom one. Linnea's pin collection. Mostly from ski areas like Vail and Aspen and Park City. Also on black velvet.

"You think these pins are a clue to where she is?"

Mel shook her head. She scooped out the pins and placed them on Linnea's nightstand. Then she dug her fingernails into the velvet and wedged it out of the drawer. A tiny notebook computer lay underneath. Mel removed an aluminum Acer Chromebook from the drawer. She handed it to me. I opened it. The screen lit up and requested a password. I said, "Do you know the password?"

Mel said, "No. I guessed at a few but nothing worked. But I think Linnea hid this here for me to find."

"Why do you think that?"

"I gave her this jewelry box. Howard hit his head on the curb a few days before Linnea's birthday. He was in the hospital. A lot slipped through the cracks. After he died, when Anne and Linnea spent the summer with us, I gave her this as a belated present. When Anne was out of the room, I showed Linnea the secret compartment in the bottom drawer. So Linnea knows I know about it. If she wanted to keep something from me she wouldn't have hidden it here."

"But she didn't give you the password."

"I bet somehow she did. I've tried everything based on our conversations. Inside jokes. Names of family members. Birthdays. Anniversaries. The date of Howard's death. Nothing's worked. I keep racking my brain, but . . ." She shook her head then placed her hand on mine.

I said, "Is it possible the password is in Craig's Bar and Grill?"

"What? Why would you say that?"

"Because Linnea stuck a dollar in the Saint Paul Hotel's ceiling before she disappeared. Just like they do in Craig's Bar and Grill."

"You mean could the password be the address?"

"Maybe. Or the phone number."

We looked up both and tried them in various combinations. None worked. We mixed combinations of words "Craig's Bar & Grill" with and without the address and phone number. Nothing.

Mel said, "Maybe it's something in the bar."

I parked the Volvo in the Engstroms' garage, then Mel drove us to Craig's in her Audi Quattro wagon and parked behind the sparkly remains of my rear passenger window.

The crowd was younger and rougher-looking than earlier. The same crap band spilled over the tiny stage. How many songs could they know? I guessed they recycled songs every few hours, but it was my first time hearing them slaughter "London Calling." I wanted to order a bottle of PBR to throw at them but settled for another Moose Drool and a glass of red for Mel. I looked for the Houshes. They had left.

We chose a booth and studied the crap mounted to the walls and extrapolated possible passwords to Linnea's Chromebook. We wrote down the names of street signs, the numbers of license plates, the weight of a mounted walleye, and the name of the angler who caught it. I even wrote down the shit name of the shit band—Time Travelers—in the slim chance that was it.

We'd filled three napkins with possibilities when Graham Peters and Luca Lüdorf walked in and sat at the bar. Both wore black and yellow Warroad windbreakers. Luca looked the same with his stiff straight blond hair. But Graham's hockey hair was gone. Someone had run clippers over his head, leaving a dome of black stubble. His beard was gone, too.

I slid out of the booth, walked up to the hockey players, and reintroduced myself.

Graham said, "Dude. I know what you're thinking, but you don't have to be twenty-one to drink pop at the bar."

"I'm not a cop and don't care what you're drinking. You want to join Linnea's aunt and me? I'll order you a pizza and buy your Cokes." Graham and Luca gave each other a *why not* look. I called in their pizza order, led them over to the booth, and introduced them to Mel.

"So I'm guessing you want to talk to us about something," said Graham.

I squeezed Mel's hand under the table. It was not a show of affection. "You guys have any idea where your hockey coach is?"

Graham kept his eyes on me, but Luca looked at his teammate.

"What are you talking about?" said Graham.

"Coach Kozjek is missing."

"Nah," said Graham. "He just hit the road like he does at the end of every hockey season. Probably took off to visit his NHL buddies."

Luca kept his eyes on Graham. I gave Mel's hand another squeeze.

"Woodbury and St. Paul Police are looking for him. If you guys are aiding him in any way, you have a problem. The NCAA doesn't put up with that shit like it used to. Scholarships could be lost."

"We have no idea where he is," said Graham.

Luca added a weak, "Yeah."

I said, "You ever notice at Doug's Supermarket, there's a camera over each register? So if you guys were in there in the last couple of days and, say, bought a mess of groceries but can't account for where those groceries are now, you could be in a shitload of trouble. It's called aiding and abetting."

Luca said in a shaky voice, "What do the police want with Coach?"

"They want to talk to him about the double murder in Woodbury. About the death of Haley Housh. And about the possible whereabouts of Linnea Engstrom."

Graham said, "He had nothing to do with any of that."

Mel squeezed my hand then said, "How do you know?"

Luca said, "He was coaching us while all that stuff happened. He takes his job super serious. And he's a good guy. He wouldn't hurt anyone. And for sure he had nothing to do with Linnea."

"Why for sure?" I said. "Have you been in contact with her?"

Luca watched the Time Travelers' guitar player crucify a solo. His straw-like blond hair didn't move. He reached into the breast pocket of his Warroad letter jacket and pulled out an envelope.

The same kid who'd brought the Houshes' pizza appeared with the same insulated bag. I gave her another twenty. Luca and Graham thanked me like polite schoolboys.

Luca handed me the envelope. I opened it and removed a letter. Mel glanced at it and said, "That's Linnea's handwriting."

We read as Luca and Graham wolfed down their first slice.

> *Dear Luca,*
> *I'm sorry for everything, I really am. It's best if you just forget about me, I'm not coming back. I know this will hurt your feelings but you need to know that I'm not in love with you anymore, I never actually was. I know I'm literally a terrible person and I shoulda been honest with you but I couldn't be. Maybe when we're old and if I see you again then I'll explain it all to you, but for now just know that I do love you just not in a romantic way. You are awesome and good and didn't deserve what I did to you and I'm sure you'll have a great life as a hockey player and a person and you'll have lots of girls who will want to be in love with you and you should let one or more than one be because you deserve it. Please don't be angry at all girls because of me. If you have to be angry just be angry at me. That is what's fair.*
>
> *xoxoxoxo*
> *Linnea*

I said to Luca, "When did you receive this?"

"Today." Mouthful of pizza. "In the mail."

I looked at the postmark on the envelope. Chicago. Two days ago. Guess Guy Storstrand forgot to tell us about mailing a letter.

Mel said, "Why would she use snail mail? Why wouldn't she just send a text?"

"It would leave an electronic trail." I said to Luca, "Have you told the police?"

"Yeah. I called the St. Paul cops."

"What'd they say when you told them?"

Luca squirmed in his chair and sighed. "Nothing. They just asked me to take a picture of the envelope and letter and email it to them."

Mel said, "I don't understand. Why would Linnea lead you on like that?"

" 'Cause she's whacked," said Graham.

Luca nodded. "It's so embarrassing."

Heads shook and faces scrunched.

I said, "Sounds like payback."

"For what?" said Luca. "I didn't do anything wrong."

"It's not about you. Guy Storstrand's from Warroad. Tell me how he ended up playing for Roseau."

Graham hesitated then said, "Dude's Tourette's. Guy was coughing and clearing his throat during team meetings. Coach thought it was a distraction so he wouldn't play him."

"Kozjek wants a state title more than anything and he wouldn't give his team the best chance just because a player's got Tourette's?"

"It was six years ago when Guy was a freshman. He ticked really bad then, and Guy wasn't the superstar he'd be a year or two later. The Canadiens drafted Guy right out of high school. That almost never happens. Even Phil Kessel played a year of college first. But when Guy was a freshman, he wasn't there yet. Coach wanted him to quit and he did. Then Guy went to skate for Roseau. But a year later, when Coach realized his mistake, Guy was so pissed at Coach he wouldn't come back to play for Warroad."

"Think it's possible Guy holds a grudge so he asked Linnea to mess with Luca during the tournament?"

"Like it was a setup?" set Graham. "Like Linnea was never interested in Luca?"

"Wait," said Luca. "You're saying that Linnea planned to disappear a few months ago?"

"That's exactly what I'm saying."

Mel wasn't buying it. Her mouth mangled into an odd shape and her forehead wrinkled. We were talking about Linnea, after all, who was like a daughter to Mel. "Come on, guys. That's awful. Linnea wouldn't do that."

"Why not?" I said. "Guy asked Linnea to date Luca and get him to fall in love with her all so that if the much-hyped and favored Warroad Warriors fulfilled their destiny and made it to the state tournament, she could disappear and wreak emotional havoc on Warroad's leading scorer. In return, Guy is helping Linnea sneak Miguel Maeda across the border."

Graham said, "Who is Miguel Maeda?"

Luca lowered his head. His nostrils flared. "I thought I was going to marry her. I was shopping for rings."

Mel said, "After dating only a few months?"

Luca shook his head. He was beating the shit out of himself without words. The band maimed Prince's "Sometimes It Snows in April." No one spoke for a while then Mel said, "Luca, did you and Linnea hang out here?"

"Sometimes, yeah."

"Is there anything in this place Linnea liked? Like one of the license plates or street signs or something like that?"

Luca fumed. "I can't think of anything. She didn't like it here all that much anyway."

I got up and went to the bar to get two more Cokes. I had just picked up the bottles when a drumroll of quarters bounced off the bar. I looked up at the dollar bill that had just released them.

I knew the password to Linnea's Chromebook.

30

I asked the boys if they wanted another pizza. They did. I said, "Order it," then told Mel we had to go. Her eyes asked why, and mine answered. I thanked Graham and Luca for the conversation, set down my third pizza twenty of the evening, then Mel and I headed out.

We stepped out of Craig's into a cool, thick fog. It was almost 1:30 A.M. Mel leaned into me and said, "I fucked up pushing Linnea away. She needed the mother Anne is incapable of being."

"I don't know if it would have made any difference. Linnea turned to Winnie Haas. That didn't help."

"Thanks for saying that, but it would have made a difference. Linnea could have moved down to Wayzata and lived with us. Roger and Anne were toxic. I didn't get her away from them, so she got herself away, no matter who she had to hurt."

We drove the 1.2 miles back to the Engstrom house guided by low beams and fog lights. Mel's dash said the temperature had risen to forty degrees. Maybe that March blizzard wouldn't come, after all.

We sat on Linnea's bed and opened her Chromebook. I thumbed through the pictures on my phone and found the snapshot of the dollar bill stuck into the Engstroms' ceiling at The Saint Paul Hotel. I typed the bill's serial number into the Chromebook, and we were in.

The only thing on the desktop was a document. I opened it. It contained GPS coordinates and a message.

Dear Aunt Mel,
You're the only person who could figure this out probably so if you did and you haven't heard from me by June then the GPS coordinates above are where I was going or leaving when something went wrong. If anyone cares you can look for my body there. But I would not. A person can't have a more natural death than in the middle of the woods or on a frozen lake. That sounds peaceful to me. That's why it's not scary. It's the way it used to be for everyone before the world got so crazy and stupid.

If I'm okay but you find this before I contact you in June then don't worry about me because I am fine. I probably have money. Lots of money. Whatever anyone says about me I didn't do anything illegal. Except help someone sneak across the border and I stole money from my dad, but he can't do anything about it because he broke the law. He's a stupid person, and he did stupid and wrong things to make money for his stupid company. He thought he was using me to carry drugs to Minneapolis and bring cash back and that I didn't know about it. But I found out so I stole the money to make my own life. I don't want to tell you where that is because I

don't want to be found. So please don't look for my
body whether I'm alive or dead.

　One more thing. No two more things. The first is
that I know you felt bad about us having a close re-
lationship and I didn't have one with my mom so
that's why you and me couldn't be close anymore.
But I hope one day we can again. Maybe if you're
mad at me you won't be in a few years. But I'd like
us to be close again. You are the only real parent I
ever had.

Love,
Linnea

p.s. I'm writing this before leaving for St. Paul for
the hockey tournament. So I only know what I
think will happen, not what really happened. Maybe
I should have waited until I turned 18 but I just
can't take it anymore. Please believe me. Oh. And
tell Ivy I love her and we'll be together again some-
day I hope.

Mel's head hung and her shoulders shook.

I said, "Heartbreaking. Who taught her how to write a sentence?"

Laughter leaked into Mel's labored breathing then it disappeared and she said, "Those GPS coordinates are where she's meeting Miguel, right?"

"Probably." I opened Google Maps and typed in the coordinates. "It's right here on the U.S.-Canadian border. It looks like Miguel will leave the Canadian side on Stony Point and cross Sand Point Bay. Then maybe another mile or so and he hits land in the U.S. That's where Linnea will be waiting for him."

"Do we call the police or border patrol?"

"Do you want Linnea arrested?"

"I don't know. Roger's funeral is Tuesday. She should go to that, shouldn't she?"

"Let's get some sleep and figure this out in the morning."

"Stay with me?"

We fell asleep in the guest room on a bed that once belonged to Mel and Anne's grandparents. We found each other sometime before dawn and made love then slept a few more hours. I woke to gray light filtering through the drapes and went into the kitchen to search for coffee. There was none. I left a note for Mel then drove the Volvo out of the garage and headed back to The Patch Motel.

A cold front had frozen last night's fog out of the air. The temperature on the dash read twenty-two degrees. I mourned the rear passenger window and thought of Kozy in the hunting cabin. I wondered if he'd light a fire to warm himself or if he thought the chimney smoke too risky and opted to shiver in candlelight.

I had suggested he turn himself in. Might as well be warm and comfortable while the truth worked its way to the surface. Kozy could afford good lawyers—he'd probably make bail—he could tell the microphones and cameras he's innocent. But Kozy feared that kind of fight. He'd skated in playoff games with broken bones and stitched-up flesh. He'd seen his own teeth get picked off the ice to be replanted after the final horn. But outside the arena, he'd lived as one of Minnesota's elite. A star hockey player. Since he was a boy. He had no intention of relinquishing his status.

Just after 8:00 A.M., I stepped into The Patch Motel front lounge. A crowd helped themselves to coffee and

not much else. I filled a paper cup for myself then turned
toward the fire and saw two surprises sitting on a leather
couch: Ellegaard and Ben Haas. Other familiar faces meandered about, including SPPD officer Terrence Flynn
and Woodbury Detective Jamie Waller. Char Northagen
talked to a Warroad police uniform whom I assumed to
be Officer Tony Stensrud. He was tall and hefty with a
1950s-style crew cut, pink cheeks, and dull eyes. The
room buzzed—it was the first place I'd been in Warroad
that buzzed.

Haley Housh would have been flattered to know so
many had ventured north to watch her casket lower into
the earth. Maybe one of them could tell the rest of us
how she ended up dead in a St. Paul cave.

Jameson White stepped into the lobby and glared at
me. I nodded, held up the universal "one minute" finger,
then walked over to Ellegaard and Ben Haas.

"Welcome to Warroad." Ben Haas looked at me with
red, puffy eyes that begged for sleep or sunglasses. Ellegaard offered a subdued smile of familiarity or perhaps
fatigue. I said, "Did you drive up alone, Ben?"

"My dad rode up with me. Didn't want me to be by
myself, plus he's meeting with Marvin about some
window thing."

"Anyone had breakfast?" They shook their heads.
"Ellie, come with me for a minute, then we'll grab some
grub."

"Cool," said Ben.

Jameson White cleaned and redressed my shoulder in
his room under white fluorescent light. Ellegaard gazed
out the window at the low heavy clouds while I told him
what had happened since leaving Minneapolis.

"Man oh man," said Jameson. "Getting kidnapped

by a hockey coach. A teenage prostitute. Drug running. People getting shot by arrows. I am not cut out for this private eye stuff."

Ellegaard ignored him and said, "Annika's doing a hell of a job at BrainiAcme."

"You don't want me on that case anymore?"

"I do, but there's no rush. Sounds like finding Linnea might clear up a lot of questions for a lot of people, especially the ones who work in the police departments of St. Paul, Woodbury, and Warroad. You know, Shap—"

I cut him off. "You think we should tell them where Kozy is."

"If a private withheld information like that when I wore the badge, I would have arrested him."

"It's my information to withhold. To my best recollection, I haven't told a soul about Kozy's cabin in the woods. Not you. Not Jameson. Not Mel Rosenthal."

A train pounded the tracks then blew its long, low whistle. Jameson's scissors snipped a piece of tape. Then the big nurse said, "Oh, I see what you guys are doing. Nils told us something we shouldn't know so now we gotta pretend he never said it. Am I involved in a cover-up or something?"

I said, "Whether you like it or not."

"All right. Then all I remember is you saying you spent the night at your lady friend's. And when you woke up, someone had busted your car window. How's that?"

"Perfect."

"Ha! Guess I am cut out for the private eye business!"

Ellegaard said, "We either tell the police where Kozy is and watch them run off in his direction, or we head toward the rendezvous spot to see if we can intercept Linnea coming or going or waiting. It's a long shot, but if we find her, maybe she can give us the information to clear Kozy. Or to nail him."

Jameson said, "You're done, Nils. Put your shirt on. If your pasty white skin's exposed to these harsh lightbulbs much longer, we'll be looking at your skeleton."

"Thanks, Jameson. We'll meet in the lobby in ten."

"All right." He put the bandage scissors and tape in his bag. He gathered up the old dressing then said, "Oh. Did you want me to leave?"

"If you don't mind."

"Mind leaving my own room? Why would I mind that?"

"Sorry."

"Well, it's official, then. You're buying breakfast. As they say in the theater, I will see you in the lobby." He bowed, turned, and walked out. When the door shut we heard a "Ba ha ha ha!" from the hall.

Ellegaard took his face out of the window. It had a big smile on it courtesy of Jameson White. He walked toward me and sat on the other queen bed. "So what do you think? Send the cops after Kozy or we go after Linnea?"

"We could do both, you know."

"I got no problem with that."

I said, "But let's leave Kozy alone for now. He's sitting in a cabin in the woods with no running water or heat. My guess is he'll come in on his own sooner than later. And I'll go after Linnea while most of the town is at Haley's funeral."

"I'll go with you."

Whatever was wrong between Ellegaard and me had just healed. I said, "It's good to see you out from behind that desk."

"Yeah. It's about time, huh?"

I stood and walked to the window, expecting to feel

cold near the glass but felt none. The locally made triple-pane windows kept it outside. An even layer of gray domed Warroad. Frost still clung to the brown grass courtesy of last night's fog. March had bent but didn't break. Spring would have to wait.

I said, "Before we go, I want to talk to Ben Haas."

Ellegaard said, "What about?"

"Ben said his relationship with Haley was just physical. But Ben's dad, Kozjek, and Graham Peters think Ben was in love with Haley. Now, it's possible, maybe more than possible, that Haley Housh spread that lie. Or, maybe Ben has been lying. Either way, I don't think he's telling us everything he knows about Linnea. Maybe he can help us understand what we're walking into."

31

Joe's Place was crowded with the good citizens of Warroad, out of town funeral-goers, and the ever-present throng of builders and designers visiting Marvin Windows. The air smelled of bacon, sausage, maple syrup, and pancakes. The din of flatware on plates overpowered the taciturn Minnesotans' conversation. I asked Jameson White and Char Northagen to sit on either side of five-foot-four Ben Haas while Ellegaard and I sat across from him. The seating chart was designed to intimidate.

We all commented on the clientele and menu, then Ben said, "I wasn't going to come up here for Haley's funeral, but my mom didn't want one. It was in her will. She wanted a memorial on a houseboat on the St. Croix in mid-October when the leaves are at peak color. We're supposed to scatter her ashes in the water. But my dad pointed out that's seven months away, and I need to mourn now."

Char said, "Your dad's right."

I said, "Ben, Woodbury PD found a few strands of Linnea's hair in the dryer's lint trap in your house."

"That's not possible."

It was possible, but not true as far as I knew. "Sure it's possible. Maybe Haley borrowed a sweater from Linnea and Haley wore that sweater to your place. Or maybe the hair just floated over to Haley on one of their drives down."

"I guess. Maybe."

"Or . . . maybe Linnea spent some time at your house."

"What? What are you talking about?"

Jameson said, "Please pass the syrup." Ben passed him the syrup.

Ellegaard said, "The thing is, Ben, it doesn't seem likely that your mom hid all that money in the laundry chute. And you say you didn't hide it in there. . . ."

"I had no idea it was in there. I told you that."

"Okay, then. Who did hide it? Roger? Possibly. If he knew someone was coming and that person was after it. But we think the more likely scenario is Linnea hid it in there. She was in contact with your mom. When she stole the money from Roger, she visited your mom and hid it in the laundry chute."

"What are you talking about? Linnea didn't know my mom," said Ben. "Linnea never even met my mom. If she did, my mom would have told me. We talked about everything."

I said, "You don't know that, Ben. You and Winnie talked about a lot of things. But you don't know if it was everything. I'm pretty sure your mom and Linnea were friends."

Ben forked a piece of waffle and said, "No. They weren't friends. She would have told me."

"Maybe Winnie was like a second mom to Linnea and

felt guilty about that so she hid their relationship from you."

Ben put the forked waffle back on his plate. He looked sick. This is how Ellegaard and I had planned it. I'd beat Ben up until he rolled over and exposed his soft underbelly. Then Ellegaard would go for the kill. No one expects Ellegaard to go for the kill. That's what makes him so good at it.

I said, "Did your mom date?" Ben looked at me without moving his head, the way a dog does when chewing a bone. With just his eyes. Nothing but his eyes. He didn't respond. "You don't know, do you? She didn't tell you she dated. But she didn't tell you she didn't, either. Right? So maybe she did date while you were with the band or at your dad's or otherwise occupied. Or maybe she didn't date and instead spent time with Linnea Engstrom."

In a flat, defeated tone, Ben said, "Are you saying—"

"No. Not at all. Your mom's relationship with Linnea was strictly mother/daughter like. I'm just saying you weren't around all the time. Your mom had time to see Linnea." Ben's face had gone pale, not easy for a pasty white Minnesotan in March. He dropped his fork and it clanked off his plate.

Ellegaard said, "Did you know Haley Housh was a prostitute?"

Ben's eyes closed. His chin trembled, then he grabbed his stomach. "I—I don't . . . I feel sick." He pushed his chair away from the table and ran toward the bathroom.

Jameson sighed, put down his fork, and said, "You guys have a strange way of making a living."

Char said, "What in the hell was that about?"

"We were trying to get an honest reaction out of our young friend."

"And did you?"

Ellegaard said, "I think so. Ben's been lying. He was in love with Haley."

"You didn't have to do that. I can tell you if he was in love with Haley," said Char. "I'll just ask him when he comes back. No matter how he answers, I'll know." Ellegaard and Jameson and I caught each other's skeptical glances. "You guys wouldn't understand. But trust me. I'll know."

Jameson said, "Why does it matter anyway?"

I said, "Because missing Linnea Engstrom and dead Haley Housh and the arrows at Crestmoor Bay and the arrow in my shoulder are tied together. We're looking for the thread."

"I told you," said Char, "when Ben comes back, I'll just ask him if he was in love with Haley. You didn't have to do that to the kid."

But Ben didn't come back. Ten minutes later, I walked into the men's room. He wasn't there. He wasn't anywhere in the restaurant. Ben Haas had run.

The Patch Motel was used to hockey teams and ice fishermen and contractors, all of whom stayed in clusters and knocked on each other's doors for meetings and drinks and dinner. The Patch Motel was not used to thinking about security. So when Char Northagen asked the front desk clerk which room was the Hasses', the front desk clerk told her.

I knocked on the door. No one answered. Then Char found the housekeeper and asked for more towels in room 128. She waited at the vending machine. When the housekeeper delivered the towels, Char entered the room as if it was hers. The housekeeper left. I knocked on 128 while Ellegaard stood watch in case Ben or Raynard Haas returned.

Housekeeping had cleaned the room. The queen beds were made. The trash was empty. Architectural drawings lay on the small table next to an architectural model of a flat-roofed house with clean lines. It looked like a rectangle, except for one side that curved from one corner to the other. A wall of windows looked out on something beautiful, I supposed. Maybe it would be built on the bluffs of the St. Croix River or in the hills above Duluth looking out on Lake Superior.

Char said, "It must take them forever to build those models."

"Haas probably has a junior architect do it. Unless he likes the smell of glue."

A black suit, size thirty-six short, hung in the closet next to a starched white shirt and dry-cleaned tie still in its cardboard holder. Ben Haas's funeral duds. A wool, charcoal herringbone topcoat and that damn Sgt. Pepper's–looking thing hung next to it along with a few more shirts in dry cleaning bags. Raynard Haas's runway model clothes.

A mandolin with a small, wooden, peanut-shaped body rested on the credenza. It had no sound hole but did have an electronic pickup, a couple knobs, and a quarter-inch output. It looked good for travel and quiet practice in a motel room with thin walls.

I checked the pad of paper on the nightstand between the beds. Nothing. Nor were there any indentations on the top sheet. If anyone wrote anything incriminating on a pad of paper and had seen a detective movie since 1930, they knew to remove the indented sheets below.

Char said, "So what exactly are we looking for?"

"No idea. A bow and quiver of arrows would be a good clue."

"I don't see anything unusual."

We checked the dresser and nightstand drawers. They were empty. Neither Ben nor his father had unpacked for the short stay. We checked their bags, but found nothing of interest. I returned to the closet. A few dirty clothes sat in a pile on the floor near Ben's blue Jack Purcell sneakers. I picked up an oxford button-down shirt and checked the breast pocket. Nothing. I picked up socks and underwear one by one. Nothing there, either. I picked up a well-worn pair of Levi's with a twenty-eight-inch inseam. I checked the pockets and removed a folded lavender Post-it note, stuck to itself with its own adhesive.

On it, two long numbers were written in red ink.

Char looked over my shoulder. "What's that?"

I put the Post-it note in my pocket. "The GPS coordinates of Linnea and Miguel's rendezvous point."

32

We drove north on Highway 313 for six miles, turned right on Warroad's 410th Street, which wasn't much of a street, then stopped cold when we saw Ben Haas's Toyota Highlander parked on the shoulder of frozen mud and sand. It was 10:30 A.M., half an hour before Haley Housh's funeral, and the outside temperature on the Volvo's dash read sixteen degrees. I looked at my phone—it still had a signal. It was a mile and a quarter on foot to the rendezvous point through fields and woods. He had half an hour on us and was probably there already.

Char and Jameson stayed back at the hotel. Jameson said the mile plus on frozen, uneven ground might wreck his knees forever. Char said she knew how to perform an autopsy and save the life of someone shot by an arrow, but she didn't know how to hunt someone when they might be hunting her back.

"If Ben returns to his car before we do," said Ellegaard, "he'll see the Volvo and know we're onto him."

"Yeah. Shit." We drove back a quarter mile then took

a left on 580th Avenue. Warroad had a couple dozen streets. I don't know how the hell it numbered them up to 410th Street and 580th Avenue.

We got out of the car and stood at the Volvo's open hatch. Minnesotans who embark on a road trip between November and April do so with winter gear in the car. Natural selection has taken care of those who don't.

We geared up with a base layer of Kevlar. It would do little to stop a broad-head arrow, but you never knew what projectile might be flying your way. Ellegaard body-holstered his Glock 22. I shoved my Ruger LC9 in my pocket. The Ruger is small and light. A lot of cops carry it when off duty. I'd been off duty seventeen years. We threw on parkas and hiking boots and each slung a pair of binoculars around our neck. Mine were normal. Ellegaard's were thermals. I shut the Volvo and locked it, despite its missing rear passenger window.

We walked back on the gravel road and Ellegaard said, "Lay it out." It was a game we played studying for exams when we were Minneapolis police cadets. We kept to the facts or at least what we thought were facts.

I said, "Haley Housh and Linnea Engstrom disappeared from outside the Xcel Center Tuesday night after a Warroad hockey game."

Ellegaard said, "Haley Housh was found dead in a downtown St. Paul cave the next morning."

"Roger and Anne Engstrom hired us to find Linnea."

"You were shot with an arrow outside the cave where Haley Housh was found dead."

"Linnea was dating Luca Lüdorf."

"Haley was sleeping with Graham Peters and dating Ben Haas and sleeping with men for money."

"Roger Engstrom and Winnie Haas were killed with arrows in Winnie's home on Crestmoor Bay."

Ellegaard said, "We found about a hundred thousand dollars in cash in Winnie Haas's laundry chute."

I said, "Linnea Engstrom disappeared during the hockey tournament and upset Luca Lüdorf. Guy Storstrand was cut from the Warroad team by Gary Kozjek. Linnea and Guy are close friends."

"Joaquin Maeda hosted Call of Duty private lobbies so he, his cousin Miguel in Mexico, and Linnea could chat online."

"Linnea left a note for her aunt, Mel Rosenthal. It gave the GPS coordinates of where we might find her body if she doesn't contact Mel by June."

"Linnea gave Guy Storstrand money to buy Miguel Maeda outdoor winter gear. He's sneaking across the border. Linnea plans to meet or has met him at the rendezvous point designated by the GPS coordinates."

"We found the same GPS coordinates written on a Post-it in Ben Haas's room at The Patch Motel."

We returned to Ben Haas's Highlander and scanned the field for a bow hunter in wait. If he'd camouflaged himself, he'd be tough to spot, even if he lay in an open field. In the woods, he'd be invisible. I put my full faith and trust in Ellegaard's thermal binoculars.

He panned the landscape then said, "Clear."

I looked at the map on my phone and pointed. "That way." We headed for a forest of tall pines through a field of frozen dirt clumps and wheat stalk that had been churned into the soil.

Ellegaard said, "We have pieces of the puzzle. But we're missing some. Big ones."

"Like how could Ben Haas have the GPS coordinates?"

"Maybe he knows the Instagram code."

"What about the timing? What are the odds Linnea and Miguel would have planned to rendezvous now?"

"They can't be meeting at a time," said Ellegaard. "Too many variables. It has to be a window."

I stepped into a pile of thatch. I heard a rustling, then a bird popped into the air.

"Hen!" said Ellegaard. The pheasant flew straight away from us. Its wing beats sounded like peeping baby chicks. It stopped flapping after a hundred yards and glided into a descent and turned to land near the forest's edge.

I looked at Ellegaard. "Hen?"

"Sorry. Pheasant hunting habit. You only shoot the roosters, so when a bird flushes, someone yells out the gender before anyone pulls the trigger."

"The things I learn from you."

"You've never been pheasant hunting?"

"No one's ever invited me."

Ellegaard laughed. "You're going to regret saying that."

Ellegaard grew up hunting with his father and grandfather and brothers. Last year he sat in the duck blind with Emma for the first time. He'd bought her a 20-gauge shotgun for her birthday. She downed a male wood duck on its descent toward a flotilla of decoys. She wouldn't stop talking about how beautiful it was, the thing she'd killed.

My father grew up hunting in the Upper Peninsula of Michigan, but he'd quit before I was born and never offered to take me. Returning to his rural upbringing never interested my father. He spoke fondly of his childhood and the people he grew up with. He visited once every summer. But he strived to never relive it.

"Shap?"

"Yeah."

"Why'd you stop walking?"

"Sorry. Didn't realize I had."

"You okay? You look like you're somewhere else."

"I'm good. Let's keep going."

"Wait." Ellegaard unzipped his coat and withdrew his Glock. "We're almost in archery range from the edge of the forest." I pulled my Ruger out of my pocket. Ellegaard said, "You got to get a bigger gun, Shap. That thing's ridiculous."

"If it's big and heavy, I'll never take it with me. Just like a camera."

"You never take it with you anyway."

"And," I said, "it's the perfect weight for a guy with one functional arm."

Ellegaard had forgotten about that. He said, "Can you shoot?" It wasn't a straightforward question. What he was really asking was *Can you cover me?*

"I'm right-eye dominant. I've always held a gun with my right hand."

He thought about that for five seconds then said, "Let's pick up the pace. We're too exposed in this field."

We continued toward the forest. The shooting range at the Minneapolis Police Academy provided my experience with guns. I know how to load my Ruger, shoot it, clean it, and, to a lesser degree, aim it. I have a permit to carry it but rarely do. But I was content to feel it in my hand as we lumbered across the frozen field.

Ellegaard lifted his binoculars to his face and panned the forest.

I said, "You want a second pair of eyes?"

"Please."

I focused my binocs on the forest's edge. "What are we looking for?"

"An archer. Or at least a deer stand. Your opticals can see it better than my thermals. About twenty feet up from the ground. The bow hunter's favorite spot, because deer rarely look up."

"So hunters sit up there and wait for a deer to just walk underneath them?"

"Or at least come into range."

"Challenging sport."

"Not now, Shap."

When we entered the forest the ground underfoot felt softer, and Ellegaard said something about the trees holding heat. I checked my phone. The rendezvous point was less than half a mile away. Couldn't get a cell signal on one side of the coat factory but I got one in the woods near the Canadian border. We walked in a hundred yards then crouched and looked through our binoculars. The pines grew close to one another. The trunks had gray bark and few branches except for the fifty-foot-high tops that formed a canopy of green needles. The treetops blocked most of the sunlight. Dead pine needles, fallen branches, and pinecones covered the ground, creating a sepia-tone world. The density of trees made it impossible to see far, fifty yards at most points with tiny windows of greater distances. The dense forest also made it impossible to shoot far, whether with gun or bow.

We saw no one through our binoculars then walked in another hundred yards, knelt, and panned the forest again. We repeated the process for twenty minutes until the GPS coordinates on my phone matched those of the rendezvous point. A strip of land running east-west and the width of a two-lane highway had been cleared of trees.

This was the US/Canadian border. It's known as the slash—it runs from Maine to Alaska.

The forest opened up on the Canadian side to make room for several small lakes. Their dull, gray frozen surfaces sucked what little light seeped through the cloud cover. It was an unremarkable spot. Just like a million others in the north woods. I pointed and said, "Footprints." We saw a few, half covered and half imbedded with pine needles. Ellegaard knelt and swept away the debris. He crawled around like an archaeologist, exposing a circle of bare ground ten feet in diameter. Footprints everywhere. Not just a few but hundreds made in soft earth then frozen hard like fossils.

But no sign of Linnea Engstrom or Ben Haas or Miguel Maeda. "Maybe they're in Canada."

Ellegaard said, "It's possible." We looked through our binocs to the Canadian side but saw no one.

I said, "This has to be some kind of soft spot in the border. The canopy is thick here. It could block out the drones' optical and infrared cameras."

"What about the slash? The drones have that covered."

"Yeah, good question. I don't have the answer."

We spent a few more minutes thinking and saying nothing then started back toward the car. Each hundred yards we knelt and panned the forest with binoculars. The third time we spotted them.

A person lay on the ground, dead still, about 150 yards ahead of us. It wore olive green pants, a camouflage jacket, and hiking boots. A camouflage pack lay on the ground, blocking a view of its head.

Another person stood over the fallen person. He or she wore a long gray hooded coat and carried a backpack. Tubes like those to carry fly rods were strapped to each side of the pack. The hood obscured the person's face. The density of trees between us made it difficult to see much detail. Ellegaard dropped to his belly, keeping the binoculars pressed to his eyes. My slinged arm prevented me from doing the same so I moved behind a tree for cover and leaned out to look. We spoke in whispers.

Ellie said, "Can't ID either one of them."

"Impossible to guess a height and build with the coat and backpack from this distance."

"How far is Kozy's cabin from here?"

"I don't know. I wasn't conscious on the trip there and it was pitch-black on the way back. I saw the gravel road in front of us and that was it."

A breeze pushed the treetops around, but the air on the ground remained still. My breath condensed in front of my face then hung in a cloud before disappearing. The standing figure turned and revealed a small compound bow in its hand. A red arrow with yellow fletching was loaded but not drawn. The figure knelt near the fallen person, but the trees prevented us from seeing what was happening.

Ellegaard said, "That's our archer, Shap."

"I'm trying to see if there's an arrow stuck in the person on its back."

"Me, too. Not seeing one."

The bow looked small in comparison with the archer. Either the archer was huge or the bow was tiny, maybe eighteen inches long. That was small enough to fit into the pack, and I understood how the shooter could carry it through a city without anyone noticing. Maybe under a jacket or in a day pack or even in a large messenger bag.

Ellegaard said, "They're a hundred yards out of range. We can try to sneak up on them, but if the archer spots us, we'll be in his range well before he's in ours."

"We should have brought rifles."

"You're gun's smaller than your phone. Now you want a rifle?"

The archer stood, adjusted his pack, and started toward the road.

Ellegaard said, "Let him go. As long as he's holding that bow, we can't take a chance. If Ben Haas's car is gone when we get to the road, we'll call the police. He won't get far."

We waited for him to walk out of sight then headed toward the fallen person. The camouflage pack continued to block our view of its head. Not until we were fifteen feet away did I see the auburn hair. Linnea Engstrom lay motionless. Her torso looked rock still. Ice clung to her clothing.

"Good Lord," said Ellegaard.

I ran to her and put a hand on her neck. It felt like winter.

33

I kept my hand on Linnea's cold neck and shut my eyes. The wind jostled the treetops. A pinecone bounced off the needle-covered earth a few feet to my right. I felt her pulse beat weak and slow. "She's still alive."

Ellegaard said, "Get her pack."

I grabbed the camouflage pack and slung it over my right shoulder. Ellegaard scooped Linnea Engstrom off the ground and into his arms and we headed toward the road, Ellegaard twisting his shoulders left and right to weave Linnea's body through the trees. We reached the clearing and stopped. Ben Haas's Highlander was gone. Or he'd moved it and was waiting for us. If we wanted Linnea to have a chance at survival, we had no choice other than carrying her across the open field.

Ellegaard dropped to his knees. "Take my thermals."

I did and panned everything in front of us. Nothing warm registered. "Clear."

We continued over the frozen field. I told myself Ben Haas had left Linnea to die. He had no idea we were in the woods. He'd most likely moved forward. But I kept checking with the thermals. We reached the road then continued to 580th Avenue. I started the Volvo and cranked the heat. Ellegaard lay Linnea across the backseat, found a space blanket from my winter travel kit, unfolded the three-inch square package, and draped the shiny sheet over Linnea's body. He got in back, cradling her head and pinning the space blanket against her body so it didn't blow away.

I pulled a U-turn and sped back toward Highway 313. My first call was to Jameson White.

He answered the phone. "What's all that noise?"

"Sorry. Missing a window."

"Little early for your second changing, isn't it?"

"We found Linnea Engstrom. She's unconscious and barely has a pulse. Probably hypothermia and frostbite."

"Damn."

"So here's my question: small town urgent care or you?"

"I'll call urgent care and see what equipment they have. Call you back in two."

I took a left on 313 and floored it. Mel Rosenthal answered the phone on the first ring. I filled her in and said I'd call her back when I knew where we were taking Linnea. She hung up to call Anne and get her on the first flight north.

Jameson called back. "Take her to urgent care. I'll text you the location and meet you there."

The speedometer said ninety-five miles per hour, and the Volvo wasn't even breathing hard. I called back Mel. She'd meet us at urgent care in five. I had a minute with nothing to do but drive. I caught Ellegaard's eyes in the review mirror. He was far away from his office on the thirty-second floor of the City Center Building.

I said, "Any change?"

He caught my eyes in the mirror and shook his head. "She barely has a pulse."

"Maybe that's what they used to cross the border."

"What are you talking about?"

"A person could walk across the slash undetected carrying a big heat-blocking umbrella. Like a patio umbrella, but lined with a space blanket and covered in thatch. That could fool optical and thermal cameras, especially at night. It'd be a pain to carry, but it's only a twenty-foot expanse."

"Maybe," said Ellegaard. But he wasn't thinking about how to cross a border without being detected. He was thinking about Linnea Engstrom and whether she'd die in his arms.

We turned left on Mom's Way—yes, that's the name of the road—followed the bend to Gladys Street—yes, that's the name of the road—then took a quick right on Main Street. I pulled into urgent care where Jameson White, Char Northagen, and Mel Rosenthal stood waiting next to a dark-skinned woman wearing a white doctor's coat. Two paramedics rolled a gurney toward the Volvo as I parked. They moved Linnea inside urgent care in less than a minute.

Dr. Sana Bhatt was about thirty years old, had caramel skin, bright brown eyes under heavy lids and spoke with an East Indian accent. She wore gold rings in her ears and stood four feet ten inches tall. She and the behemoth nurse practioner and giraffe-like medical examiner looked like cartoon characters working together. Most of the hospital's support staff were attending Haley Housh's funeral.

Linnea Engstrom had a pulse of eighteen beats per minute and a body temperature of sixty-two degrees. I didn't know someone could survive those vitals, but Jameson said he'd seen worse. Dr. Bhatt hooked Linnea up to a machine that removed her blood and exchanged the carbon dioxide for oxygen, warmed it, then pumped it back in. She gave Linnea a fifty-fifty chance of survival. I looked at Jameson for confirmation. He didn't have to say a word for me to understand Dr. Bhatt was being optimistic. There was nothing for Ellegaard or Mel or me to do, so we left Linnea and sat in the urgent care waiting area on plastic chairs near vending machines filled with food that will kill you. Ellegaard wandered away to make a phone call. Mel couldn't stop crying. I offered a shoulder but she didn't want it.

Ellegaard said, "I just got off the phone with Warroad PD. They'll look for Ben Haas's Highlander and contact border patrol, state police, and nearby municipalities. We'll get him."

Mel said, "I don't understand. Ben Haas did this to Linnea?"

"No," I said. "But he found her just before we did. He either thought she was dead or knew she was close and left her to die."

"But why would he—"

"I don't know. It doesn't make—" My cell rang. It was Waller. I stepped away and answered it.

Waller said, "Why's my phone blowing up with APBs for Ben Haas?"

I told her what happened in the forest while Ben Haas's Highlander was parked on the shoulder of 410th Street.

"Are you sure it was his Highlander?" said Waller.

"I don't know his plate number. Why?"

"Because Ben Haas has been at Haley's funeral since 10:45 A.M. He sat in front of me at the service then went to the reception. I'm looking at him right now."

I stepped outside through the automatic doors. The gray overcast had given way to pockets of sunshine. The snowplow-made mountain of ice and dirt in the corner of the parking lot had darkened the pavement with a few feet of wet. I couldn't see my breath anymore. The temperature was on the rise.

"Are you sure?"

"Of course, I'm sure. You think he has a twin?"

"Is his blue Highlander in the parking lot?"

"I don't know. Flynn's outside checking right now."

"Don't let Haas leave. I'll be right there."

"Warroad Police just escorted him out."

"Son of a bitch."

"You're upset that he's in police custody?"

"I'll see you at the police station."

"Go to hell, Shapiro."

I walked back inside. Ellegaard said, "What was that about?"

"Ben Haas has been at Haley Housh's funeral and reception since 10:45. Warroad PD is bringing him to the station right now."

"There's no way he could have got there by 10:45."

"Then we had eyes on someone else in the forest. Mel, are you okay if we leave?"

She nodded. "I hired a private plane for Anne. She'll land at the Warroad airport within the hour."

"If there's any change with Linnea let us know."

She nodded.

"If Jameson comes out, tell him Ellie and I are at the police station."

I drove north on Mom's Way and called Char from the Volvo. "How are things with you and Officer Stensrud?"

"I'm playing my part," she said.

"Good. Meet us at the police station. It's a two-minute walk from the motel."

Ellegaard and I got there a few minutes before Warroad Police pulled Ben Haas out of a squad car. He wore handcuffs and the black suit I saw hanging in his room at The Patch Motel. Waller ran ahead with Flynn and met Ellegaard and me at the door.

Waller said, "Get out of here, Shapiro. You found your girl. Your job is done."

Flynn said, "You had no fucking right going into those woods this morning without calling us first."

I said, "Either of you assholes ever hear of gratitude? If it weren't for us, you'd be eating lukewarm funeral food while sitting on an ice-cold case."

Stensrud led Ben Haas toward the front entrance. Ben's eyes and mouth were small. His face was red. Stensrud stopped a few feet in front of us. Ben Haas looked at me with darting eyes. His pupils looked too big. His chin trembled. He made eye contact with no one else. Just me. Stensrud said, "He hasn't said a word. He's eighteen years old and thus a legal adult. And that's all I got to say. Could you please move out of the way?"

Officers Terrence Flynn, Jamie Waller, and Ellegaard stepped aside. I stayed put and said, "Let me talk to him."

Flynn said, "Don't fucking listen to Shapiro."

Waller said, "He's not here to help us, Tony."

"Out of my way, please," said Stensrud.

"Give me five minutes."

Char walked toward us through a field of dormant grass. She called out to Stensrud. "Tony!"

Stensrud glanced at Char then looked away. His mouth contorted into something angry. Someone had told him, probably Waller or Flynn, after he ran his giddy mouth about having drinks with the tall, beautiful medical examiner from St. Paul. Stensrud gave Char an expression she'd grown used to seeing. Maybe she deserved it for letting Stensrud believe she was the person he wanted her to be. But all people are guilty of that when they're after what they want, whether it's a favor from a cop or a paycheck or a warm body. Stensrud just shook his head and led Ben Haas around me. Flynn looked like he wanted to hit me. He restrained himself then followed Waller into the police station.

Ellegaard said, "We have to walk away, Shap. Let the police do their job."

"Ben Haas didn't stick an arrow in me or anyone else, Ellie."

Char arrived and said, "Who told Stensrud?"

Ellegaard ignored her. "You can't be sure Ben didn't do it."

"Yeah I can. And I'll prove it."

34

I spent fifteen minutes searching the internet and making calls before I found her living in a "deluxe" condominium in Duluth, Minnesota. She took my call and believed my story. I told her I was a reporter for the Minneapolis *Star Tribune* writing an article on Minnesota's greatest achievers. The proud mother was eager to talk and did so for forty-five minutes. I heard all I needed to hear.

Roger Engstrom's NorthTech occupied a 1920s building on Main Street in Warroad. It was two stories of yellow brick with a shed roof that slanted toward the back. The NorthTech logo was painted on the side in the style of an old advertisement like the ones I'd seen along the Mississippi for Gold Medal flour and Pillsbury and Grain Belt beer. No one was there because it was Sunday or because Roger Engstrom was dead or just because.

"We shouldn't do this," said Ellegaard. I walked under

the NorthTech logo on the north side of the building then around to the back door. He trailed two steps behind.

You can tell how serious a business venture is by the quality of its locks. We were inside in less than two minutes and I didn't even take off my gloves. I wasn't worried about the police. They were busy with Ben Haas. And I don't think anyone else in Warroad much cared. The old building reminded me of the coat factory. Worn, undulating wood floors with brick walls and awning windows. The first floor was open with workstations scattered about. Computers and papers and headphones on messy desks. There was a kitchen along one wall and an adjacent lounge that had a pinball machine and one of those dartboards with plastic holes for plastic-tipped darts that keeps track of the score electronically. I prefer a bristle dartboard and real darts and a chalkboard and chalk and third-grade math and a pint of Guinness, but I suppose those things aren't best for productivity.

A spiral staircase led to the second floor, and nearby, a fireman's pole offered another way down. It was as if Roger read an article about how to inspire workers with a fun work environment and took every shit suggestion the article offered. We wound up the staircase to find the second story lit via large skylights. There was a big conference room and small conference room, both walled off with glass, and Roger's office, which was also walled off with glass but hidden by drawn blinds. I knew it was Roger's office because the glass door was embossed with: ROGER ENGSTROM.

The door was locked with an Abloy Protec. They're made in Finland. I could walk to Finland in less time than it would take to pick that lock.

I said, "You might want to leave, Ellie."

Ellegaard didn't look angry or sad, just disappointed. "I am going to leave." He waited for a response, but I didn't give one. "I got too much cop in me, Nils. Or maybe it's just the way I am. It eats me up, buddy. Remember what you used to call me at the academy? Boy Scout."

"Used to?"

The clouds gave way. Sun shined through the skylights. Ellegaard had a sad smile in his baby blue eyes. "I'm just not cut out for breaking the rules. I'll go back to the police station and tell 'em what we know."

I said, "You think they're going to listen to you?"

"I think they would've if we'd been straight with them from the beginning."

"Maybe, but that hasn't been my experience."

"Still, I'm going to give it a shot. Then I'm going home."

I nodded. Ellegaard wound his way down to the first floor. The metal staircase rung like a dampened bell, then the old wood floors creaked as he made his way to the back door. I waited until I heard it open and shut. Then silence. Not even the radiators made a sound.

I considered taking a throw pillow from the lounge to muffle the Ruger but that could lead to me prying a slug out of a brick wall, and I didn't want to take the time. I went downstairs and explored and found a granite bookend holding up a collection of tech manuals. It was carved to look like a statue from the Easter Islands. I carried it back upstairs, stood in front of Roger's office, and bemoaned my left shoulder. So I did something I'd practiced as a boy. It was part of my twelve-year-old self's plan to become an ambidextrous pitcher. I abandoned the plan before I turned thirteen. But I got enough behind the right-handed throw to send the bookend through the glass wall. The entire pane of tempered glass fell to the floor like an emptied sack of gems. I pushed aside the blinds and walked straight into Roger's office.

I found what I'd expected. A safe. About waist high. Not big enough for a rifle but bigger than most document safes. I didn't need to open it to know what was inside.

I pushed the call history button on Roger's phone and scrolled down about twenty numbers and found what I was looking for. I scrolled down a bit more and found it again. Then a third time. And a fourth. Then I used my cell to call a cop who cared far more about justice than interdepartmental politics or justifying her job.

35

Jameson White took a fifteen-minute break to redress my shoulder then returned to helping Dr. Bhatt treat and monitor Linnea. I sat in the waiting area with Mel Rosenthal. We spoke little over the next hour, then Anne Engstrom walked in. She wore black cigarette pants, metallic pink Doc Martens, and a pink cashmere sweater. The stupid, shaking dog sat on her lap. Anne's affectations provided identity and comfort. With her husband dead and her only child fighting for life, she held them more tightly than ever. Mel greeted her with a hug.

Anne went in to see Linnea. A few minutes later she returned to the waiting room and informed us Linnea had stabilized but was still unconscious. Both Dr. Bhatt and Jameson had changed their prognosis. Linnea would survive. Dr. Bhatt was most concerned about gangrene in Linnea's frostbitten toes, fingers, and nose.

A steaming cup of shit coffee and a vending machine Salted Nut Roll sat on the plastic chair next to me. Lunch.

I said, "Do you want to do this here, Anne, or somewhere more comfortable?"

Anne said, "What do you mean?"

Mel said, "Now's not the best time, Nils."

I ignored Mel Rosenthal and looked at her sister's tired eyes behind the big glasses. "How often did Roger go on his little hikes?"

Mel said, "You don't have to talk now, Anne, if you don't want to."

Anne stroked the little dog's tiny body and said, "Once a week or so."

"Where's his backpack?"

"In the back of our Lexus, I think. It's parked at my parents' house in St. Louis Park."

"Does it have plastic tubes strapped to the sides?" She nodded. "Do you know what's in those plastic tubes?" She shook her head. "Really? You weren't curious. You never looked?"

"Once in the garage, I saw him put something in it. It looked like a shiny stick."

"And you never asked him about it?"

"No. We didn't talk about those things. We talked about the house, mostly. How we were going to redecorate it. And where we were going to go for our winter trip. We always took a trip to somewhere warm. Usually over Christmas. Last Christmas we went to Cancun. It was just me and Roger. Linnea refused, so she stayed here. Why a girl would want to be in Warroad, Minnesota, in the dead of winter I couldn't understand."

I caught sight of Mel. She scrunched her forehead and pressed her fingers over her lips.

"We stayed at one of those all-inclusive places. It was lovely. Just the two of us. The way it used to be. The water is the prettiest shade of aquamarine. We took long walks on the beach at sunrise and sunset so we didn't burn. During the day we read and napped in hammocks under palm trees and one day we took a tour of Chichen Itza. Roger climbed up the big pyramid. He was in shape enough because of his hikes. But I didn't go. He said it was scariest coming down. I was so proud of him . . ." She trailed off and removed her windowpanes to wipe her eyes.

Mel looked sick. She placed a hand on Anne's as if Anne were old and feeble and in need of reassurance.

I said, "But you never asked Roger about the shiny stick?"

"No. We never talked about that."

"It was a collapsed umbrella made out of a heat-reflecting plastic. Kind of like Mylar. The stuff shiny balloons are made of. He carried it so he could walk through the woods near the Canadian border without thermal cameras detecting his body heat." Anne said nothing. Mel looked at me with concern. "Did you ever wonder, Anne, why Roger needed a big pack to hike for only a couple hours?"

"He said it was to practice carrying weight in case we ever went hiking in the Appalachians or California or Switzerland. I've always wanted to go to Switzerland. Or Austria. It's so beautiful in *The Sound of Music*."

"You went for long walks on the beach together in Mexico, but he never invited you to go on his hikes near home?"

"Roger said he needed his thinking time." She smiled, then the smile faded. "I knew he was doing something on those hikes. Once, last summer, he came back from one. A bee had stung him on the cheek. It was red and swollen so he made a paste out of baking soda and aspirin to put on the sting. He'd left the pack in the garage, so I looked in it. There were packages wrapped in brown paper. I opened one just enough to peek underneath the paper. It was a plastic bag of white powder."

Mel looked like she might throw up.

I said, "Did you ask Roger about the powder?"

"No. I didn't need to. I knew what he was doing."

"What was he doing?"

"He was selling drugs. It was just temporary. To fund NorthTech. Once NorthTech took off, he wouldn't have to do it anymore."

"Did he say that?"

"No. But I knew."

"And you were okay with it?"

"Roger was a brilliant businessman. He had real vision. Like that Mark Zuckerberg. But people didn't understand Roger, so they'd lose patience with him and pull funding or fire him. That's what happens to geniuses and that's why he had to take matters into his own hands. So he could prove once and for all that he knew what he was doing. But I knew. I always believed in Roger."

Mel peered at me through her frameless teardrops. The rosiness of her cheeks had faded. I said, "Anne, do you know why Linnea went to the Twin Cities some weekends?"

"Yes," said Anne. "She had an internship at the public TV station."

"That's what she told you?"

"Yes."

"Do you know she drove the white powder to Minneapolis and then drove cash back to Roger?"

Anne sat with her knees together and scratched between the dog's ears. "I don't believe that's true."

"I don't think Linnea knew that's what she was carrying. At first anyway. But at some point she figured it out. Do you know what the white powder was?"

"I don't want to talk about this anymore."

"You don't have to say another word." I crossed my legs and slid on the plastic chair. It gave me a shock. I hate plastic chairs. "The white powder is something called W-18. It's a synthetic opioid. Ten thousand times more powerful than morphine. When it's in pills, there are other ingredients mixed in to hold the pills together and give them bulk. But Roger bought pure W-18 from a Canadian supplier then sold it to an American buyer in the Twin Cities. Roger took a nice cut in the process."

"To fund NorthTech," said Anne.

"Yes, to fund NorthTech."

"NorthTech was going to change everything for us."

"Down in St. Paul last week, Linnea helped herself to about a hundred thousand dollars from Roger's W-18 sale. When you and Roger hired me to find Linnea, did you know that Roger also hoped I'd find the money as much as your daughter?"

"Roger needed to raise money. It was his fiduciary responsibility."

Mel removed her glasses and buried her face in her hands.

"Thank you for taking time to talk to me, Mrs. Engstrom. I hope Linnea wakes up soon."

"Me, too," said Anne. "Me, too. It'd be nice to hear her voice."

My phone buzzed in my hand. It was my old friend Jamie Waller. I ignored the call and stood. Mel lifted her tear-stained face. I looked at her, said nothing, then left.

36

The police station had the same plastic chairs as the urgent care. Waller appeared, said "come on," then led me to a small conference room with a white table made of smaller tables that fit together like a puzzle for idiots. A large TV hung on the wall behind one end of the table. A video conferencing camera was mounted over it. Stensrud and Flynn were already seated, each at one end of the table. I sat in the middle, facing a wall of high-quality windows. Waller sat across from me. Fluorescents buzzed in the suspended ceiling.

Officer Tony Stensrud said, "Anders Ellegaard stopped by here a little while ago and recommended we speak to you. I appreciate you taking the time to come in." I said nothing. The silence hung, then Stensrud continued. "Ben Haas seems to be in a state of shock. He hasn't said a word, and I'm not sure he's understanding the words we're saying to him. Paramedics are examining him now."

Another silence. Then Waller said, "Do you know what may have caused Ben to act like this?"

"I do. And he's not acting. His life is shattered."

Fat Flynn exhaled something tired and frustrated. "You want to share with us what you know?"

"You sure, Officer Flynn? Last week outside the cave, you didn't seem too eager for me to participate."

"Don't be an asshole. We're doing our jobs. We got pressures from brass and the press. We got procedure. We got jurisdictions. We got interdepartmental politics. We got to account for every second of our time. We don't have the freedom you have, you motherfucking private asshole. We can't sleep with victim's aunts and get precious insights during drunken pillow talk. Give us a fucking break here. We want the same thing you do."

"You want a little more than that," I said.

"Yeah, we do. We want to cover each other's backs and get promoted to make a little extra cash. We don't have Ellegaards out there raising money and putting our fat asses in fancy offices and shiny new lady station wagons."

I tried not to smile, but failed. Flynn was growing on me. I needed a pasty white fat fuck cop friend in St. Paul and had finally found one. I stared out the triple-pane window behind Waller's head then started talking. About Haley Housh and Linnea Engstrom, their Warroad activities, and their weekend trips to the Cities. Stensrud squirmed when learning a teenage prostitute serviced builders and designers who visited Warroad on Marvin Windows business. He'd had no idea and blushed right through his crew cut.

"One of Haley's customers was Gary Kozjek. That's why Kozy ran after getting ejected from the hockey game. He had slept with Haley at The Wabasha Hotel after the Tuesday night victory. He noticed the large police presence at the game, felt the eyes on him, and figured someone had found out. Maybe not the biggest crime in the world to pay an eighteen-year-old girl for sex, but when she turns up dead, you can understand why he got a little jumpy."

Waller said, "How do you know about Haley Housh and Kozjek?"

It was one of those dilemmas that arise when you're a private. I call it collateral information. Not what you're looking for but something you learn along the way. Something that could ruin a person's life, deservedly so maybe, but I didn't like holding the lever. "Doesn't matter. I'm only telling you so you understand why Kozjek ran. And that he didn't shoot any arrows."

I told them about Roger Engstrom and his Canadian W-18 business and that Linnea unknowingly muled the drugs down to the Cities and cash back up to Warroad, where Roger used it to keep NorthTech in business. I told them about Guy Storstrand asking Linnea to break Luca Lüdorf's heart during the tournament and, in return, Guy helped Miguel Maeda prepare to sneak across the Canadian border.

Stensrud said, "Where is Miguel Maeda now?"

"That, I don't know. Only that Linnea Engstrom nearly froze to death waiting for him. Maybe he never crossed the border. Maybe he crossed in the wrong spot."

Waller said, "So how did that bag of money end up in Winnie Haas's laundry chute?"

"At some point, Linnea learned what she was carrying down to the Cities and back. Then last week, either she or Roger made a drop while in St. Paul for the hockey tournament. Roger received a little over a hundred grand. He hid the money in the hotel suite. Or, more likely, put it in the suite's safe. Linnea figured out the code, took the cash, and ran. Winnie hid Linnea in her big house on

Crestmoor Bay. Ben had no idea." I looked at Waller. "Did forensics check the lint trap in Winnie's dryer?"

Waller ignored the question because she'd ignored my suggestion. She said, "Why would Winnie Haas hide Linnea Engstrom?"

"Linnea was her supplier."

Flynn said, "Of what?"

"W-18. Winnie Haas was an addict. The first time I met her, she was glassy-eyed. I knew she was on something but I didn't know what. I have friends who work at 3M. I made some calls. Winnie was in a car accident two years ago. T-boned. Busted up her whole left side. My guess is doctors prescribed pain meds, and Winnie got addicted. Then they took 'em away. Happens every day. Ben probably told Haley, and Haley told Linnea on one of those long drives to or from the Cities, if for no other reason than to have something to talk about. Linnea saw an opportunity, stole small amounts from the packages Roger gave her to deliver, and sold the drug to Winnie. It didn't take much to do the job. The W-18 had no excipient."

They looked at each other but no one spoke. Then Flynn said, "Okay. We're idiots. Tell us what that means."

"The excipient is the inactive part of a pill, the part that gives it bulk and holds it together so you can swallow it. Usually it accounts for at least two-thirds of a pill. If you crush a pill with excipient and snort it, the stuff gets stuck in your nose. If you inject it, the excipient can find its way into your lungs and kill you. But you can do whatever you want with pure W-18. And it's easier to transport without the added bulk."

Flynn said, "Thanks for the lecture, professor."

"You're welcome. Winnie paid Linnea with cash and friendship. Actually, more than friendship. Mothering.

Linnea didn't get much of it from Anne. She got a taste of it from her aunt Mel, but Mel felt guilty about it and cut her off. I guess you could say both Winnie and Linnea were in need of a fix."

Waller said, "So why would Linnea hide the cash in the laundry chute?"

"It's just a guess, but I think Linnea was in the house when Roger came over. She panicked and stashed the bag and ran."

Terrence Flynn rubbed one of his chins with his forefinger. "How did Roger know about Linnea and Winnie Haas?"

"Winnie must have got in contact with him. She probably knew of Linnea's plan to run but not that Linnea had taken Roger's drug money. Winnie called Roger out of concern for Linnea and herself. She was an addict, and Linnea had supplied a cheap fix with no paper trail. Winnie wanted to make sure that wouldn't end. She assumed Linnea would be out of the house by the time Roger got there or maybe she was just careless or high. But when Roger showed up, Linnea was caught off guard and hid the cash and ran and figured she'd come back for it after Roger left. But Roger never left, not alive anyway."

Stensrud said, "Because Ben Haas killed his mother."

"I already told you he didn't do it. The only thing Ben Haas did wrong was ignore his mother's addiction. But that's hardly a crime."

Waller looked angry. I'd begun to suspect that was her resting face and she had no fat on it to soften her intention. She said. "Well, this is all very informative, but if Ben Haas didn't kill Roger and Winnie—"

"Or stick me with an arrow. I know you're equally concerned about that."

Waller forced a smile. "Right."

"First I'd like to talk to Ben, if that's okay with you."

Stensrud sighed. "I'll go get him." He stood but stopped when seeing the look on my face. "You want to see him alone?"

"I think it would be better. I don't care if you listen in or watch via camera or one-way mirror, but he should think it's just the two of us."

"All right, then. Fair enough."

37

Ben Haas sat where Waller had sat, directly across from me, his hands cuffed in front of him and resting on the table. He wouldn't look at me. He didn't seem to be looking at anything. Stensrud didn't bother covering the red light that indicated the video conferencing camera was on. Ben Haas didn't notice the light. Ben Haas didn't notice anything.

I said, "Ben. Are you okay if I take off the handcuffs?" He stared at something that wasn't there. He sat still. "I'm going to do that, Ben. I want you to be more comfortable." I'd asked Stensrud for the keys. I stood and walked around the table. I removed the cuffs and carried them back to my seat. Ben rubbed his wrists but remained mute.

"You hungry?" He shook his head. "You want some water or coffee or anything?" No reaction. "Ben, I'm sorry for what you're going through. I want to tell you what's going on. If you're feeling up for it." He looked at me for the first time since being led into the conference room. I took that as a yes.

"You know I'm a private investigator. I've learned the best way to do my job is pay attention to the little nagging questions that stick in my head and won't go away. I found a couple at your house in Woodbury.

"One was the first time I visited. Remember that? My friend Ellegaard and I, we showed up kind of late for a weeknight. The police had found Haley in the cave that day. Your dad was there to see how you were doing. And your mom couldn't have been nicer. She acted like our visit wasn't an inconvenience at all, even though she was ready for bed. She acted as if our visit was a happy surprise, as if we were old friends or relatives she hadn't seen in a long time. Seemed a bit strange at the time. I made note of it but let it go because she gave us what we needed, which was access to you at 10:45 on a Wednesday night.

"Then, the day I found your mom and Roger Engstrom, I noticed another little thing that bugged me. Those architectural models in your room downstairs. Architectural models used to be made of foam board and they were just walls with cutouts for windows and doors. Maybe a roof. But the models in your room showed the frames of the houses. Studs, headers, floor joists, everything. And I thought, *Who in the hell has time to cut out all those little pieces and glue them together?* Kind of weird, isn't it? I find your mom and Roger with arrows in them. I find a paper bag with a hundred grand in it, but the images that stick with me are of those architectural models. They were houses your dad designed. One-off custom designs. So I knew they weren't mass-produced."

I had Ben Haas's attention. He wasn't in his own world anymore. A dozen bottles of water sat on the credenza. I walked over, got two, returned, and twisted off the caps. Ben Haas and I became drinking buddies.

"Then Char Northagen, the tall blond medical examiner you may remember seeing at your house that day, told me that the arrowhead that went into my shoulder had a fingerprint on it. And you know who it belonged to? Warroad hockey coach Gary Kozjek."

Curiosity flashed across Ben's face.

"I was shocked. Kozy shooting me didn't make any sense. He had no reason to. And for one of Minnesota's favorite sons to sneak around downtown Saint Paul unnoticed in broad daylight, it just didn't add up. So I wondered if someone faked his fingerprint."

My phone lit up. Ellegaard. I ignored the call.

"Faking a fingerprint isn't hard. Especially with a high-resolution digital camera. You find a clean print on a glass or other hard surface and take a picture of it. Then you print it. But not on a regular printer. On a 3-D printer. Except you print with silicone instead of hard plastic. So it's like making a little silicone fingertip. Then you rub it on the oil of your nose and press it onto wherever you want the fingerprint to show up. Simple."

My phone lit up again. Ellegaard texted *CALL ME!!!* I said to Ben, "Hey. I got to make a quick call. Sorry. Looks like an emergency." Ben didn't respond. I didn't know how far away Stensrud, Flynn, and Waller were, so I wasn't comfortable leaving the room. I pressed call and headed toward the credenza while waiting for Ellegaard to answer. He did on the first ring.

"I'm following him, Shap. He's headed southeast on Highway 11 toward Baudette."

"What?"

"I was pulling out of The Patch Motel parking lot to head home when I caught a glimpse of the blue High-lander heading east out of the Marvin Visitors Center. I called Stensrud. He put the word out. Baudette police are setting up a roadblock. We should be hitting it any minute."

"I'm having a little chat with Ben. Call me when it's over."

I hung up and walked back to the table. Ben said nothing. I picked up where I'd left off. "So then the two weird things from that day, the architectural models and the possibility of a fake fingerprint, became not so weird. In fact, they made sense, not in spite of each other but because of each other. Those architectural models in your room, nobody spent a million hours gluing those together. Not even close. They were printed on a 3-D printer. Just like the silicone stamp to make the fake fingerprint."

Ben shook his head.

"The question I couldn't get past was: How did a persnickety, highbrow, high-fashion-wearing, manicure-getting Lilliputian architect named Raynard learn to shoot a bow so well?"

Ben shut his eyes.

"I spoke to your grandma Catherine today. She told me something about your dad you might not know."

Ben gulped some water but it didn't help. His voice crackled. "What?"

"Your grandpa Frank was always out of work. And for the most part, drunk. Your grandma said whiskey was his preference. The cheap Canadian stuff. He bought it by the jug. So your dad didn't have it easy growing up. That part of the country was depressed enough. All the mining and lumber jobs were gone. The Haas family was on welfare most of the time. But they lived in Northern Wisconsin. They liked meat. Lots of meat. But meat's expensive. Yet the ironic thing is it's running all over the place.

"You know what someone in a bar told me, Ben? Something like twenty-five thousand Wisconsin deer get killed by cars every year. I didn't believe the guy so I got out my phone and looked it up. The actual number was over twenty-six thousand."

"But the hunting season is only a couple months a year, and licenses are expensive. And even then, you're only allowed one deer, even though they're overpopulated and getting hit by cars all the time.

"So your dad learned how to poach. Your grandma said he became quite skilled at killing deer and gutting them in the field and burying the entrails and head and everything they didn't want then cutting up the meat and packing it into plastic bags and backpacking it out of there along with his bow and arrows.

"He never used a rifle because rifles made too much noise. He'd buy a couple arrows a year. That was it. He was famous in his family for never losing an arrow because he almost never missed his target. And if he did, he wouldn't leave 'til he found the arrow, and if it got dark he'd mark the spot and go back the next day. The arrowheads were expensive 'cause he needed the ones that sliced right through so the deer would bleed out in minutes. He couldn't have a deer run off with an arrow in it. Not out of season anyway."

"Wait," said Ben. "Grandma Catherine told you all this?"

"She did. I told her I was a reporter doing a story on how successful your dad's become. She had so much to say, I had a hard time getting off the phone with her."

"I don't believe my dad grew up like that. I would have heard about it."

"No, Ben. You wouldn't have. Your dad is about image. His business and reputation depend on it. Your mom said he had to hold his nose to even step into her McMansion. You think he's going to tell you he had to poach deer to eat? You think he would have told your mom? He wanted to keep that well buried."

Ben took a sip of water, but said nothing.

I said, "Your grandma said when your dad was in high school he invented the smallest bow she's ever seen. Apparently, he's great with mechanical stuff like that. I guess that aptitude is part of what makes him a good architect."

Ben dropped his eyes and played with his water bottle. I stole a glance at the video conferencing camera hanging over the TV. The red light was still on. Without looking up, Ben said, "My dad would never kill my mom. Never. There's no way he'd do that to me. He's a great dad. Plus, he was in Chicago. He couldn't have."

"The police checked that out. He being the ex-husband. He definitely flew down to Chicago a few days before the murder then flew back when hearing the news. He must have come back up to Minneapolis and flown back to Chicago in between. Probably on a private plane. They're reviewing flight plans right now."

Ben shook his head.

"Ben, you know your dad did it. You know it's true. I'm sorry. I'm terribly sorry."

Ben burst into tears. My phone lit up again. I excused myself and answered. "Yeah, Ellie?"

"Police just pulled him out of the car."

"Good."

"Not good," said Ellegaard. "It isn't Raynard Haas."

38

An hour after I spoke to Ellegaard, Ben Haas was back in his cell and Gary Kozjek sat in Ben's chair. Stensrud, Waller, and Flynn rejoined the party. Ellegaard was headed home. Again. Poor guy couldn't get away from me. Before he left he'd filled in Kozjek on why the coach had run into a roadblock. Kozy seemed both relieved and insulted it wasn't intended for him. We settled in with new bottles of water. Kozjek poured water into his mouth rather than drinking directly from the bottle, an old hockey squirt-bottle habit.

Kozy said, "I'm not talking without a lawyer."

Stensrud said, "You're not under arrest. We just want to know how you ended up driving Raynard Haas's car."

"Yeah, I hear you. I want a lawyer."

Waller said, "You got one in town?"

"Not for criminal defense. But I know one in St. Paul. Let me call her."

Flynn said, "Jesus Christ."

I said, "You don't need to call her, Kozy. I'll tell you what she'll say."

"Oh, you will, asshole?"

"Hey, I thought we were friends."

"Friends don't drag friends into bullshit like this."

"That lawyer's going to tell you to keep your mouth shut until she gets up here. Soonest that'll be is two hours. That's if a private plane's available on a Sunday afternoon. One just flew Anne Engstrom up here, so that's one less available. Maybe your lawyer will fly commercial, but chances are her quickest way up here is to drive. That'll take six hours." I looked at the clock on the wall. "That'd get her here about 10:00 P.M. Then our conversation will have to wait until morning. I'm sure officer Stensrud will be happy to put you up in his finest cell. But waiting until tomorrow will give the Twin Cities reporters plenty of time to get wind of the story and be up here by morning."

"Reporters? I thought I wasn't under arrest."

"You're not," said Stensrud, "yet. But we may have to arrest you for solicitation of a prostitute to keep you here overnight."

Well bullshitted, Stensrud. Well bullshitted.

Kozy said, "I didn't kill anyone."

Waller said, "Then you have nothing to worry about."

I said, "Other than the press."

Stensrud said, "With everyone's permission, I'd like to offer Coach Kozjek a deal."

Flynn said, "Jesus Christ."

Waller said, "Let's hear it."

Stensrud said, "We agree not to file charges if Coach here tells us all about his connection to Raynard Haas."

Kozy poured more water into his mouth, swallowed, then said, "You won't charge me for anything?"

Waller said, "I'll agree to that. Except for rape or murder."

"Rape?"

"I'm not saying you raped someone. I'm just not letting you walk for it if you did."

Stensrud, "Works for me. Officer Flynn?"

Flynn nodded his wide head. We all looked at Kozjek, who squirmed then said, "All right. Deal." The hockey great didn't seem to understand cops can't cut deals. Only prosecuting attorneys can do that. But he was sure of himself the way other arrogant masters of one field tend to be arrogant about all things, even those they know nothing about.

Kozjek said, "Haas knows a lot of pro athletes. He's designed homes for some Minnesota Vikings and Twins and Timberwolves. Done a couple homes for guys on the Wild, too. I met him at a charity event and talked to him about designing me a new place up here. Something I could age into. He had this idea for a single-story house made of poured concrete walls and aluminum windows that don't look like metal or nothing. Zero maintenance for life. So I hired him to design the place.

"One day, we're walking my land to pick a site, and he can see I'm in pain. I tell him anyone who played nineteen years in the NHL is in pain. He asks if I'm on anything for it. I tell him no. Doctors told me to manage it with Advil. He says he knows someone who can get me something stronger if I want it. I ask how much stronger. Like oxy? He says way stronger than oxy. I tell him no thanks. I'm a fucking hockey player. Opioids are for pussy football and baseball and basketball players.

"Then I tell him when the pain gets too bad"—he glanced at Waller—"and I apologize for being a smidge crude here, I find one of my local admirers to play a little hide the lamp shade. Takes my mind off my knees and hips. Haas figures we're buddies at this point, and we kind of were, even though the man dressed like a freak. Anyways, he says he knows a young woman in town with all the body and can-do attitude I could handle. Available most anytime I want. For a price.

"So I ask who is this young woman, and he tells me it's Haley Housh. Fuck, I know the Houshes. Generations of 'em. So I think no way. Plus the girl's only seventeen. But I see her around, you know. Small town. She's at all the hockey games. A guy can't help but let his imagination get the best of him. Then she turns eighteen. Raynard's up here. We have a few cocktails and I go against my better judgment. Tell him to make the call. Then once it started, I didn't feel much like stopping it."

Kozy poured more water into his mouth. I said, "You told me the other night no one else knew you were sleeping with Haley. But obviously, Haas did."

"Yeah, well. I didn't want to get him in trouble."

Flynn said, "You ever sleep with Linnea Engstrom?"

"Fuck no."

"She drove down to the Cities all those weekends with Haley. Were they in the same game?"

"I don't know, but I never slept with her or heard about anyone who did other than Luca."

Stensrud said, "So, Kozy, how did you end up in that Highlander?"

"I have a burner. Used it to communicate with Haley. But last night I used it to call Raynard. Told him I was hiding out 'cause the cops were after me 'cause of Haley. He told me to hold tight. Then today he calls me back and offers me a way out. Says I can take his car to Hurley,

Wisconsin. He's got a cabin there and it's stocked. I'm getting stir-crazy hiding here so I accept the offer. He picks me up. Asks me to drive north 'bout a mile shy of the Canadian border. I think that's kind of weird, but hey, he's giving me wheels to get out of town. So I drop him where he wants then head east."

Stensrud said, "When did he call and offer you the Highlander?"

"Hell, not much more than a couple hours ago."

I said, "Did he have a backpack with him?"

"Yeah. How'd you know?"

"You didn't ask why he wanted to be dropped near the border?"

"No. Like I said. He gave me my ticket out of town. Or so it seemed that way at the time. 'Cause look where I'm fuckin' sittin' right now."

Waller looked at me and said, "So Raynard Haas's son is sleeping with Haley Housh, and Raynard knows she's pay to play. Fucking father of the year."

I said, "Anything else you want to tell us, Kozy? Now's your chance."

"Yeah. You think the press will find out about me and Haley?"

Waller said, "Were there other hookers?"

"No. Never. Plenty of women wanted to sleep with me. In every town I played in. And plenty of women did." He looked off, as if he were deep in thought. The fluorescents overhead reflected off his scars. "But there was something about that Haley. Maybe 'cause she was so young. Maybe 'cause she acted like she liked it so much. Whatever I dreamed up, seemed like she was already thinking it. Kind of took the fire out of me, in a good way. Helped me relax. I've been fighting my whole life, on and off the ice.

But for that hour or so, I didn't have to fight for nothing. I'm going to miss her."

Flynn said, "Jesus Christ."

I said, "Any idea how Haley wound up in that cave?"

Kozy shook his head. "I was with her until 11:00. She left my room at The Wabasha. That's the last I saw or heard from her."

The five of us looked at each other, waiting for someone to say something else. Anything else. Stensrud hosted this gathering and figured he had to step up. He pointed to the big fish-eye lens over the TV. "See that camera, Kozy? It just recorded everything you said."

"You fuckin—"

"Take it easy. No one's ever going to see it. Unless you run. I don't care if you're here or in the Cities. But don't leave the state. And answer your phone. Got it?"

"Yeah, I got it."

"As soon as we have Haas, and this is all settled, I'll delete it. You have my word."

"Guess that'll have to do. I don't have much of a fuckin' choice." Kozy stood up and headed for the door.

"And leave us the keys to the Highlander. We need it for evidence."

Kozy tossed the Highlander key onto the table then left. We waited until we saw him walk through the parking lot to wherever he was going.

Waller said, "I got a double murder on my board, and my killer's in the wilds of Canada. Might as well have written it in permanent marker."

Flynn said, "Jesus Christ."

"I'll make a few calls," said Stensrud, "but Canada has a lot of square miles and not a lot of people. I'm sure Haas's friends got plenty of places to hide him."

Raynard Haas wasn't in Warroad. He wasn't in St. Paul. He wasn't in Woodbury. He was in none of my all-of-a-sudden-friends' jurisdictions. But I wasn't so sure he was in Canada, either. Was there any value to sharing that information with my new friends? None than I could see.

39

I drove to the corner service station and asked if they could cover the space where my rear passenger window used to be. They had plastic sheeting and tape and said no problem. I left the car with them then walked to The Patch Motel. I sat in my room on my soft bed and thought in the stillness of a small town on a Sunday. The answer was close.

A framed color photograph of a wolf standing in a snowstorm hung on the wall. The wolf stared at the camera. Snowflakes fell except for those resting on its coat. The amped-up intensity of color and the yellow oak frame made the photograph feel cheap. If the photographer had left the washed-out hues of a snowy day, and the frame had been simple and black, the picture might have been beautiful. But it's hard to leave things simple. For artists. For designers. For people living their lives.

Raynard Haas designed simple homes. Straight lines. Flat roofs. No molding. Muntin-free windows. Not many people in Minnesota wanted homes like that. There were

a few around the lakes in Minneapolis, a few more out
on Lake Minnetonka. Modern masterpieces studded the
prairie near colleges like Carleton and St. Olaf. The few
people who did want homes like that often built them
large and filled the space with quality materials. Expensive homes.

Architects don't make a fortune unless they become
builders, as well. But Raynard Haas should have made
enough money. He was the little man with the shaved
head and stubbly face and funny clothes and blue-framed
glasses. When you hired Raynard Haas to design your
home, you got not only the dwelling, but you also got
the artist. And most people like to be in the presence of
a *real* artist.

So why was he pedaling W-18 with Roger Engstrom?
Maybe Haas took too big of a hit during the Great Re-
cession and couldn't recover. Maybe he was just afraid
of revisiting the poverty of his childhood. But I guessed
it had more to do with being needed. Raynard Haas was
a luxury item, the subjective desire of fickle taste. He
could toil for months on a home only to see his design
scrapped for something cheaper to build, more tradi-
tional, or worse, arbitrarily different.

When Raynard Haas was a boy, it must have felt pretty
good to provide meat for his family. Maybe if he'd been
a locksmith or cobbler or baker, he would have felt more
useful. But he wasn't. He designed homes for the few, isolated by his refined taste.

None of the *why* mattered, of course. Other than it led
me to believe Raynard Haas wasn't in Canada. He knew
we'd learn of his connection to Roger Engstrom and their
business. He knew we'd be on the lookout for Ben's
Highlander. He knew we'd find Kozy, and Kozy would

tell us he'd dropped Raynard near the Canadian border right near where Ellegaard and I had last seen Raynard. He'd left a trail of crumbs to the land of maple syrup and round bacon. It was a trick Raynard had used over and over—lead the eye to where you want it to go. Just like he had with that bouquet of arrows in my hospital room.

It would make perfect sense if Raynard had fled to Canada. Unless you thought he was the type to hold on dearly to what gave him meaning. Even if it doomed him. Like Steve Jobs trying to cure his cancer by drinking fruit juice instead of undergoing surgery.

When I called Ellegaard he was halfway home. I filled him in on what he'd missed, starting with the NorthTech break-in and finishing with the sour expressions of Waller, Flynn, and Stensrud as they realized Raynard Haas had escaped to Canada.

He didn't respond. I said, "E, you still there?"

"Yeah. And Raynard Haas isn't in Canada."

"That a boy, partner. I'll be on the road in half an hour."

"I'm going to check out a possible location," said Ellegaard.

"The same location I'm thinking of?"

"Does it have gold and platinum albums hanging on the wall?"

"You know it does," I said. "Wait for me, will you?"

"I'll get the address from Bemidji Police. Tell them what's going on and drive by. See if there's any sign of Haas."

"Use the thermals from the road."

"That's my plan. I'll take a look and give you a call."

I texted Char. We packed up, met in the lobby, picked up the Volvo, then drove to urgent care for Jameson. On

Jameson's suggestion, Anne and Mel had decided to medevac Linnea down to Abbot Hospital in Minneapolis because Linnea hadn't regained consciousness.

I asked Jameson if he wanted to drive back to the Cities with us. He insisted on staying with his new patient, though I wasn't sure if it was for medical reasons or for the quick flight back home. He changed my shoulder dressing and said to call him when I got back to the coat factory. He'd swing back to redress my wound later that night.

Char pummeled me with questions on the drive south. I told her what I knew and what I guessed to be true. She said, "What I don't get is how Roger Engstrom and Raynard Haas even knew each other much less got into the W-18 business together?"

"No idea. But Warroad's a tiny town and Haas visited Marvin a ton for business. Somehow they met. Maybe Roger was interested in Haas designing a building for NorthTech. Or a home for Anne. Maybe Roger tried to get Haas to invest in NorthTech. Haas saw the desperation on Roger's face and invited him into the drug business. Who knows? But when we catch Haas, we'll ask him. I'm sure he'd love to tell the story."

"Boring. I thought you'd have it all figured out by now." She smiled.

"At least I'm more fun than hanging out with dead people."

"Meh."

Ellegaard called an hour later. He said, "I went straight to Bemidji Police and filled them in. Most of their officers are busy patrolling the Spring Ice-Out Festival. They gave me a kid who can't be much more than twenty. I told them to keep the kid and called Robert Stanley. He's meeting me there in fifteen."

"Perfect. He'll get the part-time detective work he wanted. But just a drive and look, Ellie. Nothing more."

"Oh, now you're Mr. Conservative?" I could hear the smile on his face.

"If I don't look after you, who will?"

"I appreciate it, Shap. Even though your policy of looking out for me is a tad inconsistent."

"Well, I can't care about you all the time, Ellie. That'd be exhausting. Text me the address. We'll be there in an hour."

"Will do."

Char said, "Who's Robert Stanley?"

"A retired Minneapolis cop. His daughter, Leah, works for us. She's headed to law school in the fall. Robert fishes every day and will only step foot in the Cities for newborn babies, funerals, and graduations."

"I thought the old Minneapolis cops hate you and Ellegaard for not returning after the layoff."

"Most of 'em do. But Robert Stanley never blamed us for getting laid off."

The sun dropped in the west, painting the sky pink. The temp hovered around thirty-six degrees. I smelled rotting leaves and new green life. Maybe the blizzard would come in April. Maybe in May. I wouldn't take the giant toothbrush out of my car until June.

Ellegaard called back twenty minutes later. "Graham Itasca's summer house is on an unnamed lake about twelve miles southwest of Bemidji. It's not a big lake. House is on the north side. I'm on the south side. I parked half a mile away and walked in. As far as I can tell, Itasca's house is the only structure around. I wouldn't be surprised if he owns the lake, too."

I said, "Keep a safe distance."

"I will. Stanley should be here any minute. Left a

message for him to walk in. I dropped a pin on my phone where I parked. I'll text it to you."

"Any sign of occupancy?"

"A few lights are on. Not seeing any sign of a person in there with regular binocs or the thermals. When Stanley gets here, we'll work our way around to get closer. Pretty sure if anyone's in that house they won't be able to see us."

"Unless they have thermals."

"Yeah, well. I suppose there's always that chance. I'll stay out of archery range, just in case."

We pulled in behind Ellegaard's Navigator and a 1990-something Ford something, which I assumed belonged to Robert Stanley. Char and I dimmed the screens on our phones. I gave Char my Kevlar, pocketed my Ruger, grabbed two extra ten-round mags, then we set out on foot.

It was a perfect Minnesota night. Thirty-four degrees. No wind. No bugs. No snow nor mud. No clouds. A sliver of moon. A star-filled sky city dwellers forget exists. Ellegaard wasn't kidding about the lake. It was small, more of a pond by Minnesota standards. Maybe a hundred yards in diameter. Still frozen. But even at night you could see the gray water below had worked its way into the soft, dying ice.

Itasca's house was massive. At least ten thousand square feet. The entire south side was black with windows other than an occasional rectangle of yellow light. If someone was in there, they'd be looking right at us. But with no moon or snow, the night hid us well.

Ellegaard and Robert Stanley stood on the south end of the lake. Char and I found them crouching behind a copse near a massive pair of binoculars fixed atop a tri-

pod. After introducing Char, Robert Stanley said, "This
time's no charge. Next time I'm on the payroll."

Both former police officers carried scoped rifles, courtesy of Robert Stanley's personal collection.

I said, "Either of those rifles have thermal scopes?"

Stanley said, "Ellegaard's does."

"What do you hunt with that?"

"Assholes."

Ellegaard said, "The lights switch from time to time.
Off in one room. On in another. Probably on timers. Some
of the rooms are under construction. We've seen ladders
and unpainted Sheetrock and work lights. But no sign of
a person."

Char said, "So he's not in there."

"Or he is. Come here," said Stanley. He led us to the
binoculars. "Have a look."

I looked through the binocs and saw the control panel
of an alarm system. Stanley said, "Steady red light. The
alarm system is armed."

I looked at him. "So?"

"It's on Home Mode. You don't set it on Home unless
you're inside. When it's on Away Mode, it gives you time
to get out of the house and time to get in and put your
stuff down and enter the security code. But when it's on
Home, there's no time. If something triggers the alarm,
it goes off. End of story."

I looked again at the alarm pad. I could see it but
couldn't read the buttons. "I assume you're familiar with
this model alarm pad."

"Hell yeah I am. You know how many calls I responded to because homeowners set the god damn
alarm wrong then forgot their password when the alarm
company called. Those damn things give people nothing

but a false sense of security. If a pro wants in, they're going to get in. The only people who can't get past 'em are the people who god damn own 'em."

Char said, "Does that mean someone has to be inside?"

"That's what we're thinking," said Ellegaard. "You can't accidentally set it on Home Mode when you leave. It's impossible. You can only set it on Home Mode when you're home."

"But you haven't seen anyone."

"Not yet," said Ellegaard. "If Haas or anyone else is in there, they're in a room not facing us. We need to make our way around the house, see if we can pick up something with the thermals."

"And if we see someone?"

"We call Bemidji PD. Sighting an intruder in Graham Itasca's house should be enough to convince them to abandon the Ice-Out festival."

I looked through Stanley's binoculars again. "I got a better idea. Let's shoot out a window to trigger the alarm and let the cops come flush him out."

"If that's your attitude," said Stanley, "what in the hell are we doing here in the first place?"

"Raynard Haas nearly killed me. He succeeded in killing his ex-wife and Roger Engstrom. He wanted to kill Linnea, too. He just figured he got lucky when he found her near death. No reason to tie himself to that murder. He figured he could kill her by just leaving her there. I don't know about you, but I feel obligated to find him. If Raynard's in that house, we did find him. But we don't need to risk our lives bringing him in. The police can do that."

Robert Stanley stared at me like I was a dog taking a shit on his lawn.

"Listen. The question I keep asking is why. Why did Raynard kill Roger Engstrom and the mother of his son and intend to kill Linnea? Why did he try to stop me from finding her? It wasn't because of the money Linnea took. He could always get more money. The only reason is because they knew about his W-18 business."

Stanley said, "What are you making a speech about, Shapiro?"

"Haas has had opportunities to run but he hasn't done it. He loves his life. He loves his status. He's come a long way from poaching deer for dinner. He has killed and will kill to preserve his place in the world. So yeah, I think the cops should handle this. You know, after they're done policing the Ice-Out Festival."

The night lay still, unmoved by my sermon. Two rooms in the house traded light and dark. The new lit-up room gave us a glimpse of scaffolding and bare studs but nothing alive.

Ellegaard said, "Raynard Haas has lost his place in the world, regardless. He killed two people. He can't go back to being who he was. It doesn't make sense."

"Haas isn't thinking clearly. Another big reason to let the police handle this. St. Paul PD is probably issuing a statewide APB right now. That will get the police here in minutes."

Ellegaard bit his upper lip then said, "Let's just walk the perimeter. See if the thermals pick up anyone. Then call the police."

Robert Stanley said, "I got two Kevlar vests in case he's got a gun. That leaves two of us unprotected."

I said, "Give me your extra vest. I gave mine to the tall blonde."

"Which one?"

"The pretty one."

"That could be any one of you fuckers." Robert Stanley tossed me a vest from his pack.

"Ellegaard's wearing his. We're all covered."

Ellegaard said, "You got a gun, Char?"

She shook her head.

"Ever shoot a pistol before?"

"I grew up on a farm. I shot plenty."

Ellegaard handed her his Glock. She dropped out the mag and popped it back in. Then we started, moving counterclockwise. Ellegaard kept his thermals on the house the entire trip. It took us forty-five minutes to work our way around to where we'd started. No one saw any sign of life inside the behemoth structure.

"That's impossible," said Robert Stanley. "Someone has to be in there."

Char said, "Maybe there's an interior room or one in the basement that the thermals can't penetrate."

"That's got to be it," said Ellegaard.

Someone was thinking of what to say next. Then we heard the whoosh, and something unprecedented happened. Raynard Haas missed.

40

The arrow flew between Char and Robert Stanley. Its fletching brushed the upper arm of Char's jacket then lodged into the base of a birch tree a yard behind us. Ellegaard yelled, "Get down!"

We scattered into the trees behind the gravel road. Char lay flat on her belly to my left. She said, "He's on the far side of the lake, based on the angle that arrow stuck in the tree."

"Char says far side of the lake," I called to Ellegaard and Robert Stanley.

"He can't come straight across," said Stanley from somewhere to my right. "Ice won't hold him. Eyes on the edges of the lake. Safeties off."

"Nothing on the thermals," said Ellegaard. His voice came from the right of Stanley. "I don't get it."

I said, "He could be on the far side of the house now."

"Or he's back inside," said Stanley. "The construction could have left a door or window unprotected by the alarm. If anyone would know, it's the goddamn architect."

Ellegaard's rifle went off. In the gunshot's decay, I heard falling shards of glass followed by a piercing, electronic alarm. Help, in theory, was on the way.

Raynard Haas had miscalculated. He assumed we'd take the bait that he fled north. And almost everyone did. But Haas hadn't considered the possibility his son, Ben, would mention that The Fiveskins opened for Graham Itasca at Graham's summer house in Bemidji, a party to celebrate construction crews breaking ground on a Raymond Haas–designed remodel and addition. A party where guests drew on the walls that would soon be knocked down.

That led Ellegaard and me to the same conclusion: Haas had a place to hide. Maybe we wouldn't have remembered if I hadn't taken a genuine interest in The Fiveskins and got off topic. I was a fan. That was just dumb luck. So when I saw the signed pieces of Sheetrock in Ben's bedroom, the existence of Graham Itasca's summer home rooted deeper in mind.

One thing had bothered me about this case. Lying on my belly in the woods that night, it suddenly made sense.

There was a timing problem. Haas shot an arrow into my shoulder about an hour after Roger Engstrom hired us. An hour wasn't enough time for Raynard Haas to fake a fingerprint. Either he'd been planning on shooting me for a while or the arrow was prepped and ready for another victim. But that person wasn't available to get shot, so I got it instead.

I don't know if the intended victim was Roger or Linnea, but Raynard Haas had planned on framing Kozy for whoever got shot. It made sense. Kozy paid Haley Housh for sex. Kozy was screwing a high school student. His character was shot. He was the perfect patsy.

Haas might have been delusional, but he wasn't stupid. Outmanned and outgunned, this time he'd run. In order to get away, he'd just have to stick one of us to divert our attention. Even missing human flesh and sticking the arrow into a birch tree had diverted our attention. Maybe he'd already left.

Ellegaard must have been thinking the same thing because he said, "Let's go around. One rifle and one pistol each direction."

Stanley said, "Come on, Shap. You cover directly ahead. I'll focus on the house."

I said, "Got it," then joined Robert Stanley, moving counterclockwise around the lake from our position.

Char crouch-walked over to Ellegaard and they started clockwise toward the house. I led with the Ruger. Robert Stanley followed without taking the thermals away from his eyes. We saw and heard nothing before reaching the house then crept up to its east side and stood against the concrete wall of the walkout basement. My phone buzzed. Char had started a group text. She and Ellegaard had made it to the west side of the house. *Spread to the corners. One person per corner.* It was Ellegaard's strategy and a good one. Haas couldn't escape unseen.

Front corners peek around the front edge of the house at exactly 7:45. Another good strategy so we didn't accidentally surprise and shoot each other.

In old heist movies, people were always synchronizing their watches. You don't have to do that with cell phones. I took the northeast corner. Robert Stanley took the southeast corner.

Ellegaard updated BPD. On their way.

Raynard Haas was trapped. *If* he was in the house. If he'd run north and was looking back at the front of the house, we were exposed.

At exactly 7:45, Ellegaard and I stuck our heads around the front edge of the house. No sign of Haas. We each stepped out a few feet, Ellegaard's rifle with its night vision scope and my Ruger trained on the house. The four garage doors, service door, and double front doors were shut.

Char: *My corner clear.*
Ellegaard: *Clear.*
Stanley: *Clear.*
Shap: *Clear.*

There was nothing to do but wait for Bemidji PD.

My gut. My understanding. My horror. They surfaced in such rapid succession I can't remember which came first. The house belonged to Graham Itasca, Minnesota's third favorite music icon behind Bob Dylan and Prince. Prince had lived in a compound before leaving us too soon. Dylan lived mostly in Los Angeles. When he visited Minnesota, no one knew where.

But everyone knew Graham Itasca spent from late May to December in Bemidji. First cast of fishing season to last blast of duck hunting season. Summer thunderstorms and fall color. The guy couldn't live without them. There was a recording studio in the house we'd surrounded. Musicians flew in from Los Angeles, New York, Chicago, Nashville, New Orleans. From Europe, Asia, Africa, and South America. Talents like Mick Jagger, A Tribe Called Quest, Lana Del Rey. The list was deep. Graham Itasca was world famous. And so were his visitors.

So why wasn't the entire property fenced? The front side of the house was gated at the road. But we'd just walked straight up to it from behind. That meant Graham Itasca was either foolishly trusting, just plain foolish, or the security panel we'd spied through the big glasses was just the beginning. Pressure sensitive sensors in the ground. Thermal sensors hidden in bushes. Solar-powered wireless cameras mounted in trees. Microphones. A safe room inside. And probably—and this is the part that twisted my stomach—an underground escape route.

I texted the group: *Check the other side of the lake with the thermals.*

A second passed. Or maybe a minute.

Ellegaard shouted, "Got someone! Back across the lake!"

I heard the pop of Char's pistol. Then the loud crack of rifle shots. I didn't know if they were Ellegaard's or Stanley's. I ran back down the side of the house toward Robert Stanley. More gunfire. Then police sirens. I could smell the cordite of Stanley's rifle. But I didn't see Stanley. He must have run after Haas. But why would he? He had a rifle.

I tripped and flew forward. Before I hit the ground, I realized what I'd tripped over.

Robert Stanley.

He was down. I scrambled back toward him on my hands and knees. I reached for my phone but was afraid to turn on the flashlight. Maybe Haas had night vision. Maybe he didn't. On the chance he didn't, I couldn't risk making us visible.

More gunshots. Ellegaard yelled "Man down!" I thought he was referring to Stanley.

"Stanley? Are you hit?"

He didn't answer.

I reached out and felt the cold ground. I crawled on my right hand until it found him. He was on his back. I ran my hand over his legs. Nothing. Then over his Kevlar insulated torso and felt the arrow. I yelled, "Stanley's hit!" I woke my phone and used only the light from the screen. The arrow stuck in Robert Stanley's chest. It had sliced clean through the Kevlar. I brought the phone up toward Robert's face as Char and Ellegaard arrived with flashlights shining.

Robert Stanley looked at me. He blinked. He made no sound. He opened his mouth, but only a bubble of blood escaped his lips. Then Robert Stanley found the strength to shut his eyes so he could die like he'd lived. With dignity.

41

Neither Ellegaard nor I would leave Robert Stanley's
body. Bemidji police arrived. Char walked them through
what happened.

When we were cadets, the grisly Minneapolis Police
sergeant made the two of us his favorites. That didn't
mean he showed us kindness. Far from it. He said we had
the potential to be the best cops in the class. He showed
us no leniency. In our physical training, intellectual training, or emotional training.

Robert Stanley said the emotional training was most
important. So much of the other police work could be
learned in books or at the gun range or on the driving
course. We took classes on interrogation and community
policing and evidence gathering. But the emotional part
of the job could only be learned in the physical presence
of victims.

One Sunday Robert Stanley called us at our homes
around 4:00 A.M. He said it wasn't mandatory, but he
highly suggested we join him at a crime scene in south

Minneapolis. Ellie picked me up and we arrived unshaven and half asleep. Robert Stanley waited for us in the driveway of a small home, the flashing lights of emergency vehicles pushing away the darkness. It wasn't his case. He didn't have to be there. He dragged himself out of bed for our benefit.

He led us into the home. Three victims lay dead in the kitchen. A woman and man had each suffered gunshots to the chest. There was blood everywhere. A second man died from a single, self-inflicted gunshot. He had stood with his back to the refrigerator, put the gun in his mouth, and pulled the trigger.

Much of what used to be inside the man's head had sprayed out the back and onto the refrigerator. That's what Robert Stanley showed us. Not the man. Not the brains. But the children's artwork on the refrigerator.

"This bullshit," he said, "the blood, the bodies, how it all went down, that shit's in the past. We'll piece it together 'cause that's part of our job. But now the thing that really matters is the fate of whoever drew that dog. Or that flower. Or that house."

I could barely make out the crayon drawings under the blood and gray matter. Then Robert Stanley led us into a bedroom where two children had slept. Social Services had taken them away. Their beds were unmade and dresser drawers askew from clothes being hastily removed.

"Now we'll go downtown," said Robert Stanley. "Meet these kids. Then you'll know what it means to be a cop."

Nearly two decades later, Ellie and I stayed with Robert Stanley until the county coroner slid him into the back of the truck.

In the next hour, we'd come to understand Raynard Haas was also dead. Ballistic reports indicated that

Stanley shot Haas in the thigh, just before or after Haas launched the fatal arrow. Two of Ellegaard's rifle shots dropped Haas. One lodged in Hass's rib cage, puncturing a lung, and one found the back of his head, which killed him. The bald little man in the funny blue glasses had finally turned to run.

My guess was right. A secret tunnel ran underneath the pond. It connected Graham Itasca's safe room to a camouflaged hatch in the very copse behind which we'd first gathered. Haas knew our plan because he saw and heard the entire thing. The woods behind his house had more security devices than Disneyland.

Haas launched his first arrow from the house-side of the lake to draw us forward, then ran inside and traveled via tunnel to where we'd just come from. It was a clean getaway plan if Robert Stanley hadn't looked back across the pond through the thermals. Or, more specifically, if I hadn't asked Robert Stanley to do so.

Three days after Bemidji and two days before Robert Stanley's funeral, I walked into Linnea Engstrom's hospital room at Abbott Northwestern. Jameson's insistence on medevacking her down to Minneapolis turned out to be the right one. The doctors there amputated half her ring finger on her left hand and a worthless toe on her left foot. That was it. She'd been conscious for over forty-eight hours and had suffered no brain damage. Or, as I'd later tell people, no "additional" brain damage. I visited with Anne's permission. Mel Rosenthal insisted on being present, but I don't know if her concern was for Linnea or me.

Mylar balloons, stuffed animals, flowers, cards, and banners filled Linnea's room. They weren't all get-well messages. Some wished Linnea a happy birthday. The former runaway turned eighteen that day. Wrapped gifts littered the room.

Linnea sat up in bed, wearing jeans and a T-shirt. She put on a new sweater, baby-blue angora, a gift from Anne, she said. She forced her head through the tight neck hole. Her hair frizzed into a mess. She took a sip of something from a lidded plastic cup with a bendy straw, then looked at me with clear, gray eyes and said, "Thank you."

I said, "For what?"

"Saving my life. If you and Mr. Ellegaard hadn't found me . . ." She shrugged.

"Don't thank us yet. You may have wished we hadn't."

Mel said, "Nils."

"I'd like you to tell me the whole story."

Linnea said, "Aunt Mel said you figured it out."

"Not all of it. Do you know where Miguel is?"

She nodded then hung her head. "Guy Storstrand's family has a hunting cabin right near the border. I didn't tell Guy I was going to hide out there, because I already asked him to lie a lot for me. And I knew where they hid the key, so that's where I went.

"When it was time to meet Miguel, I hiked a few miles through the woods to the spot. Miguel was so close to me. We literally spoke to each other. It was like he was across the street. He was standing right there. He started to run toward me, then he disappeared. It was night so I couldn't see but he had this big umbrella that—"

"A giant Mylar umbrella? Like your dad used?"

"Yeah. How'd you know?"

"Keep going."

"I could hear the umbrella, you know, like the shiny stuff getting scrunched up. I could barely see though.

Then I heard Miguel splashing. It was awful. I tried to crawl out to him, but I couldn't. The ice was mush. I don't know how much time went by." She cried and squeaked. "Maybe a minute. Then it was quiet. And he was gone."

She sobbed and sniffled and sobbed some more. I ran out of patience.

"Have you told the police?"

She shook her head. "They're coming this afternoon."

"How about Joaquin?"

She shook her head again.

"This is the first I'm hearing it," said Mel, whose adorable cheeks had turned gray.

I said, "Is that true, Linnea?"

She nodded. "You're the first two people to know."

Mel said, "Linnea, why didn't you tell your mom about the W-18?"

"My mom? Are you kidding? She wouldn't have done anything. She bought my dad's bullshit all the way."

I said, "Your dad put you in a terrible situation, transporting his drugs to the Cities, transporting the cash back. But once you realized what you were doing, you played along with it. You skimmed a little W-18 and sold it to Winnie Haas. You became part of it."

Linnea scowled. "So what? I had to get away. I fucking hate my parents. I don't care that my dad's dead."

Mel said, "Linnea, you don't mean that."

Linnea slid off the bed and walked to the mirror above the sink. She fussed with her hair. The bandage on her left stub of a ring finger got caught. She used her right hand to free it. She left her hair disheveled but more to her taste.

I said, "After you disappeared, you called your dad and told him you stole the money, didn't you?" She leaned on the sink and said nothing. "You thought you were in the clear. You thought you were untouchable. You had over a hundred grand. You had Guy Storstrand helping you. Winnie Haas hid you. She hid you so well Ben didn't even know you were in the house. You were off to help Miguel then start a new life far away from Minnesota. So you told your dad you stole his money, just to rub it in and be a little shit."

Linnea Engstrom looked back up and glared at me.

"He said you wouldn't get away with it. He told you he was going to hire me to find you. Then you told Joaquin Maeda, hoping he could intimidate me into backing off."

"So what? So what if I did?"

"You didn't think it through. That's what got people killed."

Linnea shook her head with hate.

"Don't fucking get mad at me. Because once your dad told Raynard you knew about the W-18, Raynard was exposed. Your dad wasn't the brightest man. He probably told Raynard not to worry. Roger was about to hire me. But the last thing Raynard wanted was for you to be found. Alive anyway. So Raynard waited outside the Saint Paul Hotel then followed Ellegaard and me as we walked to the cave. That's when the first arrow flew.

"Raynard knew he couldn't trust your dad. So Roger had to be next. And of all the places your dad might go, he went to Winnie's. Raynard went around back and scaled the deck. He broke in and overheard what they were talking about, which was you and W-18. That was all he needed to hear. Winnie couldn't live either."

"Shut. Up."

"You were there, weren't you? Hiding in the one of the guest rooms on the second floor. You heard the conversation between your dad and Winnie while they ate breakfast. You stashed the money in the laundry chute, went downstairs, and slipped out the front door. You didn't even shut it behind you."

Mel Rosenthal grabbed tissues, wiped her tears, and blew her nose.

"Stupid drug addict was going to turn me over to my stupid dad."

"You should have gone to the cops. You would have got a slap on the wrist. Instead you got four people killed, including Raynard Haas, who got off easy with a bullet in the back of his head. If he'd been arrested and faced trial, it would have destroyed him. He knew it. That's why he killed the people who could bring him down and he would have killed you, too, if he thought you weren't as good as dead lying frozen and unconscious in the woods."

She sat in a chair near the window, the one you're supposed to pull up when visiting patients. "I didn't get any sympathy from anyone else so I sure as fuck don't expect it from you."

"How did Haley Housh end up in that cave?"

The smugness left Linnea's face. She couldn't rationalize that one. "I told her to meet me there after the game. Said I'd give her some W-18. She'd been asking to try it. I always said no. I saw how addicted Winnie was. I told Haley if she wanted some she'd have to get it from Raynard. Know what Haley said? She said Raynard creeped her out too much."

"Then why did you change your mind?"

"I didn't. I never intended to meet Haley in the cave. I just wanted her to tell everyone I did, to throw off the people looking for me, make them think my plan was to stay in the Cities."

"So she just sat there waiting for you, getting sleepy and not knowing why. Five people. That's five fucking people who died because of you."

"Shut up!"

Mel hid her face in her hands.

"Then you went to Madison before you went north. Same idea, to throw people off your trail?"

"I never went to Madison. Joaquin did."

"But the fingerprint—"

"I just added his fingerprint to my phone and my bank account. Simple. Someone would have figured it out eventually. I was just trying to buy some time."

"If you didn't go south, how'd you get from St. Paul to Warroad?"

"I paid someone to drive me. And I'm not telling you who."

Linnea said it as if she were smarter than the whole world.

When I was eighteen I was dumb. All of us were dumb because we could only be as smart as our life experience would allow. But in the information age, kids can be smarter than their life experience. It's a false kind of smarts, of course. It's not learned the same way. It's learned through words and images on electric screens, not through joy, pain, and shame.

Linnea's generation is not ashamed. Of anything. And shame, really, is the seed of decency. But it's not their fault. How could they be ashamed? They've grown up in a shameless world.

Linnea Engstrom was just too fucking smart in her brain and too fucking stupid in her heart. That's what made her dangerous.

I couldn't stand being in that room one more minute. I walked toward the open door and said, "Good luck with the rest of your life, Linnea. You're going to need it. And happy fucking birthday."

I walked out feeling nothing but regret for finding the

girl with auburn hair, never knowing if she was one of the
dead bodies on the kitchen floor, or if she were the kid
who drew the pictures on the refrigerator.

I attended two funerals in two days. The first was Roger
Engstrom's. It was open casket, and Anne had him looking better dead than he'd looked alive. I didn't pay much
attention during the service. I mostly watched Linnea,
who cried like a child. Guess she wasn't so happy her dad
was dead, after all. Maybe she missed hating him. Maybe
she missed the future they'd never have. Maybe she was
just plain sorry. For everything. And all that remorse
gushed out at once.

Mel Rosenthal and I smoldered like a doused campfire.
We'd admitted we'd always be in love with others, and
she'd witnessed my unpleasant conversations with Anne
and Linnea. That didn't give us a great start. We remain
friends, though, and every so often the bellows of lone-
liness stokes us into something more. For a night. Sometimes a long weekend. We share respect and attraction
and laughter. But we're not kids. When you're looking to
share a life you've already built rather than find a partner
with whom to build your life, the bar gets terribly high.

It's sad.

Robert Stanley only returned to Minneapolis for babies, graduations, and funerals. His funeral was held at
Fellowship Missionary Baptist Church in North Minneapolis. It's big and old and made of stone and stained
glass and wooden pews.

The place was full of cops. Minneapolis PD, St. Paul
PD, half the Woodbury force, and dozens from other

agencies around the state. Leah sat with her mother and siblings in the front row.

I sat between Gabriella Núñez and Micaela. We were flanked by Ellegaard and his wife, Molly, and Annika Brydolf. Char and Jameson sat together a few rows behind me. Mel was there with Anne. Linnea stayed away.

I barely remember the service other than it broke Leah Stanley. All that smarts and toughness yielded to raw grief. Leah Stanley wailed. Her pain infiltrated my bones like the cold of Minnesota in January.

Micaela held my hand through the entire service. Afterward, she drove me back to the coat factory and lay next to me on the cold bed. I drank no alcohol and fell asleep in my suit pants and shirt. Whenever I woke, I'd reach out and find her.

Read on for a preview of

THE
SHALLOWS

MATT GOLDMAN

Available in June 2019
from Tom Doherty Associates

1

Police floodlights lit the backyard, insects flew crazy squiggles in the faux daylight, and I followed a lackluster cop down to Christmas Lake.

We stepped onto a dock of fiberglass planks. It jiggled underfoot. A red rowing shell lay at the end, overturned and chained to a galvanized post. It was 4:30 A.M. The eastern sky had lightened to gray with a breath of purple. I looked down. Todd Rabinowitz's body lay on the sandy lake bottom under a couple feet of water. It wore khaki pants and a white T-shirt. He looked like he'd lived to about fifty. Fish nibbled on dead Todd's face and fingertips.

I said, "You're leaving him in the water?"

Detective Mike Norton said, "There's a complication." Norton was midfifties, tall, white, and doughy. He had light brown hair and a forehead so big he could rent it out as a billboard. Dress pants and a dress shirt but without jacket and tie. A badge hung on his belt. He said, "When Mrs. Rabinowitz found her husband, she wasn't sure he was dead. She was using her phone as a flashlight.

That's how she spotted him. So she ran into the water and tried to pull him up on shore. She moved him a couple of feet then the body stopped. It was hung up on something. She was freaking out, which hey, you can't blame her for. She wanted to see what he was caught on but didn't want to look too close. Most people don't spend a lot of time around dead bodies."

"I thought you said she didn't know if her husband was dead."

"Yeah, well. I'm just telling you what she told me. So, Mrs. Rabinowitz walks out closer to the body and sees there's a cord underwater that leads to the dock."

I looked at the dock. A red nylon cord was tied to a post.

Norton said, "Only it's not exactly a cord."

"Looks like a fish stringer."

"Yep. But instead of the spike running into a fish's mouth and out its gill, it runs it into the vic's mouth, under his tongue, and out his lower jaw. The killer then ran the spike through the ring-end and tied the cord to the dock."

"Like a caught fish."

"Yep."

"But Mrs. Rabinowitz didn't untie him?"

"Nope," said Norton. "She said she was too upset. And by then she was pretty sure her husband was dead. That's when she called nine-one-one."

I wiped the back of my hand across my face. The August air was so humid I couldn't tell if I was sweating or moisture had condensed on my skin like I was a hunk of cheese. I said, "Get him out of the lake."

"We're holding off, Mr. Shapiro. CSU is unloading now. We're waiting for them so it's done right. We don't want to mess up any evidence."

I watched the fish feeding on Todd Rabinowitz's body.

Sunfish, crappies, perch, and pike. Might have been a few small trout in there. Then the body rolled faceup.

"Shit!" said Norton. He jumped back. "Sorry. Just surprised me."

"Like you said: most people don't spend a lot of time around dead bodies." I glanced without favor at the country club cop. Then I returned my attention to the water. Todd Rabinowitz stared at the starry sky. The fish had eaten away his eyelids.

My day started at 3:27 A.M. with Anders Ellegaard's phone call. He was my best friend and business partner, although "partner" is a misleading term. Ellegaard ran our private investigative firm. He assumed the important responsibilities like paying bills, bringing in new business, and purchasing our health insurance. I assumed other tasks like, during one of our slower weeks, making a catapult out of coffee stir sticks and a rubber band.

Ellegaard told me his wife, Molly, had just received a call from a friend named Robin Rabinowitz. Robin found her husband dead in their lake, and she requested I go out to see her. Not anyone from the firm. Me. She said it had to be me.

When Ellegaard called, I was sleeping next to my exwife. We had a bad habit of falling into bed together. For her, it seemed just that. Bed. But for me, Micaela was a spring trap—I'd have to chew my heart out to get away. I'd tried cutting off all contact. That lasted a year and did nothing to help me move on. So, for the past six months, I woke in her bed as often as my own. We had both just turned forty. I'd heard women hit their sexual peak in their forties. Based on our recent frequency, that appeared to be true. Happy birthday to us.

Everything you need to know about Micaela Stahl you could tell by looking at her side of the bed. It looked more sat-on than slept-in. No strewn sheets. No twisted duvet. No mangled pillows. Micaela slept rock-still, her dreams and worries never creating enough turmoil to toss or turn her. When she told me about a dream, even a bad one, even right after waking, she'd already analyzed it. It was as if she'd not experienced the dream but had seen it like a movie and had written the review before it ended.

Her low stress level helped Micaela succeed at whatever she set her mind to. Or maybe it was the other way around. The companies she ran. Her foundation providing apartments for homeless women and children. And she was a black belt in yoga, or whatever the hell they call a person who's really good at yoga.

Micaela's one failure was her marriage to me, but perhaps failure was my definition. To her the marriage was a house she never quite felt comfortable in or a pair of eyeglasses her eyes never adjusted to. It made perfect sense to move on. Except we didn't move on, not at night, anyway.

I put on my jeans, entered Micaela's master bathroom, brushed my teeth, and pushed my hair around. The face in the mirror did not care for what it saw. Forty Minnesota summers and winters had taken their toll. On my way back through the bedroom, I stopped to look at my ex-wife. She'd get up soon for an early flight to New York. Meetings with money people, she said. I did not kiss her good-bye. There was no point.

Christmas Lake sits across the road from St. Alban's Bay. One of dozens of bays that make up Lake Minnetonka. Unlike its gigantic neighbor, Christmas Lake is small and cold. Trout breathe in its oxygen-rich depths.

Wealthy people live around it and commute half an hour to work. Or their money works for them, and they commute nowhere at all.

The Greater Lake Minnetonka Police Department protected and served a handful of municipalities near the lake. They had secured the area. Yellow police tape crossed the narrow street. A GLMPD uniform stood next to it with a clipboard.

I rolled down my window. "Nils Shapiro. I'm a private."

"Got you at the top of my list, Mr. Shapiro. Mrs. Rabinowitz and the detectives are expecting you."

No argument. No attitude. Just welcome aboard. Once in a lifetime it goes like that. She moved the yellow tape, and I drove the half mile to the Rabinowitz house. It was low, long, modern, and sided with white stucco. Big windows revealed an interior of wooden antiques and overstuffed white couches and artsy chandeliers, the kind with a lot of glass balls filled with vintage-style filament bulbs. It looked homey and happy, but if that were true, I wouldn't be there. A flashlight with an orange cone told me where to park. I did, and walked around back to the lake side of the house. That's where I met Detective Norton, who led me down to the dock and showed me the body.

Detective Norton and I left Todd Rabinowitz underwater. I followed him up from the lake and toward the house on a path of crushed limestone. The white-blue LED floods revealed a lawn of deep green. Hydrangeas and lilies grew in planting beds topped with mulched cedar. It smelled fresh and good. The frogs and crickets couldn't stop singing about it.

Norton led me to a screened-in porch attached to the back of the house. Inside, a man and woman sat on big furniture made of more white cushions. A dozen single-filament bulbs hung from individual cords and illuminated the porch in a soft yellowish-gold. The people inside looked hazy through the screens, like in an old photograph.

Detective Norton opened the porch door and said, "Mrs. Rabinowitz, Nils Shapiro is here."

A woman's voice said, "Please send him in." A man stood. Another Greater Lake Minnetonka PD detective.

Detective Dale Irving said, "Thank you for driving out, Mr. Shapiro." Midthirties, dressed like his partner, and had orange hair. Why do they call it red hair? It's orange. Get the big box of Crayola crayons and find the one that matches. It'll have the word "orange" on it. Not red. Red is for punk rockers and baristas and kids who are pissed at their parents. "Please let us know what we can do to help. Anything at all."

Weird. The cops acted like they were working for me.

I turned my attention toward the woman, who had remained seated. Norton the Forehead said, "Nils, this is Robin Rabinowitz."

Robin Rabinowitz looked up at me and said, "Hello, Nils. Thanks for coming out here so quickly." Her brown eyes met mine then looked away. She said nothing more, as if it had taken great effort just to greet me. She swallowed, and I wondered if she was in shock.

I said, "It wasn't any trouble. I understand you're a friend of Molly Ellegaard."

She brought a hand to her cheek and felt it, as if she'd just been to the dentist and her face was still numb. "Yes," she said. "I know Molly. I called her to ask for you."

Robin turned toward me again then stood. Thin and tan with short hair and long, lithe fingers.

Ellegaard would have brought a contract and insisted on receiving a retainer before getting further involved. I didn't have his business skills. I said, "How and when did you find him?"

She looked at me again. High cheekbones seemed to push up the bottoms of her eyes, elongating them into something Asian. But she wasn't Asian. Just a dark-haired Jewish woman who'd received a perfect complement of Semitic genes. If anything, she looked like a model who was supposed to pass for Native American while wearing something made of calfskin and fringe by Ralph Lauren.

"Todd was home last night," said Robin. "We ate dinner, then he worked in his study for a couple hours. I went into the bedroom to read. I fell asleep early, but I woke when he came in."

"Do you know what time that was?"

"A little after ten thirty. Then I woke up again around two, and Todd was gone. I didn't think anything of it. But I heard a motorboat on the lake, which is unusual after midnight. Then I heard a bang, like a gunshot. I told myself the motor just backfired, but something felt wrong. So I left the bedroom to look for Todd. He wasn't anywhere in the house."

Robin walked over to the screen, and looked out on the lake. She wore old jeans and a white gauze top. "Sometimes when Todd can't sleep, he takes out his rowing shell . . ." She paused. ". . . *took* out his rowing shell." She walked back toward me. Her neck looked longer than her head. She didn't wear a necklace. A necklace would have wrecked everything. She said, "Todd liked to row when the water was glass. So I walked down to the dock to see if his shell was there." Robin spoke evenly and in a matter-of-fact tone. "That's when I found him." She shook her head as if discovering her husband dead was more of an inconvenience than a tragedy.

I said, "What were you wearing when you tried to get your husband out of the water?"

"Excuse me?" said Robin.

"Detective Norton said you told him you tried to drag your husband out of the water but were stopped by the stringer. What were you wearing when that happened?"

"Oh," said Robin. "Just a T-shirt. That's what I sleep in."

"Where is it?"

"It's in the laundry room sink. Why?"

"Irving, have CSU check it for blood and pay attention to whether it's a smear or a splatter or nothing. If there's no blood, I want to know if just the bottom of the shirt is wet or if it's all wet. You know, like she washed it."

Irving nodded.

Robin said, "What?"

"Why didn't you untie the stringer from the dock, then pull your husband up on shore? Oh, and, Mrs. Rabinowitz, I'm going to need a five-thousand-dollar retainer if you want me to work for you." I guess Ellegaard had rubbed off on me more than I realized.

Robin Rabinowitz sat down and said, "Did you just imply that I killed my husband then ask me for five thousand dollars?"

"I didn't imply anything. I'm trying to clear you as a suspect. Not that you couldn't have hired someone to kill your husband, but I assume you asked Molly Ellegaard to send me here because you want this solved sooner than later."

Robin squeezed her knees together with her hands then took a deep breath. I'd made her uncomfortable so I continued. "You could want the case closed because you have a keen sense of justice or you loved your husband or you want suicide ruled out ASAP so you can collect the life insurance. Or it could be because you know you'll be a suspect."

She stared at me without expression. Detective Irving fidgeted with his watch. Voices carried from the dock to the house the way voices do around lakes before daybreak. CSU officers pulled Todd Rabinowitz out of the water, barking instructions to be careful with each other's end as if they were moving a couch.

Robin said, "Huh. Molly said you were nice."

"I am nice. But I'm a private detective, not your lawyer. If I were your lawyer I would have told you the police will look hard at you and not to lie about anything because you've left a trail whether you realize it or not. Lawyers give good advice like that, so if you have one, you may want to give him or her a call. You know, after you settle down and aren't crying so hard about your dead husband."

Officer Irving scratched the back of his orange-haired head and looked at Robin Rabinowitz with expectation. He'd become my toady and had that *yeah what he said* look. I was a bit hard on the new widow—the bizarre crime scene stirred up something in me. The only reason to tie a dead man to his dock by a fishing stringer through his jaw is you have something to say. I guess I was trying to ferret out if Robin had something to say.

She stood, stared something cold at me, and walked into the house.